THE LUCIFER CUT

A Novel

MATTHEW HART

PEGASUS CRIME
NEW YORK LONDON

THE LUCIFER CUT

Pegasus Crime is an imprint of
Pegasus Books, Ltd.
148 West 37th Street, 13th Floor
New York, NY 10018

Copyright © 2024 by Matthew Hart

First Pegasus Books cloth edition June 2024

Interior design by Maria Fernandez

Library of Congress Cataloging-in-Publication Data is available.

ISBN: 978-1-63936-674-3

10 9 8 7 6 5 4 3 2 1

Printed in the United States of America
Distributed by Simon & Schuster
www.pegasusbooks.com

for Ellen

LOU

Someone dies in New York City every 9.1 minutes, so the dog walker was the thirty-ninth that day. It was just before 6:00 A.M. when she finished checking her makeup in the window of the Prada store on Madison Avenue. She dropped the lipstick in her purse and snapped it shut, turned her head this way and that. She adjusted her fedora. It looked cuter now, especially with the Wayfarers. She hoped the girl with the beautiful lips would be in the park again today. The dog walker smiled to herself as she went along Sixty-Eighth Street and collected a pair of sheepdogs, a King Charles spaniel, and three corgis. That made it six on the dot when she stepped into Central Park through the gate at Sixty-Ninth, turned into the greenery, and got a bullet in the ear. The girl with the beautiful lips dragged the body behind the Japanese maples, put on the dead girl's fedora and Wayfarers, and collected the dogs.

A few blocks away, Lou Fine stared at the diamond while his coffee went cold. The stone throbbed with light. It paced around inside the diamond like a caged animal. A top white. Absolutely colorless. Its grade, a D: the most perfect white color. A sixty-carat D, cut into a heap of facets. No living person had ever seen anything like it. The light slithered and dashed around inside the cage that Lou had made. Sixty million easy. He felt a surge of elation, then caught himself.

"Bullshit," he said out loud.

He leaned back and ran his hands through his thick black curls just as Angus, Coco's West Highland terrier, dashed through the dining room and skidded to a halt at the French doors, wagging his tail and looking back at Lou. Lou shoved the diamond in his jeans, got up, and opened the doors. Angus shot outside, and Lou stepped out after him.

A high brick wall covered in ivy enclosed the garden. Most mornings this was the moment he took a deep breath, inhaling the scent of the flowers and reminding himself how good things were. Not this morning. This morning he wasn't thinking that. Because things weren't good. Things were bad.

He stepped down onto the patio. The tiles were cool under his bare feet. They were travertine, a color called Persian red that had swept through the townhouses of the Upper East Side like a pathogen. Your neighbor caught it: you caught it too.

"Why not just pave it in thousand-dollar bills," he muttered as Coco rustled up beside him in her dressing gown, stifling a yawn. She squeezed his hand and leaned her head on his shoulder and bumped him with her hip.

"What's the matter, babe?" she said. "That big white getting up your nose?"

Lou sat down on the wicker sofa and put his feet on the glass-topped table. He stared at the bank of blue hydrangeas. Only a faint hum betrayed the presence of the city. Buffered by walls and the surrounding buildings, the garden was a sanctuary in the raucous jungle of New York. Or was. No sanctuary can keep out what you bring in yourself.

"I told them I don't like these stones just showing up," he said. "Why haven't I heard about them before? This one was eighty carats, and the polish comes out at sixty! A rough so good I got a seventy-five percent yield? Please."

"You think there's something wrong with the stone," Coco said, digging a pack of cigarettes out of her dressing gown.

"The machine says it's good. I ran it twice. Like the Geneva stone."

Coco tapped out a cigarette and lit it. She sucked in a lungful and blew it out into the garden while Lou scowled at her. She waved at the smoke to disperse it, sat down, and took Lou's hand. It was like a block of wood. He had muscular arms, and the thick, scarred hands of a diamond cutter. He'd left the cutting bench a long time ago, but he made sure his clients noticed his hands. It was part of the Lou Fine shtick—the bad-boy cutter who could tame any diamond and who always showed up at his Fifth Avenue store in old jeans and a T-shirt. And no bargaining. Any movie star or billionaire chokes on the price—hey, take it or leave it. The problem was, they'd been leaving it. You get into a little trouble, people pick up the scent like bloodhounds.

Coco stroked her husband's thick fingers with her thumb and studied his face with affection. The travertine had been for her. She couldn't have cared less. Lou could have paved the patio in asphalt as far as Coco gave a damn. She came from the same tough Flatbush neighborhood Lou had come from. But he couldn't stand for her not to have everything that people like Rachel Lowenthal had—another Flatbush brat, but one with a husband on Wall Street and a patio in Persian red.

"Babe," Coco rasped in her hoarse, smoker's voice, "listen. Do what's right. You don't like something about this stone? Tell them to stick it up their ass."

He fished the stone out of his jeans and rolled it onto the glass. "Nobody's seen a cut like this. In the old books, only a description. It's the only cut you can ever attempt without a plan. You can't have a plan," he said, his eyes fixed to the stone. "Only the diamond has the plan." The jewel flashed and stormed. He held the stone to the loupe. "On a good day, eighty million," he murmured. "A hundred."

Coco got mad. The truth was, she didn't give a hoot about diamonds. She loved Lou because he'd been the tough, kick-ass kid next door. Who else was she going to love? She took a deep drag and let the smoke out through her nostrils, her lips pressed tight. Lou shot her a disapproving look. "Before you even have breakfast."

"Don't change the subject," Coco snapped, just managing to smother a cough. "It's not the first time with them. The diamond bothers you. Louis Fine"—she glared—"it's not going to get better by doing it again."

Upset by the tension between them, Angus whimpered and looked anxiously from Coco to Lou and back again. "Ah, baloney," Coco muttered when Lou made no reply. She stubbed her cigarette into a planter and went inside.

Lou usually walked to work. Eighteen blocks straight down Fifth Avenue from Seventy-Third to his store at the corner of Fifty-Fifth. Twenty minutes. Less if he stepped on it. He liked to get in first.

He pulled on his HOKAs and was looking for his leather jacket when the doorbell rang. He shoved the diamond back into the front pocket of his jeans and glanced at his watch. Ten past six. He stepped into the foyer and looked through the peephole.

"Isn't this early for the dog walker?" he called, unhooking the chain and shooting back the deadbolt. By the time he opened the door, the pistol with the silencer was out and pointing at his head. So that day Lou was number forty.

"Are you kidding me?" said Coco, heading into the front hall. "It's not 'til seven."

Forty-one.

4

1

I sat on the fire escape to cool off after my run, and that's when I read the message about Lily. Then I read it again more slowly. I put my phone inside on the windowsill and made myself sit still. A breeze came down West Ninety-Fourth Street and added a flurry of grit to the news. I reminded myself that deceit was always in the wind. It had been the first thing between us. Our purpose. Soon we had another purpose, but it was deceit that had set the ground rules, not what came after. For us, deceit was the natural habitat of love.

I showered, put on a plain white shirt, jeans, quick-draw rig at the small of my back. Holstered the little SIG Sauer, grabbed my blazer. All good. It happens. Fifteen minutes later I stopped at Zucker's on Columbus, ordered a coffee and a bagel. "BEC?" the cashier said. I nodded. "Bacon, egg, and cheese!" she shouted. Five minutes after that I was walking in the front door of the Santa Clara. Lily had the penthouse, and the private elevator opened directly into it. She was waiting for me outside on the terrace. In her hand she had a steel gardening fork. Her bare feet were caked with mud. She wore a T-shirt sewn with diamonds. She did a little twirl and grinned. My phone buzzed.

"I'm taking this," I said. The smile wilted. She stomped off into the runner beans. "What's up?" I said into the phone.

"The cops are trying to get you," Tommy said. "Murder on the Upper East Side. Diamond guy."

"That's it?" I stretched out and popped the lid on the coffee and took a sip.

"I've asked for details. You should get them in a minute."

We ended the call. Lily was at the other end of the terrace, storming around in the beans. They grew on tall frames made of poles that leaned together and were fastened at the top, like wigwams. The three-story penthouse had multiple terraces. Most of them had flowers. This one had the runner beans, two wooden cribs of cucumber, and a lettuce garden. An ingenious system of hoses and timers kept everything watered.

Clumps of earth littered the terra-cotta tiles. Lily came stalking out of the beans with the fork. She had smudges of dirt on her nose and forehead, and there was a fresh swipe of mud across the diamond shirt. With her bespattered skin, her slim athletic body, and her pointy, elvish ears, she looked like a bedraggled leprechaun, except Russian. Her enemies called her Slav Lily.

She stopped to examine the lettuce. "Baby Butter," she said, fingering the pale green leaves. "Do you have any idea what they charge for this in the supermarket?"

I took a bite of the bagel. You didn't want to get into it with Lily about the price of vegetables. She was a multimillionaire diamond thief with the soul of a Russian peasant. She bought a new Porsche every year without a blink but went ballistic at the price of a beet.

"Did you get a tuxedo?" she demanded.

I was still at work on the bagel, so I just made a sound that could have been yes. I didn't have one. I'd forgotten. No one would be looking at me anyway. We were going to the Met Gala. Lily and her business partner, Xi Mei, were sponsoring this year's blowout. They owned a diamond mine. Lily watched me chewing, then pointed her steel fork at my stomach.

"Say something about this shirt or I'll gut you."

My phone pinged. I couldn't make out the message in the sunlight. "Lab-grown," I said, getting up and walking around the corner of the terrace into the shade. It was the NYPD report. I scrolled through its antiseptic sentences. Two victims. A townhouse on East Seventy-Third. I had a feeling the location should mean something to me. Lily's apartment was on the Gold Coast—a pricey stretch of Central Park West. The crime scene was more or less directly across the park. I leaned on the parapet and gazed over the expanse of trees and thought about it for a minute. It was right there—trying to click into place.

My phone pinged again, but I let it go. Two NYPD helicopters were coming down the park from the north. Flying low. I stood at the parapet for a better look. Lily came and stood beside me, twinkling like a Christmas ornament.

"How did you know they were lab-grown?"

"Just a hunch based on the news that you and Mei have decided to expand into lab-grown diamonds, according to the story that the *Wall Street Journal* will break this afternoon."

She pulled out the hem of her shirt and wiggled it in the sun, spattering my face with dots of light while she tried to decide whether I'd been spying on her or on the *Journal*, or more likely, both.

"Mei thinks we have to get into lab-grown. That it's just another part of the diamond business and we shouldn't let competitors have it all to themselves."

"Yes. That's what you told the *Journal*."

She dropped her chin to examine the arabesque of tiny stones. "Do you think it's vulgar?"

"Absolutely."

Her face took on a look of predatory satisfaction. "Good. Vulgar is the new chic. They'll fly off the shelves."

One of the choppers took up a stationary position above Fifth Avenue. The other started to make a slow circle low above the park, marksman in the open door. The rifleman was sweeping the ground with his telescopic sight. The roof lights of cop cars flickered in the trees beneath the helicopter.

"You've got egg on your lip," Lily said, swiping at it with a mud-stained finger.

My phone pinged again. This time the message had the names of the victims in the townhouse.

When Lily saw my face, she said, "Alex, for God's sake, what?"

2

T V trucks lined Fifth Avenue. The NYPD had Seventy-Third Street sealed off. Reporters and camera crews swarmed around the steel barriers, lenses pointed down the block. The Upper East Side of Manhattan is not the murder part of New York City. It's the masters-of-the-universe part. Kill somebody in Jackson Heights—it happens. Kill a rich man, every crime reporter in the city is pitching the book to her agent on the way to the scene. One of them was watching as I stopped at the barricade and pulled out my Treasury pass. She caught a glimpse of the ID.

"Why is the Treasury here?" she demanded, jabbing a mic at my chin. "Why is the federal government involved? Is this a terrorist event?"

"Spot tax audit," I said as the cop pulled the barricade aside. "I hope you kept all your receipts."

"Get a tight shot of smart-ass, here," she said to her cameraman. "Especially that gunk on his lip."

Crime scene techs in hooded white suits were going back and forth between their truck and the townhouse. I stopped and collected a pair of booties, put them on, and headed for the door. A sergeant glanced at my pass again and nodded. They were expecting me. "For Inspector DeLucca," he said to the cop in the entrance, who stood aside to let me in.

Anthony DeLucca had gone up a couple of ranks since we'd last met, but it hadn't cheered him up. He had the same gloomy air that followed him around like the chance of rain. A tall, sad-looking man, staring down at the mess that had been Lou.

The body lay on its back. Entrance wound between the eyes. The impact had caved in his face. On the way out, the bullet had mushroomed and taken off the back of his head. His brains were scattered across the foyer. Bright red paw prints were all over the white marble and across Lou's body. The linings of the pockets were pulled out.

"What did you find in his jeans?" I said.

DeLucca turned to a kid in a sharp gray suit. He had a gold detective's badge clipped to his belt. Blue latex gloves. His hands were planted on his hips, and his chin was tilted up so he could sight me down his nose. "You go through the pockets?" DeLucca asked him.

"Perp," he said tersely.

DeLucca pursed his lips and nodded, and after a few seconds of stone-cold silence, he moved his eyes from the body and dragged his gaze slowly up the detective until it rested on his face. "Mr. Turner's with the Treasury, Detective," he said. "I asked him to come. He knows about diamonds. He's here to take a look and maybe give us a hand. That work for you?"

"Yes, sir," he said, giving me a hard look. "So what it looks like is, the perp went through his pockets. Left a wallet on the floor. We bagged it already."

"Detective McCormick is the homicide lead," DeLucca said.

"What's the story with the paw prints?" I asked.

"Man's best friend," McCormick said. "There's a security camera at the front door. We checked the tape. Shooter posed as a dog walker."

"After killing the actual dog walker," DeLucca said.

"Right," said McCormick. "Phony dog walker rings. Vic opens. Single tap to the forehead. Shooter is off-camera when he comes inside, so we don't see him kill the woman. But he doesn't go anywhere else in the house. Thirty seconds later the tape picks him up leaving. The dogs do what dogs do when they find something dead with lots of blood."

Coco's body lay about ten feet away, paw prints on her back.

"So who called it in?" I said.

"Nobody called it in. Looks like the shooter didn't close the door all the way. It swung open. Dogs with red muzzles wandering in and out. Some guy heading to the park for his morning jog spots the action and stops for a look, and suddenly it's all over Instagram. That's where we picked it up. Welcome to New York."

"Let's take a look at Coco," I said.

When I spoke her name, his head snapped up. "You knew these people?"

"We were friends a long time ago."

He shot an angry look at DeLucca, then back to me. "If it's not too much trouble, maybe you could fill me in."

"I'll put a file together."

He just stood there breathing through his nose. Sure, he was mad. It's his crime scene, and suddenly here's this fed. He's pretty sure we're going to hijack his case. He shot another look at DeLucca, then stepped to the body. Coco lay on her stomach at the end of a bloody smear. McCormick squatted beside her.

"Way I make it," he said, "she's coming to see what's going on. Perp gut-shoots her." He pointed a latex finger at Coco's lower back. The wound was the size of a dinner plate. "So that's the exit." He darted a look at me. "Hollow point. In small, out big." He turned his face back to Coco. "She tried to crawl away. That's why the smear. Then he shot her in the head."

He pushed aside Coco's matted hair to show where the shooter had placed the kill shot. There wouldn't be much left of her face when they turned her over. I remembered the day I'd met her. I could see her getting off the plane at Cape Town airport.

It was the first time Lou brought her. We drove straight from the airport to my apartment below Table Mountain. It had a great view of Table Bay and the South Atlantic and the long curve of the beach at Bloubergstrand. Coco stood on the balcony with a big grin and her cotton dress rippling in the breeze—a New York girl on her first trip anywhere.

We were young, but Lou and I had already cut so many corners, our lives had become a straight line, and we were hurtling down it at the speed of damnation. Who doesn't want to take that ride?

Lou had just opened his first store and was looking for an edge. The edge was what I had for sale.

My rough diamonds came from the Namibian diamond beach just north of the Orange River. That beach leaked like a sieve. The way they mined it—they scraped the sandy overburden off with giant bucketwheel excavators until they got to the bedrock. That was the pay dirt, where the diamonds were. The rough stones sat there in cracks and crevices, and the miners sucked them out with industrial vacuum cleaners that fed the rough into secure containers. That's how it was supposed to work. How it did work was, they didn't vacuum everything.

When the guards were looking somewhere else, a miner would stamp the heel of his boot on a stone. The diamond stuck there. Later he would pry it out and drop it in the gas tank of a service truck. The gang retrieved the diamonds later when the trucks went in for servicing.

Smugglers took the stolen rough across the Orange River at night, into South Africa and down the coast to Port Nolloth. I went up once a month and bought top goods from the Portuguese, who ran the smuggling. It didn't take Lou long to find me.

I was twenty. I had a Mercedes 190 SL in the garage—white with black leather interior. Italian furniture. Handmade shirts. Girls so tigerish their eyes glowed in the dark. I thought it was one of them coming back when I opened the door one night, but it wasn't a girl who walked straight in. It was the rest of my life.

He sat on one of the chrome-and-leather chairs and waited for me to stop snarling. Then he dealt out a series of eight-by-tens onto the glass-topped coffee table. The photos documented my last diamond buy. He didn't say a word until I'd had a good look. Then he slid them all together again and tapped them on the glass and slipped them back into the plain manila envelope he'd brought them in.

"So," he said, "I'm going to offer you a job."

"I have a job."

He smiled. "You can always say no."

I thought I'd better sit down too. He didn't look like he was going anywhere.

"And if I say no, somebody else gets a look at these."

He spread his hands to acknowledge the regretful truth. Job interview, CIA style.

Years later, when I'd transferred to the Treasury and moved to New York, Lou was already jeweler to the stars. I'd dropped in once to say hello. We had a few laughs, and that was it. The reason the address on the Upper East Side rang a bell when the phone alert came through was that when they'd bought the house, Lou and Coco had thrown a housewarming bash that made the *Times*. It couldn't have been more than a year ago. I thought about this as I left the townhouse with DeLucca and McCormick and stood outside in the street. Is that what had attracted the killer's attention? No doorman, as there'd be in an apartment building. No building security.

"The shooter didn't go anywhere else in the house?" I said.

McCormick shook his head. "In and out." He peeled off his gloves and stared back at the house. The morgue attendants were unfolding their long black bags in the hall. "There's a safe in the den," McCormick said. "Steps from the hall." He looked at me. "There's a camera in there. Shooter didn't even come in for a look."

"He found what he wanted when he checked the pockets."

McCormick nodded. "You gotta think so. But here's something you can tell me. Let's say the perp scored a diamond—something worth the hit. How easy is that to sell? I mean, he doesn't just walk down to Forty-Seventh Street and cash it in."

"I'd like to say it couldn't happen. The truth is, if a dealer thinks it's stolen, what he's mainly thinking is how cheap he can get it."

"But there's a record of the diamond somewhere—in this case at Lou Fine's store, right? A physical description in his inventory? Any buyer has to know that."

"Sure he knows it. He re-cuts it. The cut and weight are part of what defines a diamond, so now the stolen diamond's gone. You can't track it because it no longer exists."

We were still in the street when the bags came out. The morgue attendants slid Lou and Coco into the van. The black doors closed on them.

3

That's actually a woman," Tabitha murmured, leaning against me to study the screen. We were sitting at the bar in Via Carota. She was on her second vodka martini. Even her freckles looked a little flushed. Her linen suit was rumpled and her hair a wild mop. She wore dark glasses with thick, tortoiseshell frames. They kept slipping down her nose, giving me a glimpse of green eyes. The eyes had been through the wringer too. Goddess, the day after something.

I looked again at the black-and-white security footage running on my phone. The shooter's face was obscured by the peak of a fedora and a pair of Wayfarers.

"A woman?"

"Oh, come on." She reached over me to tap the screen and freeze the image. She put her thumb and forefinger on the image and spread them to zoom in on the shooter's face. "Look at those lips. I'd kiss her myself."

I shifted my stool slightly away, but Tabitha just moved closer, her flyaway hair brushing my face and stirring the smell of shampoo into the vodka fumes. She tapped the little arrow to replay the clip. The camera at Lou's front door showed the shooter walking up with the dogs. The shooter pressed the doorbell. The footage was stripped of drama by the wide angle, the drabness of the black-and-white image, and the silence.

I angled the phone so people nearby couldn't see the screen. The shooter stood motionless, dark lenses staring at the peephole. Then the gun came out and jerked as Lou opened the door, and the shooter stepped inside and off-camera.

"Not sure Fort Meade will be able to do much with that," Tabitha said. The footage would go to the National Security Agency at Fort Meade, Maryland, and be run through their facial-recognition software.

"The NYPD are getting footage from other cameras on the street and out on Fifth," I said. "The killer shot a dog walker in Central Park. They have him going into the park and then coming back out."

"Her."

I swiped out of the image and put my phone on the bar. "Any time you're ready to tell me why we're here will be fine with me."

The salad arrived. She picked up her knife and fork and transferred some glistening leaves to my plate. "This is the only place on the North American continent where you can get a decent plate of escarole," she said.

I pushed my plate aside. "Like I said."

She prodded the salad with her fork, cut off a tiny piece, and chewed it. Then she arranged the cutlery neatly on the side of the plate. She'd hardly eaten any of the octopus either, or the cacio e pepe, her favorite pasta. Tabitha normally had the appetite of a high school football team. She asked the server to bring coffee.

"I'm sorry about Lou Fine and his wife," she said, peering at me over her glasses. They'd slid down again. Her eyes were steady. "I should have said that before. I know you were friends."

"Tab," I said in a low voice, "I'm not in the mood, OK? You want me to know you can look at my file when you like and find out who I was friends with and who I wasn't. Fine. Noted. Now what do you want?"

I'd leaned close to her to make sure no one could hear. People had been sneaking glances at her and whispering since she'd swept in. You can often find a movie star on a stool at Via Carota. Tabitha looked like one—a glamorous, disheveled woman dumped by fate into a vodka martini at a bar in Greenwich Village. Plus, she'd arrived in a black Suburban. It was parked illegally, right in front of the open French doors so the two guys in blue suits and dark glasses could keep an eye not only on the street but on Tabitha too. But they weren't movie-star muscle. They were secret service. Tabitha was an assistant deputy to the director of National Intelligence.

"Simmer down, bruiser," she murmured. She waited while the bartender put down our espressos and went away. "You know about this business of Lily and Mei moving into lab-grown diamonds?"

I was grateful for the espresso, so I could pick up the tiny cup and take a sip, blow on it, sip again, then place it carefully back in its little saucer while the thought balloon that said *huh?* had time to float away. Because I wouldn't have put lab-grown diamonds on the list of worries for the DNI, where they are paid to chew their fingernails about Chinese subs and North Korean nukes.

"We're here to talk about lab-grown diamonds?" I said.

She signaled for the bill.

"Mei and Lily already own a diamond mine. What do they want lab-grown diamonds for? What's in it for them?"

"Money," I said. "Just a guess."

Tabitha snorted, to indicate the depth of my failure of imagination. The bartender placed the credit card machine in front of her. She added a tip and tapped the screen with her black AmEx card. She got up and I followed her outside. One of the agents opened the back door. She told him to wait outside until we were finished. That's how I knew we weren't. I followed her into the back seat.

"This is serious, Alex," she said the moment the door thudded shut behind us. "Xi Mei is the most powerful woman in China. She has close ties to the Chinese government. That makes her one of our top intelligence targets." She looked down at her hands for a minute. This time the glasses actually fell off and dropped to the floor. "Fuck," she muttered, leaning forward and groping around until she found them. When she sat back up, she blew the hair from her face with an irritated puff.

"Mei's hedge fund has been snapping up Chinese synthetic-diamond companies. The fund's clients are China's top generals. It's how they get rich. However, they have to be sure that what serves their own interests and lines their pockets is also serving the interests of the Chinese government, because the guy who runs *that*," she said, turning back and fixing me with her lethal eyes, "keeps everybody in line by shooting one of them from time to time." She reached across and fastened a button on my shirt that had come undone. A cool finger grazed my skin. "You know all this," she said, giving my shirt a little tug. "I'm just repeating it so you'll have it in mind when I blow up your day."

She sank back into her seat and grinned. That was the thing about Tabitha and grenades. She liked to make sure she had your full attention when she pulled the pin.

"The Chinese can make undetectable fakes."

I stared at her. She raised her chin and arched her eyebrows, waiting for me to speak the line she'd already written for me.

"I don't think that's possible."

"Apparently it is. Three months ago a Shanghai lab sent a twelve-carat lab-grown white to New York. It was a D color. Flawless." She held my gaze. "Guess who the customer was? I'll give you a hint. He's dead."

"Lou?"

She opened her hands.

"You're saying a Chinese lab grew a diamond that Lou Fine sold as real?"

"He did. We tracked that shipment to him from Shanghai. We know what was in it because we opened the package when it got to customs. It was a twelve-carat top-color white, flawless. One month after Lou received that diamond, he sold an eleven-carat D flawless at auction in Geneva for $1.4 million." She let that sit for a moment before she joined the dots. "To us that looks like Lou bought a Chinese lab-grown, re-cut it to improve the make, and sold it as a real diamond. Tell me if I'm missing something."

It wasn't Tabitha missing something I was worried about. It was me missing something. "Make" is a diamond-trade term for *cut*. A stone that good would have come with a certificate, but she'd had someone take a look. Whoever that was had also come up with the rationale for Lou re-cutting the stone from twelve carats down to eleven. But why not come to me? I'm cleared to top secret. I work for a clandestine agency.

"You know what I'm going to ask. Why am I only hearing about this now?"

"We were waiting for Mei to make her move."

"And Lily."

She frowned and started looking for her glasses. They were right beside her. She found them and held them in her lap. "Mei is the concern," she said. "She's the one putting the big diamond growers into her hedge fund. Lily would be more on the retail side. Frankly I think we can safely forget about Lily."

Always pay attention to a sentence that begins with the word *frankly*, because I guarantee it's bullshit.

"OK," I said.

"Mei is basically an agent of the Chinese state. She's buying these diamond factories because the generals agree she should. If they can simply manufacture lab-grown diamonds good enough to pass for real ones, that means they can generate US dollars at will and use them for whatever nefarious purpose they have."

"The nefarious purpose could just be the money," I said. "Sorry to keep hitting the same note." She rapped a knuckle on the window. An agent opened the door beside me while his partner climbed into the driver's seat. I got out of the car. "Who gave you the cutting scenario on the Geneva white?" I said. Her lips tightened.

"Find out how many of those stones Lou Fine was buying," she said.

"You know you can always depend on me," I told her. "Frankly." The agent slammed the door and climbed into the front. They shot out onto Seventh Avenue and disappeared downtown.

It was only a few blocks to the office. I walked down Grove and crossed Bleecker Street while I sorted through the perplexities of the moment, such as why an assistant deputy director of National Intelligence was so stoked about fake diamonds.

Somebody passes off a fake and pockets a few million—that's not a road map to world-destroying power for the Chinese state. And a stone here and there is the best they could hope for, assuming they could make a passable fake on demand. Huge volumes can't suddenly appear on the market, because the trade knows to the carat what the output of the diamond mines is going to be. It's a predictable figure.

And another thing I was wondering—how many people had to be in on it? An auction house wants to see some fancy paperwork before they put a diamond on the block. So somebody with standing certified the Geneva white. The diamond would have been tested by machines designed to catch lab-grown diamonds. If Tabitha was right that a

Shanghai lab had actually grown a stone so good it couldn't be distinguished from a real diamond, then the stone had beaten the machines. If the lab had done it once, could they do it again? And why Lou?

I just didn't see Lou peddling a fake. He might grade a stone E when it was F, but everybody tried that. The ability to make it stick—to push a jewel up from one price category to another by the sheer force of your reputation—that's part of what made a dealer like Lou who he was. But a fake? Unless it was so good not even Lou had caught it.

In some ways this was just my normal day. Trying to figure out how much of what I was being told I could rely on, and picking zero as a fairly representative number. Best line of the day: I think we can safely forget about Lily. Ask the Russian gangster found with his throat cut in a diamond lab on Long Island how that had worked. Maybe I should ask the kid with the overbite what he thought. He was standing at the corner of Greenwich and Clarkson examining the fascinating architecture of the West Village. Please.

4

Our unit of the Treasury hid behind the dignified redbrick exterior of a row of old townhouses on Clarkson Street. There were shiny black doors with brass handles, black trim around the windowpanes, and big terra-cotta pots of geraniums on the front steps. It looked like a lot of other blocks in the West Village until you got inside, where a nest of spies, forensic accountants, phone techs, and hackers toiled away on the government's dime.

The door closed automatically behind me. Only when it locked did the second door, a heavy slab of glass, hiss open. I walked through and poked my head into the guards' room. "You guys still have a camera on the corner?"

"I can toggle one onto it," she said, swiveling her chair to a control panel and grasping the little joystick in her fingers. "You pick up a tail?"

"Maybe. Tall kid, toothy, big hair."

"And if he shows up?"

"Ping me."

"OK. Tommy's looking for you, by the way. Said for you to go right up."

"Sure," I said.

I went along the hall to the stairs, but instead of going up, I went down a flight to the basement. Tommy would just want to find out what Tabitha had said so he could sneer at it. At my office door I peered into the small glass panel until the iris scan turned green and beeped. Then I pressed my right thumb against the black pad. After another beep, the lock clicked and I went in.

I wedged the door open with a rubber shim and slid up the window. It looked onto an alley, and with the door open, a cool breeze blew through. The breeze was a little dank, but I liked that.

Here's something not many people know about New York. There are hardly any alleys. People think there are because they see them in cop shows on TV. But it's all the same alley. It's in Tribeca. Film crews book it a year in advance and then decorate it with fire escapes and dumpsters. The truth is that Manhattan was designed to be alley-free, because alleys would take up room that could otherwise be filled with paying tenants. I thought of my own alley as a secret luxury, and you'd be surprised what people leave out there.

"So what did she want?" Tommy said as he came in. See? He dropped his massive bulk into a leather club chair. It was one of a pair.

"She wanted to make sure I knew that Mei is plotting world domination of the lab-grown diamond business by China," I said, unlocking my secure in-tray and pulling out a sheaf of papers. "Could be nefarious."

Tommy parked his size-thirteen loafers on a corner of the desk. "So," he said, "that guy who got topped this morning. Friend of yours, right?"

"You saw that Tabitha had pulled my file, and had a look yourself, is that it?"

"Not just me, bubba. Your dark past is making the rounds today. The murder of your old comrade in crime, plus the involvement of Lily in that lab-grown thing." He laced his sausage-thick fingers behind his head. "That's a lot of coincidence."

He was wearing one of his collection of vintage bowling shirts from the 1950s—in Tommy's view, the golden age of American couture. This one was peacock blue with navy piping. The blue glowed against Tommy's black skin. The name "Stan" was stitched in a flowing script on the front pocket.

"And what conclusion has your penetrating mind drawn from this coincidence?"

"Aw, now I've hurt your feelings," Tommy said, settling more deeply into the club chair. It creaked loudly. He was carrying a lot more weight than when he'd been a 195-pound New York Jet and the fastest line-backer in the NFL. A blown knee had ended that career, and Tommy went to law school, unerringly picking a profession where he could do even more damage than he had on the field. As a government lawyer, he'd helped our secret agency out of some difficulties, and now he ran the place.

"Listen," he said, "this thing with the murder and the lab-grown and that Geneva diamond, it's got some very important people stirred up in Washington. The secretary was asked to second you to the DNI."

Tommy meant the secretary of the Treasury, our boss. "DNI" was the director of National Intelligence. So whatever was worrying people was worrying them at the cabinet level.

Tommy seemed to notice the chair for the first time, frowned, and rubbed his hands along the armrests. "When did you get these? I don't remember seeing a requisition." He sniffed the leather suspiciously. "Jesus," he said, clambering to his feet. "Did you get these from the alley?"

"So what you're saying," I said, "is that now I work for Tabitha."

He glared at the chair, paced to the window, and stared out. "Consult as needed," he said. "Best I could do." He grabbed one of the steel window bars and gave it an experimental yank. "What I'm wondering is, why didn't she just phone you? Why the in-person meeting?"

"Tabitha? She comes to New York for the escarole. Via Carota has the best in North America. I thought you knew that."

Tommy wouldn't know a piece of escarole if it came running at him with the ball. He shoved his hands in his pockets and rocked back on his heels. He turned his attention from the alley to the ceiling pipes.

"My guess, they are worried the Chinese have figured out how to make perfect fake diamonds, and formed some understanding of the threat."

I shuffled some papers around on my desk.

"She wanted to see if you agreed," he added. When I still didn't respond, Tommy stopped studying the pipes and looked at me. "*Did* you agree?"

"No."

He leaned back to give the pipes another once-over. The ratchet inside his head went *click-click-click* as he parsed my answer. It didn't take him long to find the hole.

"Did she *ask* if you agreed?"

"No."

He raised his eyebrows at the pipes. They emitted a *clank*, as if to tell Tommy they knew how he felt. "You're just evasive by default, aren't you, Alex. It's probably something to do with your crummy childhood."

"Nothing is hidden from you, Dr. Freud," I said. "I found out this morning about Lily and Mei expanding their diamond business into lab-grown, and five minutes later that Lou Fine and his wife had been murdered in their home. A few hours after that, Tabitha told me about the Geneva white. Naturally, a detailed theory tying these events into a unified conspiracy immediately snapped into place in my mind."

That seemed to satisfy him. He just wanted to make sure Tabitha didn't know more than he did. But something else was on his mind, too. He grabbed a window bar again and tugged it, as if to make sure that it hadn't loosened in the last few minutes. He craned his head and looked along the alley.

"I don't like that you picked up a tail," he said. Obviously the guard had logged it, and a notice would have automatically appeared on Tommy's computer.

"I don't like it either."

"Could it be one of Tabitha's people?"

"I wondered about that, but I don't think so. She can find out what I'm doing just by logging in and checking the file."

"I agree. I'm going to get somebody from the pool to shadow you."

The pool was a roster of staff available for emergencies. We were a small unit, but a lot of the office people had field experience. They could pitch in when needed, usually to stake out a location or tail a target.

"I'll let you know when I leave."

He nodded and headed for the door but stopped and looked at me.

"It's too fast, Alex. This just started, and right away you pick up a burr."

"I know."

He looked like he wanted to say something more but in the end just nodded and walked off down the hall.

5

I practiced rearranging the stack of papers to see if I could make them look more completed than they were, failed, and picked one from the pile. It was a standard Treasury form, a confidential report known as a 16-B. This one was on Lily. I was supposed to analyze the meticulous data trail that described how she'd bought her $150 million penthouse, including where the money came from, and make a recommendation called an "interdiction plan." In other words, how to remedy any possible criminal activity and stop her from doing it again. The problem was we'd helped her with the criminal activity. It became part of her job when I turned her into a double agent, informing on her Russian oligarch diamond bosses. She had to be engaging in that criminal activity in order to report on it. So instead of scribbling "seize assets and deport," which was what I felt like doing at the moment, I wrote "pending" and stuck it in the outbox just as a metallic rattle sounded from the hall and Frankie from filing wheeled her trolley in the door.

"Please tell me you didn't bring more 16-Bs," I said.

"They opened one on that murder this morning." She pulled it off her trolley and put it on the desk, then stroked the leather on one of the club chairs. "These cleaned up great."

She'd helped me bring them in. She went over to the window and pulled a pack of Kools from her jeans. She leaned her hip on the sill, lit up, and inhaled deeply. With a long sigh, she blew the smoke out through the iron bars.

"It's blank," I said, leafing through the latest form. "He was shot just after six this morning. I don't see what I'm supposed to recommend."

"Don't recommend anything," she said, taking another drag and exhaling into the alley. "Mark it for attention of the deputy secretary for security. I'll flag it urgent and send it by secure courier. He won't know what it's about, but he can't admit that. He'll hand it off to somebody else. You won't see it again for months."

"Have you thought of running for president?"

"I'd have to quit smoking."

Like me, Frankie had worked for the CIA before transferring to our unit. I didn't know what she did there, but I doubted it was filing. She had capable-looking hands. Her employment record was sealed. I'd tried to look.

We'd become friendly because I let her smoke in my office. That was another bonus of the alley. Superior ventilation, plus Frankie. Running the archive, she knew everything that was going on. She tugged a folded paper from her pocket and spread it open on my desk.

"Just so you're up to speed," she said.

I leaned forward to examine it. It was a printout from MAUREEN. MAUREEN stood for Machine-Learning Algorithmic Unrestricted Engine. Pronouns: she/her.

Like all large language model computers, MAUREEN had been "trained" by programmers who'd fed her vast amounts of data. In this case the data was about financial crime, including crimes involving gold and diamonds, and countless case studies of successful crimes already committed, with the names of the criminals, their backgrounds, and psychological assessments.

MAUREEN resided on an IBM Sierra supercomputer at Fort Meade. The Sierra operated at ninety-four petaflops, and a single petaflop was one thousand million million operations per second. MAUREEN's product went into a digital folder, where it was supposed to stay until Tommy authorized its use. Until then only Tommy had access to it. And of course Frankie. Because Frankie ran the archive, and that's where the folder lived.

I looked at the page. It was MAUREEN's analysis of the sale of the Geneva white. MAUREEN had picked up the shipment from Shanghai, mapped the diamond's path through the hands of half a dozen shell companies, and finally to Lou. She agreed with Tabitha that the stone was almost certainly a fake. Or more likely, Tabitha had agreed with MAUREEN. So that was interesting. First Tabitha tells me about it, then Tommy. In another world, this coincidence might signal inter-departmental cooperation between a high-ranking officer working for the director of National Intelligence and an equally high-ranking officer in a secret branch of the Treasury. But I didn't live in that world. I lived in the one where Tabitha and Tommy would rather cut out each other's beating hearts and fry them up with onions than cooperate with each other.

"This is undated," I said. "When was the search?"

"Today. Tommy put it through a couple of hours ago."

"That's weird. Tabitha at the DNI already has this information."

"It was the DNI who requested the search," she said.

"I thought only Tommy had the say-so over what MAUREEN went after."

"So did Tommy." Frankie flicked her spent cigarette through the bars. "And then somebody reminded him who ran the government of the United States."

"You're saying the West Wing ordered the search?"

"They ordered Tommy to order it."

I tossed the last 16-B onto the trolley. I closed and locked the window and opened the drawer where I kept my gun. Then I decided against it. I was going to the diamond district. An alarm would go off every time I went through a door. I shut the drawer, got up, and grabbed my jacket. I pulled the rubber shim from the door and tossed it on a chair and followed Frankie into the hall. The steel door swung shut, triggering the dead bolt. It shot home with a heavy *thunk*.

"Take a look at this," said the guard. She tapped one of the monitors. "Don't know if this is the guy."

Wide angle of the corner of Clarkson Street and Greenwich Avenue. Basically, right outside. A figure walked into the frame. She toggled in for a tight shot.

"Some clampers, eh?"

The kid had an overbite like a snowplow. He looked like he was trying to eat his chin. He stood there for maybe ten seconds, then walked out of the shot.

"When was this?" I said.

"Soon as you got here. I didn't ping 'cause he left right away."

"Grab a still anyway and send it for ID."

I doubted we'd get a match. Fake teeth.

"You're supposed to wait for a pool agent," the guard said when I headed for the door.

"It'll be fine."

I walked up to Seventh Avenue, crossed the street, waited in Sheridan Square, ducked into a street and came back out—couldn't flush a tail. I walked out to Sixth. When I reached the West Fourth Street station, I tucked myself into the spectators watching the action on the basketball court. I had a good view of the way I'd come. My phone buzzed. Tommy.

"I told you I was getting somebody from the pool."

"Doesn't seem to be anybody on my tail now."

"Are you carrying?"

"Will you relax? If the guy wanted to shoot me, he could have tried when I was sitting in the park having lunch."

"The pool agent is drawing a weapon. Where are you now?"

"I'm going up to Forty-Seventh. I'll give you a shout."

I went downstairs and waited for the uptown B train. Only a few people got on. Overbite wasn't one of them. Five minutes later the train clattered into the station at Rockefeller Center. I took the stairs at the south end of the platform. That brought me up at Sixth Avenue and Forty-Seventh, and into the diamond quarter.

6

Every year, tens of millions of carats of polished diamonds wash through the single block of Forty-Seventh Street between Fifth Avenue and Sixth. Windows shimmer with the light. Barkers for competing dealers hustle tourists. Hasidim in long coats and tall black hats hurry by. Traders scream counteroffers into their phones as they rush to the next appointment.

Ari Bar-Lev was on the second floor of a building beside the Diamond Dealers Club. He traded polished diamonds and ran the Bar Line, a daily tip sheet on polished prices. The prices tended to be high. That was the idea. The whole point of the price list was to give traders something to wave under a customer's nose to show how much of a discount they were offering. Maybe the prices were skewed even higher for sizes and cuts Ari happened to have on hand himself. On the diamond street, they expected that. Business was business. Ari performed a service. Who wasn't there to make money?

Ari had a bony face and thick black hair. His brown eyes glittered under bushy eyebrows. He wore a black yarmulke and a starched white shirt open at the neck. A man wearing a tall, round, fur hat called a shtreimel sat across the desk from him. Ari beckoned me in.

A small parcel of diamonds lay open on the pad of white paper in front of Ari's customer. Ari tweezered a stone that the man had been examining and dropped it on the scale. The digital display gave the weight as 1.26 carats. Ari plucked up the stone and placed it in front of the customer, penciled a revised weight on the outside of the parcel, and put it to one side.

"It's until four o'clock," he said in a voice like poured gravel. He pointed at the diamond with his tweezers. "Bring back the diamond or bring back the $3,200."

"It's a matzo, Ari," the man said, using the term for a stone cut to make it look bigger than it was. "It's an L color. Maybe I have to accept lower."

"Accept what you want," Ari said. "Then bring me the $3,200."

The man sighed and gazed at the stone for a moment, then picked it up, folded it into a paper of his own, and left. A young man came in and left a tray on Ari's desk. Beside the tiny cups was a small bronze pitcher with a straight wooden handle fixed to the side. There were plates of soft, white cheese and fresh figs. Ari filled the cups with tar-thick Turkish coffee and put one in front of me. He took a knife, loaded cheese onto a fig, and took a bite. He washed it down with coffee and refilled his cup. He pointed the knife at the cheese.

"Have some bulgarit," he rumbled. "It's fresh."

It would be. Ari went home to Tel Aviv every weekend, getting there before sundown Friday and spending the Sabbath with his family. He would pick up the cheese before coming back on Sunday night with the hundreds of other Israeli diamond traders who plied their business on Forty-Seventh Street but kept their hearts in Tel Aviv.

"Lou Fine," he said, swiping a fig into the cheese and looking out the window while he chewed. He took another sip of coffee and wiped his lips with a napkin.

"You knew him well," I said.

"So did you."

"A long time ago."

"Bah," he said, waving his hand dismissively. "Long, not long—who cares? You knew the man. You sold him those beach diamonds. You think I didn't know? Those diamonds helped put Lou in business." He got up from his chair, walked over to the window, and stared down onto the busy street.

My phone pinged. It was a message from Tommy. The NSA had run the still from our street cam. No ID, but the software confirmed the overbite was fake.

"This I will say about Louis Fine," Ari rumbled. "He understood a diamond." He placed his palm against the window for a moment, like someone saying good-bye through a pane of glass. "He was a *sawyer* when I first met him. Before we had lasers. When we still used diamond saws. People brought him the difficult stones. Where there was a risk. Nothing scared him. He could saw this close to a flaw," Ari said, turning to me with a sad smile, his thumb and forefinger a hair's-breadth apart. The smile faded back into the stern face. He turned back to the window and stared grimly at the street. He jerked his chin at the teeming scene. "Today a machine says how to cut a stone."

"He wasn't on the saw for long," I said, joining him at the window. And there he was. Fake overbite. Two doors down across the street. On the phone, his eyes on Ari's building.

"The first big stones he cut," Ari said, "and I mean, not just sawed but cut and polished"—he made a shaping motion with his hand—"were for old Fischl." His face softened at the memory. "I remember one. Fischl is coming to Lou's bench in that little factory he had, and saying, 'Louis, here is a nice big twenty-carat rough. I want a ten-carat square cut, and the angles better be good.'"

Ari turned from the window with an evil grin. "You see, it was a bad stone. It had a nasty little flaw. And Fischl wants a fifty percent yield? Bah. He will take what he can get, blame Lou for not achieving fifty, and refuse to pay!" His eyes twinkled as he peered at me through his eyebrows. "Two months go by. No stone. Fischl is getting nervous. He bought the stone on memo." *Memo* meant on credit. "The man who gave the memo, he is asking for his money. After three months and nothing from Lou, Fischl is afraid. 'Louis,'" Ari croaked in a frail voice, imitating Dov Fischl, who had to have been ninety at the time, "'Louis, where is my stone?' Lou hands him the parcel." Ari put his hand on my arm. "Alex, a twelve-carat emerald cut! *Twelve* carats!" He rapped a knuckle on the wall. "Twenty percent more polished than Fischl even asked for." He cut the flat of his hand through the air like the blade of a knife. "What else? It's Lou Fine."

Suddenly fake overbite looked up and stared straight at me. He still had the phone to his ear. He said something, put the phone in his pocket, and walked away in the direction of Sixth Avenue.

Ari sat down at his desk. His assistant peered anxiously into the room, a trader in a tall hat glaring over his shoulder. Ari glanced at his watch. I sat down so he'd know I wasn't going to take the hint. And just in case:

"Tell him to shut the door, Ari."

He shot me a furious glance, and the rage boiled up before he could stop it.

"You think I don't know why you're here?" he growled in a low voice, his knuckles white as he leaned forward and placed his fists on the desk. "You are like vultures on a corpse! You want to feast on the remains of a good and honorable man!"

"The door, Ari."

His eyes burned with emotion, but he gestured to his assistant.

When the door was closed, I said, "Pull yourself together. He wasn't Mother Teresa and neither are you. I have my reasons for needing to know what was going on with Lou, and from your reaction, you can tell me. So unless you want this place crawling with Treasury auditors, start talking."

He rubbed his face with his hands and drew a deep breath. He spread his hands on the large pad of white paper that all diamond traders kept on their desks. He picked up a loupe and tapped it on the pad, then placed it to the side.

"He should not have bought that house. Is he Rockefeller?" He moved the loupe again. "The stock market was bad at the time. Those people—the Wall Street people—they were important customers of his. Suddenly they are not buying. You could see the change in Lou. He starts taking chances. He buys stones nobody else will touch. One of them was a monster he had on memo from Van Kees."

"Van Kees?" I stared at Ari. Van Kees Consolidated Mines had invented the modern diamond business, forming a cartel that had sucked up most of the world's rough for a century, and made the Van Kees family billionaires. They never gave credit.

"A 1,200-carat yellow," Ari said. "Everybody warned him about that stone. Van Kees had been trying to sell it for years. A fault plane through the middle. But he is Lou Fine!" He flung out a hand. "He will master the stone, it will not master him." Ari stared at the window in despair. "It blew up on the wheel."

"The heat," I said.

"Of course the heat. The heat from the wheel penetrates the crystal. The stone is too fragile to withstand the forces of expansion."

"How much did he lose?"

"I heard the memo price was $5 million. But there were other stones, Alex. The street is always full of rumors." He examined his hands. "Some will be true."

For an hour we sorted through those rumors. The diamond trade is like the system that allows the trees of a forest to communicate through a fungal web that connects their roots so that information collected at one place in the forest spreads to every tree. Collectively, the forest knows what's happening everywhere. The forest knew about the nightmare yellow and it knew about the memo. And I shouldn't have been surprised to learn what else the forest knew. It knew about the Geneva white.

7

Outside, I searched for overbite in the crowded street. Gone. I called Tommy.

"The diamond street knows about the Geneva fake," I said when he picked up. "Not everything, but enough to be suspicious."

"How do they know?"

"Somebody at the auction house thought it stank. It leaked from there."

"So who bought it?"

"A numbered company bought it on a phone bid. Maybe get MAUREEN on it. See if she can find who owns the company."

Then I spotted overbite's replacement. She looked about twenty. Good imitation of a tourist—shorts and running shoes, backpack, camera slung around her neck.

She wore a Yankees cap and those Kestrel sunglasses with enough room in the frame for a pinhole camera and a built-in mike. Wide-angle lens, so although she wasn't looking right at me, I was in the picture.

"Tommy, I picked up another tail."

"Goddamn it. Why the hell couldn't you have waited? Where are you?"

"Forty-Seventh."

"OK. That's not good. Street's too busy. Go to the plaza at Rockefeller Center. I'll call operations on the other line and get the pool agent up there. Go now. Stay on the line."

I gave him a description of the girl, headed down to Sixth and turned right, walked north a block and turned right again.

"Location?" said Tommy.

"Rock Center. Just coming up to the plaza."

"OK. Agent on the way. Stay on the line."

I got a coffee at a stand and found a bench where there weren't too many people. I was trying to look like a guy scrolling through his phone when I saw fake overbite again. Coming into the plaza on the far side. He checked his phone, then looked around again. The wind is always gusting around in there, and when his shirt rippled I spotted the gun. Then he saw me.

"There's two," I said to Tommy. "The other is back. They're bracketing me. The girl's feeding a visual of me to her partner. They came heavy. One has a pistol in a shoulder rig. The other one has a backpack, so I don't know what she's got. Rock Center is packed. I'm leaving the plaza now. I'll go down to the lower level and see if I can shake them, then come out on Fifth."

I heard him relay the information. I could just hear the crackle of the voice on the other line. Then Tommy came back on.

"Are you carrying?"

"No."

"OK, I'll pass it on. Stay on the line." And a moment later, "Standby pool agent is still a few blocks away. Operations says head north on Fifth."

I ran down the stairs to the sunken part of the plaza, where they have the roller-skating rink. I dashed into the lower-level mall. As soon as I was inside, I cut around toward Fifth, walked quickly down a hall and into Banana Republic. I stood behind a rack of dresses close to the door. I could jump anybody who came in before they'd see me. I gave it a minute, then went up the stairs to the street level and stepped out onto Fifth. Yankees cap was twenty yards away, looking in the wrong direction.

I wedged myself into the middle of a group of Chinese tourists heading north. The guide had a pole with a red disc on top and was keeping up a patter. We stopped at the corner of Fiftieth Street. The guide turned around to say something and saw me.

"Private tour."

"Yes," I said. He stared at me for a moment, then the light changed and he turned and led the way across to St. Patrick's Cathedral. I stayed in the middle of the group. Just before we entered the church, I shot a quick look over my shoulder. Yankees cap had me in the crosshairs. I looked for overbite but couldn't see him, and I ducked inside.

"I'm in St. Pat's. They know I'm here."

"OK," said Tommy. There weren't many benefits to having Tommy as a boss, but that was one right there. He did not get rattled. I heard him muttering into the other line.

The Chinese tourists followed the red disc into the right-hand aisle. I went left. Shrines and altars lined the aisle, each set into its own recess. The devout lit candles or knelt to pray while camera flashes flickered through the church.

I went up the crowded aisle, picking my way through clumps of people gathered at the candle racks. When I reached the main altar, a priest and two altar boys emerged for the start of a service. He genuflected, then faced the church and made a sign of the cross. The first two or three pews had filled with worshipers, who crossed themselves and bowed their heads. From the cover of people still filing into the front rows, I scanned the church.

People drifted through the dim interior. I searched for the two, couldn't see either of them, so I slipped out the side door onto Fifty-First Street. Yankees cap had been on Fifth, so I headed the other way.

"I'm going north on Madison," I said to Tommy.

"We looped in DeLucca."

"OK. There's always cops at Trump Tower. Give DeLucca the description of the tails. They might still be on Fifth."

I heard Tommy's other line crackle again.

"Alex, pool agent says can you get to Central Park?"

"I can try." The sidewalk was jammed. I dashed into the inside traffic lane and started running. Horns blared and drivers shouted at me as they brushed by inches away. I had almost reached Fifty-Seventh when I checked behind me. Yankees cap was two blocks back. She was in the street too, running. She had the backpack in one hand and was opening it as she ran.

I dashed across Fifty-Seventh against the light. A taxi screeched to a halt sideways in a skid across two lanes, and a semi coming west fast enough to run the yellow blew by with a blast of air horn. I ran up to Fifty-Eighth. When I checked behind me, I couldn't see Yankees cap, so I cut over toward Fifth Avenue. I wanted to make it into Grand Army Plaza. There'd be fewer people there than on the street, and from the plaza I could get into the park. The light had just changed against me at Fifth, but I sprinted across and made it into the plaza.

I started walking north toward the park when overbite stepped out from behind the Sherman statue with a big Glock held down along his leg. Somebody screamed. I turned and ran. I was going to head down Fifty-Eighth behind the Plaza Hotel, but the street filled with a horde of kids being shepherded across. In the other direction, Fifth Avenue was a wall of tourists. I dashed across the street and into the side entrance of

Bergdorf's. An arrow with an escalator symbol pointed to the right, and I ran in that direction.

I came into a hall filled with mannequins in summer dresses. Some of them held lacy parasols. I grabbed one and looked back the way I'd come. Where was he?

"I'm in Bergdorf's," I said to Tommy.

"Alex. Bergdorf's? Are you crazy?"

"There were kids in the plaza. I'm just trying to find somewhere with no people."

"Hang on," he said. Then: "Pool agent was coming up Fifty-Eighth and saw you go in. Can you wait?"

I heard a commotion from the direction of the door and caught sight of overbite's reflection in a mirror. He hadn't seen me yet. I ducked through a door marked POWDER ROOM.

8

Two young women were sitting on a sofa, talking across a stack of
Bergdorf bags. They turned to me, their lips opening into a pair
of perfect, bright-red Os. I flattened myself against the wall inside
the door and tightened my grip on the parasol. "Please be quiet," I said.
"There's a guy with a gun. I'm a federal officer."

One of them reached across and took her friend's hand. They didn't
look scared, just stunned. Then their heads swiveled in unison as the
door eased open and overbite stuck his head in for a look.

I grabbed his hair, yanked him in and jabbed the parasol in his ear.
He screamed and stumbled forward. The Glock clattered onto the par-
quet. I hauled his head up by the hair and punched him in the throat.
He collapsed to the floor, gasping and choking. I stamped on his head.
The false teeth skittered across the room, and he lay still. I grabbed the
Glock. The bright-red Os were staring at the teeth.

I poked my head around the door and surveyed the room. The display
of parasols blocked the view through to the next hall. I stepped out cau-
tiously and made my way to the escalator, pulling out my phone.

"I put the guy out," I said.

"Got it. Pool agent is in the building. Go to the third floor."

"I don't see the woman."

"She's in the building somewhere," Tommy said.

"How do you know?"

"She's still trying to talk to the guy you took out. DeLucca has a chopper up. They cracked the audio."

"She doesn't know he's down?"

"No. She's still talking."

"Tommy, did he tell her where he was?"

"Said he was checking the powder room."

"Shit. There are civilians in there."

I'd just started up the escalator, and turned to run back down, when Tommy shouted, "She's got you," at exactly the moment I heard cries from across the room. She was coming through the shoppers in a fast walk, an Uzi held out straight in front of her. The wall beside me exploded in a cloud of plaster. I couldn't shoot back. There were too many people. I turned and started to run up. A bullet struck the moving handgrip, peppering me with slivers of plastic. The Glock spun out of my hand and clattered down the metal steps. I'd just reached the second floor when she got to the bottom of the escalator. She fired a burst as I staggered off the steps and into a display cabinet. A woman standing at a mirror in a full-length gown gaped, her face frozen at the sound of the Uzi and the screams from below.

"Get on the floor!" I shouted as I scrambled up and ran for the next escalator.

I galloped up to the third floor, throwing myself forward at the top. As I rolled away from the moving steps, a woman's voice said calmly, "Stay down, honey." I wrenched around to see Frankie from filing rip a pink blanket from a stroller and haul out a Heckler & Koch MP3 submachine gun. She dropped to one knee and swung up the barrel, and when Yankees cap's head rose into view coming up the escalator, she pretty much just chewed it off.

I got up and went over to the body. Each arriving escalator step pushed her further into a crumpled mess. I hit the red STOP button. The blood from her severed arteries formed a sticky pool on the marble floor. I went through her backpack before the cops arrived.

"Two spare mags," I said to Frankie. "Nothing else."

"We'll ID her," she said. "She'll be in the system somewhere."

We sat down beside a rack of floor-length gowns. She lit up a Kool and offered me one. We were smoking quietly when I heard the cops arriving on the floor below. A radio crackled, then the heavy metallic stamp of someone coming up the stopped escalator. DeLucca's head appeared. He looked at me with his sad eyes, then studied the body blocking his way.

"I'll go around," he said, and clomped back down.

We didn't stay long. Tommy arrived and huddled with a deputy chief. They worked out a story for the press—internal feud in the Russian mob.

"Who knows," DeLucca said. "Could even be true."

Frankie and I took the stairs to the ground floor and went out by the side entrance onto Fifty-Eighth. The plaza was crowded with people watching the crime scene techs troop into the store and the NYPD chopper hovering overhead.

We crossed the street and made our way through the crowd. There's a fountain there and a bronze figure of Pomona, the Roman goddess of plenty. She cradles a basket of fruit against her naked body and stares morosely at the passing shopping bags, as if she'd rather be in Bergdorf's herself, getting something nice to wear, instead of standing out here with the tourists.

Frankie lit another Kool and waved the pack at me. I took one. I was getting used to them. We smoked for a while.

"So I guess you weren't always in filing," I said.

She took a long drag, blew it out, and slid her eyes at me. She let the silence sit there long enough to show she wasn't going to go there. "Some other time," she said, stubbing out her cigarette on the step.

She got up and shoved her hands in the pockets of her jeans. "Listen," she said. "We've both been around the block. In this business we might even pass for friends. So let's be straight. Something stinks. This was too crazy." She tilted her head at the yellow ribbon around the store. "When did you ever see a hit like that? Take out a United States government agent in the middle of New York City, and fuck the civilians? I don't even know who does that."

The crowd stirred as the coroner's van pulled up, and they brought Yankees cap out in a bag. Onlookers crowded the tape with their phones held up. Body bag in NYC! Straight onto TikTok.

"Where I am now," Frankie said, "in the archives, I see the traffic. Your file's been going around a lot in Washington."

"Yes."

"How did those two ID you? They got your picture somewhere, honey. It's not like we post it on the website."

I watched her push her way through the crowd and walk off down the street until she disappeared.

9

The night air poured out of Central Park onto the steps of the Metropolitan Museum. Rappers, bankers, and millionaire athletes milled around enjoying the smell of trees. Across the street, on the other side of Fifth Avenue, people who couldn't afford $300,000 for a table at the Met Gala crowded behind the steel barricades and the phalanx of cops. I was watching from the NYPD command trailer around the corner on Eighty-First, a cave of dim green light filled with the smell of too many alpha males.

DeLucca was on the phone talking to the commissioner. You didn't have to wonder why. Lou and Coco dead. Dog walker dead. Attack on Treasury agent. Shoot-up at Bergdorf's. Assassin dead. Met Gala. What mineral links all these? Exactly. Nightmare scenario—A-listers topped in front of the Met on live TV by snipers taking another crack at Alex. Hence the amassed forces of the NYPD. Hence the commissioner.

"Who's the pipsqueak with Tommy Cleary?" said McCormick, studying a monitor.

"Minnie Ho," I said.

"The fashion designer?"

"Uh-huh."

McCormick nodded. "And the knockout chick with the body by God?"

"Also a designer," I said. "Works for Ho."

"That is one hot girl."

"Also my daughter."

McCormick nodded again. He unbuttoned his jacket, then buttoned it again. He smoothed the nonexistent creases from the front. Really, what could he say?

Annie was looking around with her lips pressed tight. Still mad. I'd agreed to pick her up, and although I'd called and explained, it hadn't made things better. Annie hated what I did. She'd grown up with a dad who disappeared for long periods and came back with scars on his face.

I left the trailer and made my way through the crowd and joined Annie on the steps. She did her best not to glare at me, and even gave my arm a squeeze. We watched the latest limo spill a banker and his wife onto the red carpet.

"Ouch," Annie said. "Gucci from head to toe. For that kind of money I could have made her something nice."

"She probably didn't want a dress made out of recycled egg cartons," I said.

Annie was into zero-carbon-footprint clothing. She could reel off the statistics of the fashion industry's part in poisoning the world. Minnie Ho had let her launch a small line of her own made entirely from recycled material. You'd never guess where it had come from. I had a T-shirt made from discarded pineapples, and so far no one had tried to stir me into a piña colada.

She was wearing what I'd learned to describe as an off-the-shoulder jacquard gown in a metallic floral print. "It's the same process as weaving lamé," she explained when I told her it looked great. "Only difference—the metal filament is created from previously used sources. Basically"—she plucked out a fold and let it shimmer back into place—"old tin cans."

Then a light from a panning camera swept across my face. She leaned forward to examine my chin, stepped back and tilted her head. "I just find it sad. You told me you were getting out of that kind of life, where things like this happen to you."

I was spared having to reply when the next limo arrived. Lily erupted from the car in a firestorm of light. The T-shirt blew like a Roman candle, spewing photons into the night. Her long, flared skirt was sewn with diamonds, too, and a diamond choker blazed at her throat. She headed up the crimson carpet.

"Isn't that T-shirt great?" said Annie, completely distracted by the spectacle of Lily parading up the steps in a swirl of light. "I designed a new kind of basket stitch for the diamonds." She pressed her hands together with delight. "It really works." She rushed off with a metallic swoosh and seized Lily by the arm. I moved away. Mei had arrived in the same car as Lily. An Asian bodyguard the size of a sumo wrestler hulked behind her. Mei hung back while reporters thrust their mikes at Lily.

"Liliana Petrovna Ostrokhova," Tommy intoned behind me. "I think it's time I took a look through that file."

"Why not," I said. "It's sitting in your in-tray."

Tommy stepped down beside me and shoved his hands in his pockets. "I'm going to have to have a word with your spy in filing."

We watched as photographers and TV cameramen clamored for Lily to flash the shirt. She threw her arms wide and fired off another fusillade of light. "I asked DeLucca to put a car on the Santa Clara," I said to Tommy, "and a guy with a long lens taking head shots of everybody going in or out."

"You're just doing that to piss her off."

"That's right. And the Chinese will expect it. We want them to think our suspicions are focused on Lily, at least partly."

"And they'll be right. Where are we with the shooters?"

"The Bergdorf goofs were Bulgarian contractors. Fake teeth spilled the beans downtown."

"That was fast."

Tommy nodded. "He lacked benefit of counsel." He frowned at the cops on the roof, then looked at me.

"If I may be permitted a moment of candor, you look like shit."

"First Annie, now you."

"It's hard when nobody loves you," he said, looking around. "Have you seen Mei?"

"She arrived with Lily."

From the crowd across the street somebody shouted "Killer!"—Tommy's nickname from his days as a Jet. Tommy gave him a thumbs-up. "See if you can corner Mei. Threaten the shit out of her. Maybe you'll find something out."

"Is that your investigative plan?"

Tommy turned his body slowly to face me. His eyes flashed with the intensity of his feeling. For just that moment we were alone—the crowd and the flashbulbs a distant background.

"I'm mad, OK? Somebody sent hoods into my town to kill my friend, and now they have to find out that I will break their fucking bones. That's my investigative plan."

"C'mere, you," cried Annie, surging over and grabbing Tommy by the arm. He kept his eyes on mine for another second, then let her pull him away. I watched them go up the carpet into the museum, arm in arm. She didn't call him Uncle Tommy anymore, but Annie had adored him since childhood, when he would hold his arm straight out and let her swing from it. The people I loved most in the world were all here. I turned away with a leaden heart.

10

didn't have to look hard for Mei. She was ten feet away. Waiting for me, I think. She came over as soon as Tommy left. Her purse was open, and a tawny head with enormous ears poked out of it.

"Hello, Brutus," I said.

"Meow," said Brutus, Mei's Singapura cat.

"Hello, pumpkin," Mei said. She was dressed, as always, head to toe in blue. Steel-blue evening dress. Ditto Jimmy Choo shoes. Sapphire bracelet. Lapis lazuli clips holding her thick black hair back from her face. Even the frames of her glasses were blue.

"Have you bought a lab in Shanghai?" I said.

"Why don't you come and work for me instead of spying on me?" Mei replied. "We could use people with your skill set."

"I know you could. Didn't you just lose a couple?"

It was a stab, but it made sense. If Mei owned the lab that made the Geneva stone, and wanted to grow more, she would have to conceal what the lab could do. If I was a threat to that, trust me, she had numbers she could call. For now she just stared at me and said: "I don't understand."

"I think you do."

"Meow," said Brutus sadly. Cats always see the dark side. If they didn't, there wouldn't be any cats.

Mei regarded me placidly. Nothing unsettled her. She searched my face, ticking off the cuts. We had no illusions about each other. Mei knew who I was and what I did. It didn't frighten her. Her friends were the people who sent nuclear submarines to cruise the American coast.

A stir from the street caught her attention. She swiveled her head to watch the large blonde shape of Teddy Van Kees squeeze from a limo. He wore an old-fashioned tux, with a white bow tie instead of black. He had short blond hair and yellow eyes and a face like old leather. On his arm was his daughter, Edwina, a tangle of bones known, inevitably, as Little Teddy.

"Mei!" Teddy thundered. "So lovely of you to invite us. And Alex." He gave me his hard, square hand and squinted at my face. "Not looking so well."

"Who are you here to harass tonight?" said Little Teddy.

"I thought I'd run you downtown and hang you upside down in the cells, Edwina, until you tell me what you know about Lou Fine." They stared at me.

"Lou?" said Teddy.

"You know," I said. "Long-time customer? Murdered in his home this morning? The Lou who tried to bail himself out of debt with that 1,200-carat clunker you let him have on memo? Him."

"I know who bloody Lou is," Teddy snapped, his voice rising before he hauled it back under control behind a row of yellow teeth. "I'm just wondering why you think we would know any more than you do about his death."

Little Teddy gave me a smoldering stare. She seemed about to say something, but Teddy put out his hand to stop her.

"We are devastated," he said. "What else would you expect?"

An attendant hurried over and whispered in Mei's ear.

"They're waiting for us," Mei said.

Teddy gave her his arm. His face was flushed. "Devastated," he repeated, glowering at my hands. They'd started to bleed again. Teddy turned his back and the three of them went up the carpet. I watched them go, the imperial family of diamonds and the woman who had just launched an enterprise that promised to boost the lab-grown diamond business into orbit. So that was one thing you'd think would be preying on Teddy's mind. Another was, his most famous customer was lying in a fridge downtown. Maybe not the time to party.

I went home through the park. The old wrought-iron lamps cast pools of light onto the twisting paths. The sweet smell of vegetation saturated the cool air. Runners fled like shadows along the bridle path. I walked up onto the track that circled the reservoir and leaned on the iron fence.

On Central Park West, the twin towers of the El Dorado rose against the sky. The surface of the reservoir was puddled with orange light. The floodlit fountain sent up a silver spray. To the south, clustered above the black tree line, the supertalls of midtown raised a palisade across Manhattan. If you knew where to look, you could just pick out the skyscrapers of another age—the gleaming, scalloped top of the Chrysler Building and the barest piece, only a sliver, of the Empire State Building. Every time I stood here, the old city seemed to have receded further into the past, taking with it the dreams that had formed it.

11

At 5:00 A.M. I sat on the edge of the bed, feeling like hell. I got up and went into the bathroom and stared in the mirror. No solution there. Same guy with a mop of dark hair and a bunch of scabs and hazel eyes that were looking for somebody to punch.

I went into the living room and opened the front window and climbed out onto the fire escape. It's nice in the morning. I thought about reciting my mantra. It had been a birthday present from Annie two years before. She'd bought me an introductory session in transcendental meditation during one of her attempts to let the sunshine of self-improvement into my dark spaces. She thought I needed to clean out the debris that had built up in my mind.

"Debris?" I said.

"Dad, you are an emotional dumpster."

I gave the mantra a shot right now. No dice, unless the aim of meditation is to replace the debris in your head with a longing for violence. But I didn't think that was the idea, so I ditched the mantra and went inside and tried a four-minute plank. You don't have time to be mad when your abs are on fire. Then I got up and wandered around the apartment.

Mostly I stood in the door to Annie's old room, feeling bleak instead of angry. Maybe that was progress.

The room had been decorated in what Annie called her "lemon-yellow phase." Strictly speaking, that was her only phase. Before that, the walls had been a pale rose selected by Pierrette, my ex. At the age of twelve Annie had awakened, as if from a long slumber, and screamed, "I hate pink!"

For Pierrette, calling a color she'd picked "pink" was a deadly insult. A series of skirmishes followed, punctuated by glacial silences (Pierrette) and stomping (Annie). When Annie won, we (Annie and I) spent a couple of weeks dabbing samples from the paint store onto her walls until she settled on the lemon yellow. "It's more me."

This was around the time when the fiction that the three of us were living together in my apartment as a family drew its last breaths. Pierrette hated the Upper West Side, and the block of West Ninety-Fourth Street between Columbus and Amsterdam was not going to change her mind. There were some nice old brownstones, some that were not so nice, and a few six-story prewar buildings where people owned their own apartments. There was a Mexican food cart at the corner of Columbus, a Greek bodega that sold its own olive oil, and a Trader Joe's a block away.

In spite of these attractions, the weekends Pierrette spent at her house in Tuxedo Park expanded from three days to four, then four days to five. Tuxedo Park was a private village with restricted access and no food carts. It was about one hour and $20 million north of West Ninety-Fourth Street. At the time, Annie was a boarder at St. Mary's convent school in Croton-on-Hudson, where girls learned how to smash each other up on the lacrosse field. Worth every penny. On the downside, Croton was a lot closer to Tuxedo Park than to Manhattan.

The longest stretch that Annie spent in the apartment post-Pierrette was when she attended design school. Once she started working for Minnie Ho, she moved to a leafy part of Brooklyn called Cobble Hill, with no food carts. So I was mad (Bulgarians) and bleak (Annie). The lemon-yellow room was not going to dispel either of those feelings. Neither was the living room, where the main decorative features were the pale rectangles that marked where prints by Andy Warhol and Robert Motherwell had hung before they were removed by (first) Pierrette and (after her brief return) Annie.

I put on a pot of coffee, changed into my running clothes, and went outside. The sky in the east was just showing a tint of red. I went into the park at Ninety-Third and picked up the bridle path and headed counterclockwise around the reservoir. By the time I got over to the East Side, the sky was tigered with orange stripes. I ran downhill through the tunnel of cherry blossoms in front of the Guggenheim. At Ninetieth Street I pushed myself into an uphill sprint, then settled to a steady pace, looped up to the North Wood, came back to the reservoir, and added one more lap. The food cart was open when I got back.

I sat on the fire escape and ate the breakfast burrito with extra jalapeños. The sun splashed a golden light down the street. Even the garbage truck looked nice, but I like a garbage truck anyway. They go up the street, the street looks better. Every time. You can't say that about much.

My phone buzzed. I reached inside and grabbed it from the sill. McCormick.

"You know Leopold Rose?" he said.

"Lou Fine's bean counter."

"Friend?"

"No. I met him once when I visited Lou at the store."

"He's giving us the runaround. Any chance you can meet us at the store?"

"Nobody's trying to kill me right now, so I can probably squeeze it in."

"Nine?"

"See you there.

12

The windows of Lou's store on Fifth Avenue were dark. Yellow police tape fluttered in a dirty wind. I gave the cop on the door my name. He radioed inside. A crackle came back through his handset and the door buzzed open.

The showroom looked forlorn. At the back of the room, a staircase wound up to the second floor. I didn't recognize the receptionist.

She bounced up from her desk as if on springs. She had a short plaid skirt on and legs like an acrobat. Her pale blonde hair rippled like a silk curtain when she moved her head. Her lips were a perfect cupid's bow.

"Welcome, Mr. Turner," she said. I heard the trace of a South African accent. She stuck out her hand. "Marie." She had a firm grip.

"Do you have a last name, Marie?"

She daggered a little smile at me and kept hold of my hand. "Hout. Marie Hout. I am the assistant to Mr. Rose."

"I thought Mr. Rose was the assistant."

She let my hand go and tilted her head. The silk curtain brushed her shoulder. "Now of course he is no longer the assistant. By legal instrument effected before death, Mr. Fine raised him to partner. Now, sole partner."

"Is there such a thing as a sole partner?"

She pressed her hands together and straightened her head and let her teeth glint for a second before she said, "May I bring you a coffee?"

"Black."

She disappeared down a hall. Lou had a full kitchen back there. She seemed to know her way around. I texted Tommy: "Run Marie Hout. All entry points, dates. Query South African. Query diamonds. Query name. Obtain photo from Lou Fine store surveillance."

They were waiting in Lou's office. DeLucca slouched by the window with his hands in his pockets. McCormick sat in a chair tilted back against the wall. At Lou's desk, with his arms folded, was Leopold. He wore a starched white shirt and a silver tie. He had a face like a hammered board. He wore his dark gray hair in a crew cut with the front waxed into place. He had pale brown eyes and—so Lou had said—the brain of a Kray computer.

"Leopold," I said.

"I don't know what this is all about," he said in an injured tone. "I've told the police everything I know. This store is not the scene of a crime."

"See, that's something I get to decide," McCormick said, "not you. We have one crime scene at the house. Maybe we have another one here."

"I don't know why they have to put yellow tape across the front and station a policeman on Fifth Avenue for everyone to see," Leopold said to me. "The most famous jeweler in the world." He touched the waxed hair and adjusted his tie one micron to the left. "It's an outrage."

"My condolences for your loss," I said.

He stared blankly at me for a moment before he realized I meant Lou. "Of course. Thank you. It's terrible. I had to send everyone home.

We're all shocked." He waved his hand around, as if anyone could see how shocked they were just by looking. But the desk was neat as a pin. Stacks of papers stood at attention on the polished teak, like troops drawn up for inspection. It was neater than it was the only time I'd dropped in. Then, the desk had been littered with sketches of diamond cuts and plexi models of some of Lou's most famous stones. The eyepopper, in a silver frame, had been an original cover from *Vanity Fair* with Gwyneth Paltrow dripping in diamonds, one arm around Lou's neck and the other clutching his curly hair. He was grinning like crazy. That was gone. In its place, in what looked like the same silver frame, was a photograph of Leopold receiving a plaque from the Diamond Dealers Club. The guy giving him the plaque didn't have Leopold by the hair. But then, Leopold had a crew cut.

"We're badly shaken," he said. He laid his hands flat on the desk. "It's my job to hold the business together and then restore it to what it was. That's what Lou would have wanted. He would have wanted his business to be all that it was."

"You mean, all that it was before it went down the tubes?"

Leopold's eyes darted around the desk. "I don't know where you heard that," he said.

"I heard it from the first guy I asked."

He pressed his palms flat on the desk again, as if to make sure it stayed where it was. Leopold was a shrewd operator. He'd put together complicated syndicates that spread the risk for Lou's most ambitious diamond buys. Nothing unnerved him. But he was unnerved now.

"There's always vicious gossip on the street," he said. "You know that, Alex. The assets of this firm are unshakable. We have the best retail position of any jewel merchant in New York City. Our stones are the finest anywhere."

"Well, maybe not that 1,200-carat time bomb you got on memo from Van Kees."

"What's 'on memo'?" McCormick said.

"They gave him credit."

McCormick let his chair bang forward from the wall. He placed his hands on his knees. His eyes took on a predatory gleam. "And the stone didn't turn out so good?"

"No," I said. "It turned out bad."

McCormick leaned forward. "See, now, that right there? That's the kind of information I was looking for when I asked if there were any circumstances in Mr. Fine's life that had recently changed."

Leopold's gaze stayed locked on his hands. He raised the fingertips slightly, as if the immaculate manicure could help him decide how to answer. "That was a personal transaction. The corporate entity had nothing to do with it."

"Oh boy," McCormick said.

Marie came in with the espresso. I was pretty sure from the intense way she looked at Leopold that she'd been listening at the door. She put the little china cup down near me on the edge of the desk, then stood there with her hands clasped, looking expectantly from DeLucca to McCormick to me and finally back to Leopold.

"Was there something else?" I said.

She kept her eyes on Leopold. "Coffee?" she said. He shook his head. She touched his shoulder before she left. Leopold turned bright red. McCormick snorted.

"The yellow shattered on the wheel," I said. "That put Lou in hock to Van Kees for what, five million? He was already underwater on the townhouse."

Leopold moved the keyboard a quarter of an inch to the right.

"Maybe he hoped to dig his way out with stones like that D flawless he got two months ago from a Shanghai lab. The one he re-polished and sold for $1.4 million. As a real diamond."

Leopold's face turned white. "Shanghai?" he gargled. He cleared his throat. "We never bought anything from Shanghai." He adjusted the blotter.

This was the first DeLucca and McCormick were hearing about a Shanghai fake. DeLucca's face remained impassive. McCormick looked like a dog who'd just picked up the sound of his bowl being filled. Leopold pressed his lips together and tried to look offended.

"You can check the books if you don't believe me." He gestured at the papers in front of him. "You could audit us any time. Everything is going to be perfect."

"I'm glad to hear it, because the Treasury's pulling your accounts right now. What I'm wondering is—should we take a look at yours?"

We were already doing that too, but Leopold wouldn't find out about it until he tried to perform a transaction at an ATM and learned that his account was frozen. I'd phoned the order in from the fire escape after McCormick's call.

"I resent that imputation," Leopold said.

"It's just a formality," I said. "Like looking at the contents of the vault. You can open it, I guess?"

"I think you need a court order for that."

DeLucca cleared his throat. "You have every right to ask for a court order, Mr. Rose. We were hoping to spare you the time. But if you prefer, we'll get some officers to take you and the lady downtown while we complete the paperwork. We'd have to put you in a cell, I'm afraid."

Leopold gaped at DeLucca. "Why?"

"In case you're lying about the Shanghai diamonds and take them out of the vault while we're back at the office getting the warrant," McCormick said. "Pardon the imputation."

Leopold pressed his hands flat on the desk again, as if he was afraid it might levitate.

"You aren't going to find any Shanghai stones in there," he said. "Of that you may be sure." He shot me a defiant glance. He knew Lou was getting diamonds from Shanghai, and he also knew I wasn't going to find one in the vault.

"Did you check the computer?" I said to McCormick.

"We copied the hard drive. The forensics guys are looking through it now."

"Do you know if they found a folder labeled Dia-Vu?" I said. I spelled it out. Leopold's face froze.

Later we looked through the vault. Marie produced the logs, and started to follow us in. "No," I said. "I'm sure Leopold can handle it." She didn't tilt her head to let the silk curtain ripple. She didn't clasp her hands or offer coffee. She glanced at Leopold and smiled a cold smile, a smile as thin as a garotte. Then she turned to make sure that I could see it too.

13

I don't even know what that is," Tommy said.

We were in his office, looking at the image of a polished diamond on the plate-glass screen that hung from the ceiling.

"It's a Dia-Vu scan," I said. "Dia-Vu is the name of an Israeli company. They make scanners for examining the interior of a diamond. The scans reveal every structural flaw and impurity in a stone, even pinpoint inclusions. The software loads the scan into your computer. You can view the diamond at your desk."

Tommy was leaning back in his big black-leather chair with his feet crossed on the desk. "And that's how dealers inspect a diamond?"

"Mostly they use it to look at rough. The scan shows every fault and flaw the cutter will have to deal with to transform the diamond from rough to polished. You can rotate the diamond and study it from every angle. The machine can also tell you what cut will produce what price."

I grabbed the mouse, caught the diamond with the cursor, and twisted it to look into the stone. The lines of the cut fanned out in perfect symmetry.

"Why would Lou Fine look at a polished diamond on this software?"

"To see if he could improve the cut."

Tommy rubbed his chin as he looked at the diamond. "Leopold Rose had to know about these stones."

"Sure he did, but none of the stones from Shanghai was logged into the vault, and I think Leopold just forgot about the Dia-Vu files because he's not a cutter. He's sticking to the story that Lou must have been dealing privately, not through the company, because the company got all their diamonds from Van Kees. That's the normal route for a cutter like Lou. Buy rough at the monthly sales, take it home, polish it. As an exception, he might buy a polished stone if he thought he could improve the cut." I moved the diamond with the cursor again. Perfect from every angle.

"Did the cops take Rose and the girl downtown?"

"No. We want Rose to think we swallowed the story. The girl didn't buy it, though. I don't know where she fits in. Anything when you ran the name?"

"Nothing," Tommy said. "We couldn't find her coming in. Definitely Hout is not her name. Also probably disguised when she entered."

"She's bent, all right. McCormick has people on them. We're hoping they meet somebody."

"That had to be your idea. The cops would have taken them both downtown. You're taking a chance, Alex. She could run. That'll be on you."

"She can try. I've got notices out for the land border and the airports. McCormick has a team on her apartment. Leopold and the girl are both there now."

Tabitha blew through the door in a black blazer and a flared yellow skirt. She dropped into a chair beside me and puffed a clump of hair from her eyes.

"Go," she said.

"MAUREEN," said Tommy. "Secure the room."

The lights dimmed. The windows turned opaque. A deadbolt in the door shot home. In the hall outside, a winking red light would warn that a secure meeting was underway. The Dia-Vu image showed more clearly now.

"So what are we looking at?" Tabitha said.

"Laser scans of diamonds from Lou's computer. This is the Geneva stone."

I dragged a second image of the stone out of the box so she could see the before and after. "The image on the left—that's the way it arrived in New York. Just over twelve carats. Polished in a contemporary round cut. And the image on the right"—I moved the cursor—"is the same diamond, re-cut for sale in Geneva."

"It looks like a completely different stone," Tabitha said.

"It's called a Carré," I said. "It's an art deco cut, popular a hundred years ago. Those oversized facets—they'd magnify any flaw in the stone. So the cut draws attention to how clean the stone is."

"Don't these auction houses want to know where the stone came from?" said Tommy.

"He sold it as 'property of a gentleman.' The cut supports the idea that the stone's been around a long time, so maybe it comes from some family that's had it for generations. Another plus is that most people have never seen a stone cut like that in their lives. Even connoisseurs would be fascinated by the cut. They are paying attention to the cut instead of asking themselves how come they've never heard of this stone."

Tabitha caught her lower lip in her teeth and tilted her head. "So if it's a fake, the rare cut helps make people forget to ask questions they should be asking."

"That's my guess."

"Any other Shanghai stones?"

"They're not identified as Shanghai stones, but there were two more in the same folder. A five-carat oval, and then this." I dragged the third stone into the center of the screen.

"Jesus," Tabitha gasped.

"I know. I've never actually seen one before. It's called a Lucifer cut."

"If you've never seen one," Tommy said, "how do you know what it is?"

"I've read about it. It's only been attempted twice. The first was cut in the nineteenth century in Amsterdam. It's disappeared. There isn't even a sketch of it, only a description left by the cutter. He thought the diamond had a mind and was telling him what to do."

"And the second time?" Tabitha's eyes were fixed on the image.

"The second one was a huge piece of rough, over three hundred carats. From the old Van Kees pit in the Transvaal. The stone was packed with flaws. The family had it for twenty years before they persuaded Billy Louw, a Johannesburg cutter, to take it on. He and Sir Harry Van Kees, Teddy's father, agreed to try a Lucifer cut. Louw was just finishing the crown, the top part of the diamond, when it shattered."

"How many facets does this one have?" said Tommy.

"Eighty-nine."

"And Lou polished it?" Tabitha said.

"Looks like it. From an eighty-carat rough down to sixty carats."

"And it's not in the vault."

"No."

"So it's what he died for," Tabitha said.

"If it's what he died for," said Tommy, "that means the killer knew it wasn't in the vault, and where to find it."

Tabitha stared intently at the screen. She ran her hands into her hair and ruffled it furiously. Then she turned to me.

"Got a picture of the girl?"

"MAUREEN," I said. "Marie Hout."

A grid of a dozen images slid onto the screen. Surveillance from a subway car. Coming out of the Fifth Avenue store.

"MAUREEN," Tabitha said, "compare to Lou Fine killer." Up came a still from Lou's front step. The shooter waiting for the door to open. Tabitha turned to me and winked. Even with the fedora and the sunglasses, there was no arguing with those lips.

"Maybe time to bring her in," said Tommy.

"Not yet," I said. "We still want to see who she contacts and what Leopold does. We need to know who's running them."

No prizes for thinking China. That's where we were all going, helped by the hundreds of thousands of diamonds that spilled onto the screen as soon as Tommy toggled a key for the main part of the show.

14

For the next fifteen minutes we watched a torrent of diamonds pour through huge Chinese industrial plants. Most of the stones came out of large machines called presses, which squeezed carbon into crystals at temperatures of four thousand degrees and under pressures of almost a million pounds per square inch.

But another machine, much smaller, produced stones too. In that process, a tiny diamond called a seed was placed in a chamber. At high temperature, the chamber was flooded with carbon-rich gas. The carbon rained onto the seed, and the diamond grew.

"Jesus," Tabitha said when MAUREEN ended the presentation. "How many diamonds were we looking at?"

"From that one factory," Tommy said, "123 million carats a year. For context, that's more than the entire annual world output of natural diamonds. Just from that one factory. If you lump all the Chinese production together, it's twelve billion carats a year."

"How much of that is jewel grade?" I said.

He slid his keyboard away. The screen rose into the ceiling and the lights came on.

"Not much. Maybe six million carats. But that's more than anybody else."

"And when people buy lab-grown, it's this CVD?" Tabitha said.

"Yes. And the stones are clearly identified as lab-grown when they're sold. Some small ones get passed off as real diamonds, but until the Geneva white, nothing big."

Tabitha pursed her lips and looked at me.

"Doesn't Van Kees make a machine that detects fakes?"

"GemCheck," I said. "It's a big part of their business."

"Are they like scanners?" Tommy asked.

"No. Scanners show the inside of a diamond. GemCheck observes the way a stone behaves under certain kinds of light, and makes a call on whether it's fake or real. They update the machines constantly to stay ahead of the latest advances in lab-grown technology. It's a very secret part of their operation."

Tabitha clamped a lock of hair in her mouth and inspected her yellow skirt. "You'll have to go to London and see what they know. I'm going over for a NATO meeting. I'll give you a lift."

She got up without another word and went clacking out into the hall. Tommy tilted his head and listened until the sound faded away. Then he got up and went to the window and stared down into the street. I joined him, and we watched Tabitha come out the front door and climb into the waiting Suburban.

"Wasn't that nice," Tommy said, flicking off the lock and sliding up the window. He leaned out and inhaled a long breath. It was a beautiful day. "By 'nice' I meant her giving you a lift."

"I knew what you meant, Tommy."

He watched the Suburban cross Hudson Avenue and disappear up the street.

"At the Treasury," he said, "we worry about things like strategic enemies acquiring control of what amounts to an anonymous currency, in this case diamonds, which they can use to bribe and subvert and generally fuck things up however they want. So that's what we worry about. What's in it for her?"

"Mei is in it for her."

Tommy slid the window back down and snapped the lock into place. "And maybe you."

When I got back to my office, I put through some orders. The guys in operations got right on it, and an hour later I called Frankie. She came in and sat on the windowsill. She lit a Kool and blew the smoke into the alley. I tossed an envelope on the desk.

"I approved your application for temporary leave," I said.

"I applied for temporary leave?" She opened the envelope and pulled out the paperwork.

"Your tickets are in there too."

She went through everything carefully. "You know I'm not cleared for foreign assignments."

"That was then."

She frowned at the plane ticket. "It's not even my name."

"It will be." I scribbled an address in Brooklyn on a Post-it and handed it to her. "They're expecting you."

"They can do the passport?"

"Passport, driver's license, the whole shebang."

She parked the cigarette between her lips and shuffled through the contents of the envelope. "Tracey Ford," she read out loud. "I like it."

15

got off the subway at 125th Street and walked west almost to the Henry Hudson Parkway. At the Dinosaur Bar-B-Que, I cut over to the stone steps that led up to Riverside Park. It was the longest way to come, but that's how he'd set it up. He loved a complicated arrangement, the more elaborate the better.

If I'd got off the subway one stop before and walked up from the south, he'd know I had a tail and the meeting would be canceled. I'd just keep walking. Instead, I came up the steps and approached from the north. I crossed Riverside Drive and came around the side of Grant's Tomb. The plaza was dotted with tourists taking pictures with their phones, and a heavyset guy was down on one knee framing the dome against the trees. He had an old Leica and waited for people to get out of the way before he snapped.

I checked my watch exactly twice. That was part of the routine too. Then I crossed the street and stepped into the little park. He was sitting on the far side, on a bench, with a paper bag in his lap.

As I followed the paved path, he took a cherry from the bag and put it in his mouth, chewed for a moment, then dropped the stone into a bush. He was fastidious in everything.

He wore a summer-weight blazer with a white shirt open at the neck. His face was shaded by the brim of his Panama hat. I sat down at the far end of the bench. He thrust the paper bag in my direction.

"Have a cherry," he said. "My neighbor grows them."

"You don't have any neighbors, Hassan."

He gave me a smile that went no further than his mouth. His teeth were very white, his skin like polished mahogany. He had pale brown eyes and never blinked. He gave the bag a little shake.

"You should eat more fruit, Alex."

Hassan Crawford had been telling me what to do since the night he'd appeared at my door in Cape Town and recruited me into the CIA. I was a tough kid, and also a crook. That's what he liked.

He'd grown up in South Africa, the illegitimate son of a US naval attaché and a local girl who was pure Cape Malay. He had her features—the chocolate skin and almond eyes of the Muslim people brought as slaves to the old Dutch colony on the Cape. From the naval attaché—a spook—he got deceitfulness. He joined a gang and became an accomplished criminal. The CIA had snapped him up for the same reason he'd recruited me. They didn't have to bend us. We were already bent.

"I was sorry to hear about your friend," he said. "Do you have a suspect?"

"No."

This time Hassan's smile spread all the way to his eyes. He liked it that I'd lied. As if I'd agreed to play chess with someone who loved the game and had been missing it.

"And that attack on you, coming so soon after," he said in his clear, dry voice, every syllable enunciated. "The two have to be connected. You must have a theory."

Hassan didn't have an accent. He had squeezed out every trace of it in the long struggle to create a new person from the raw material he'd been left with. Ignored by his dad and suffocated by the love of a mother young enough to be his sister. You had to know Hassan well to see the bitterness that ate at him.

He plucked another cherry from the bag and put it in his mouth and looked away across the park, pretending not to notice that I hadn't answered him. He took the cherry stone from his mouth and dropped it in the bush.

"I've been talking to friends," he said. "You know we get together from time to time."

I tilted my head in a noncommittal way. I was interested to hear what he had to say but I wasn't going to help him get there. His clearance had lapsed years ago. Sure—he had some buddies from the old days, and some were still at Langley.

He picked another cherry from the bag, held it for a moment in his thin fingers, then dropped it back. He scrunched up the bag and held it in his lap.

"A lot of things are happening, Alex. My friends have opinions. This Chinese tycoon Xi Mei and your friend Tabitha. Some people at Langley are not completely sure about the exact nature of their relationship."

"Langley's not sure? I must remember to write that down as soon as I get back to the office. Everyone will be astonished."

Hassan had no reason to love the agency. He'd retired a few years ago with a rotten package. But the friends he had at the CIA were his only friends. He still met them. They fed him small jobs. Spoon-feeding me this crap would be one of them.

"That operation in the Canadian Arctic last year," he continued. "The one where we took out Mei's twin brother. My friends didn't like that operation." He turned to look at me with his straw-colored eyes. "My friends think MI got taken by the Ministry."

MI was US Military Intelligence, and the Ministry meant China's Ministry of State Security.

"I don't think MI got taken by China, Hassan. It was MI's plan to get rid of the brother, and they got rid of him."

"Was it their plan? The Chinese generals were looking for a way to dump the brother so Mei could take over. Tabitha helped it happen."

"Your friends are sliming her, Hassan. They're jealous because she's a star."

He shrugged. "Even if they hate her, it doesn't mean they're wrong."

"So Tabitha's a double agent; is that the takeaway?" I was getting irritated. Hassan gave me a thin smile and touched my hand with fingers as dry as twigs.

"She's a smart girl. She must have realized how much she was helping Mei. Well, so did other people. The Chinese might try to compromise her."

"They'd have help from your friends." I looked at my watch and got up. "I'll walk you to your car."

Hassan dropped the cherries in a garbage bin. We headed for the steps that led down onto Claremont Avenue, but he stopped before we got there.

"They call this Sakura Park because of the trees," he said. "Sakura is the Japanese word for a cherry tree. In 1909, on the three hundredth anniversary of Henry Hudson's discovery of the Hudson River, Japanese residents of New York donated hundreds of cherry trees to the city. They brought them over from Japan. You can find them blooming here every spring, and in Riverside Park and Central Park too." He looked at me. "That's the love this country can inspire in people."

I knew what was coming.

"In 1942 the United States repaid that love by interning 120,000 Japanese Americans—citizens, Alex—in concentration camps." The pale eyes were as cold as ice. "It's something I keep in mind."

We went down the steps. Hassan's old Saab 900 sat at the curb. Spotless as always. He got in and took off his Panama hat and placed it carefully on the passenger seat. He started the car and rolled down the window.

"That woman has a lot of enemies, Alex." He waited until I met his eyes before he added, "Don't make them yours."

I watched him drive away, then walked back up the steps to the park and across the plaza in front of Grant's Tomb. The guy with the Leica was sitting on a low stone wall, cleaning the lens. I crossed Riverside Drive and headed back down the stone steps.

16

D id you go through that song and dance at Grant's Tomb again?"
Tommy said when I got back to the Dinosaur Bar-B-Que. There
was a line out the door but he had a booth to himself. They
always treated him like a king.

"What's your problem?" I said, picking up the menu. "So he has his
rituals." I was still annoyed. I didn't like Hassan slandering Tabitha for
his friends at the company, and I didn't like his warning. Tommy picked
up on my tone.

"Simmer down, muchacho. He was your rabbi, not your friend."

"Something to drink?" the waitress asked. The question was for me,
but she had her hand on Tommy's shoulder. Her fingernails blazed with
an intricate, jewel-like design that looked like something by Fabergé. The
nails went well with the foot-long eyelashes and the permed red hair.
Her name tag said *Shawna*. I said I'd have what Tommy was drinking—
a sledgehammer brew from the Bronx called Now Youse Can't Leave.
She waited a second longer, gazing down at Tommy. Then she gave
his shoulder a squeeze and went away to get the beer.

Tommy was polishing off his starter, a plate of fried chicken skin
called Ode to Buffalo. It came with Hello Buffalo sauce and blue cheese

dressing. For a guy who shoveled down food the way Tommy did, he managed it neatly. He handled cutlery like a surgeon. He wore a cream-colored bowling shirt. Not a speck.

When Shawna came back, Tommy ordered a full rack of ribs. I went with the Big Ass Pork Plate. It sounded like a macho portion but it was smaller than the full rack, a fact made clear by Shawna. My order earned a sigh. Tommy got fanned with her eyelashes again and collected another squeeze, although that might have been for his sides. He went with barbeque beans and mac and cheese. I asked for coleslaw. She shook her head as she wrote it down.

"I don't know why you bother with Hassan," Tommy said. "It's just those buttheads from Langley trying to feed us bullshit."

"He gets a retainer. He needs the money. Plus, we find out whose back is getting stabbed this week."

"And it's Tabitha's, right? He gave you chapter and verse about how she was corrupted by the Chinese when we ran that Canadian op. Tabitha helped get rid of Mei's brother, who even the Chinese couldn't control. Ergo Tabitha got suckered and China owns her ass."

"I bet you never said 'ergo' in the NFL."

Tommy grunted. "You hate it that I was right."

Tommy had predicted what Hassan would say. He enjoyed making fun of him, but the truth was he didn't mind the meetings. They were always in the same place, and that meant Tommy could debrief me in his favorite restaurant.

The ribs and the Big Ass Pork arrived. Tommy neatly converted a four-rib section into a pile of bones while I got started. The pork was good; the coleslaw, not so much. I took a forkful of Tommy's beans.

"We should ask ourselves why the CIA is pitching this corrupt-Tabitha stuff right now," Tommy said. "How often does Hassan arrange these meetings? Three times a year? So why now?"

"Don't say CIA. This isn't the agency. Twenty thousand people work there. A few of them hate Tabitha because she's young and smart."

He concentrated on the rack for a minute. I eyed the beans again, but he moved them out of reach.

"Don't kid yourself, Alex. The guys he sees—they have bosses. Sometimes I think you don't understand the civil service. You just said Hassan needs the money. OK, that means he's getting paid." He finished the ribs and put them aside. "Somebody signs off on those payments, and more likely two people." He polished off the beans and laid his cutlery precisely on the plate.

"Let's look hard at this," he said. "Lou Fine gets murdered. Who pops up immediately? Tabitha. She has a line on this stone from a Shanghai lab. Turns out to be a very high-grade fake. Alarm bells ring, because the Chinese can now make undetectable fakes, which is the same as counterfeiting US dollars, except—oops—we can't check the serial numbers. Capisce?"

"I'm managing to hang on."

"Yeah? Well, what happens next? What happens is, we're just getting up to speed on China's scary diamond powers when—ping!—you get a call from Hassan. His old pals at the CIA feed him that claptrap about Tabitha being compromised by the Chinese." He stared at me. "Come on. You see where I'm going."

And I did. When he laid it out like that, it was obvious. "It's too fast."

"Exactly. It's too fast. How does the CIA know what Tabitha's doing? They know because they're briefed. This isn't two clandestine departments each running an operation. It's one op. Hassan—that's the fake in the backfield to distract you so you won't see where the play is going."

"The CIA points me in the wrong direction while Tabitha gets on with whatever the real operation is."

"Unless pointing you in the wrong direction is actually part of it."

A busboy cleared our plates. Shawna appeared and put her hand on Tommy's shoulder. "I hope you saved room for dessert."

"You know it," Tommy said. "Help me out."

"*My* personal favorite," she confided, removing her hand and spreading it over her heart, "is the banana cream pie."

"Hit me, baby," Tommy said.

"Two forks," I added. Shawna rolled her eyes.

"Bring him his own damn pie," Tommy told her. Shawna gave him a pat.

"I hear you, sugar."

"Another thing that doesn't add up," Tommy said when she left. "Why make these fancy stones if the whole idea is to just get a source for US cash. Grow too many stones, or make them too big, they risk attracting attention. Wouldn't it make more sense to grow two- or three-carat stones, easy to sell, no fuss? That's what bugs me about the Lucifer cut. What the fuck is that even about? You make a stone so crazy the whole world is going to be peering at it through machines and asking where you got it? Plus then you kill the guy who polished it?"

My phone buzzed. I didn't recognize the number, so I sent it to voicemail.

"Maybe it's time to pull in Leopold Rose and the girl."

The phone buzzed a second time. Same number. I sent it to voicemail again.

"I think we should," I said. "Rose had to know how the scam was being run and who they were dealing with."

When the phone buzzed a third time, I answered. It was McCormick. "We'll be right down," I said, ending the call and pushing back my chair. "Sorry, sugar," I said to Tommy. "Have to skip the pie. Marie just shook her tail."

17

W hat about Leopold?" Tommy said as we got into the vintage Caddy.

"They think he's still in the apartment. They're waiting for us. Twenty-Third and Ninth."

We shot out of 125th Street and onto the ramp for the Henry Hudson Parkway. The Eldorado convertible flew into traffic like a rocket fired from the 1950s. The coachwork gleamed under a fresh coat of Dakota Red. We cannoned into the left-hand lane while Tommy shot me a satanic grin. I avoided meeting his eye. I didn't want to be hearing about the Hydra-Matic transmission and the 364-cubic-inch engine all the way downtown.

"Feel that thrust?" he bawled anyway, shouting over the rush of air. "Three hundred and twenty-five horsepower." He patted the wheel. "Curb weight of two and a half tons—better be something under the hood."

The Hudson River sparkled in the sun. Ferries and water taxis crisscrossed the waterway. A lumbering Circle Line boat loaded with tourists wallowed downriver.

Traffic stayed light down the Upper West Side until we passed Seventy-Second Street and hit the tailback from the turning lanes at Fifty-Seventh. By the time we reached the point where the Henry Hudson became the West Side Highway, the road had fused into a solid mass of creeping metal that stretched south as far as we could see.

Tommy leaned on the horn and bulled his way into the exit lanes. A huge man with eighteen feet of car and a glare perfected in the NFL—even in New York City those were tactical advantages.

We took Eleventh Avenue, hit another bottleneck at the Lincoln Tunnel, and reached Twenty-Third Street twenty minutes after leaving Shawna stranded with the pie. Han Solo could not have got there faster in the Millennium Falcon.

Two unmarked Ford Interceptors were parked just west of Ninth Avenue. McCormick and two other detectives, a woman and a man, waited on the sidewalk. A truculent-looking bald guy in jeans and a dirty T-shirt stood beside McCormick with his arms folded. Tommy double-parked and we got out. Truculent's expression tried to stay in place, but good luck with that. You could see him thinking he'd seen Tommy before, and then remembering where. On TV, wrecking the skeletal structure of other large males while people like the truculent guy sat at home watching the game and getting balder.

"I'm the super," he said. "My boss says you gotta have warrants."

"Did you hear someone make a noise?" Tommy said to McCormick, and when the super disappeared down the steps to the basement: "What happened?"

"She comes out of the building," McCormick said, "walks down to Seventh, gets on the uptown 1 train. My guys are on her. At Penn Station she gets off the 1 and changes to an uptown 3 express. Gets off at 116th."

"And straight into a pickup car," I said. McCormick nodded. The two detectives looked chagrined.

"And we already checked out the car she got into," McCormick added. "Stolen plates."

"I better get back to the office," Tommy said. "See if we can find her."

"We should've taken her downtown," McCormick said as Tommy drove off.

"I wanted her to run."

"Yeah, that's what Inspector DeLucca said. And I'm here to tell you that is some fucked-up spook shit, my friend, because I don't think we are going to like what we find inside."

"Leopold still in there?"

"Oh, I think so." McCormick signaled the detectives. The woman grabbed a small breaching ram. No one put on a Kevlar vest. No one even thought of calling for backup. Not for Leopold. We climbed the steps to the front door and went inside.

It was a high-end reno that had converted an old townhouse into overpriced, furnished short-term rentals. Thick carpet began at the entryway and continued up the stairs. Tasteful sconces cast a warm glow on the striped wallpaper. The building was so quiet I could hear someone running a bath.

At the top floor, McCormick led the way to the back and knocked on a door. When there was no answer, he knocked again and said, "Police. Open up." He didn't shout. It was more a formality than anything else. We knew what we were going to find.

McCormick nodded at the woman and stood aside. She stepped to the door with the two-handled ram and swung. Those little rams weigh less than twenty pounds, but one good tap and you're in.

Leopold was still in bed. His face was gray, his brown eyes open in wonder, as if surprised to find that the side of his head was gone. That's the kind of criminal Leopold had been: still learning. Now he had forever to work on it.

A pistol with a silencer was in his hand.

"Yeah, right," McCormick said, snapping on blue latex gloves and looking at the body. "Like I'm buying that."

He made a call to order in the crime scene techs, then told the uniforms to secure the building and start on the door knocks. "Anybody hear anything, see anything, did they ever talk to her." You have boxes to tick, you tick them. He didn't expect to find that Marie had talked to anybody. And nobody would have heard a thing. Not from Marie and not from the pistol. And sure as hell not from Leopold, who had been staring death in the face and thought it was just a pretty girl.

"Asshole," McCormick said to Leopold, then to one of the detectives: "And dig that super out of his hole. If he gives you any lip, cuff him and put him in a car." Then he called DeLucca.

Leopold's clothes were folded on a chair. I started going through them. McCormick finished with DeLucca and asked me to wait for the techs.

"Won't take me long," I said.

He didn't like that. He put his blue latex hands on his hips and stood right next to me. "I made her for bent," he said, "but I didn't make her for a stone-cold killer."

"No."

He was breathing loudly through his nose. Just keeping his temper. "First your friend and his wife and that dog walker" he said, "then this chump. You, they missed. Way this is going, you're not clear, not by a long shot. But hey"—he spread his hands—"what do I know? I'm just a dumb cop trying to solve three murders." He looked at Leopold. "Four."

I found what I was looking for behind a narrow strip of Velcro sewn into the shoulder. Folded the way only one kind of paper package is folded. I took it to the window and flipped it open. It was a pretty stone—high color. A five-carat oval. The third stone in the Shanghai folder.

McCormick logged it on his phone and took a snap. He watched me drop it in my pocket. Crime scene protocol—that stone goes straight into a Ziploc bag. But he was learning fast.

I left the building and walked to the corner and took the same trains Marie had taken after murdering Leopold. Maybe with the same cheerful expression she'd worn when she'd brought him coffee or let her fingers brush his arm.

Like Marie, I changed at Thirty-Fourth and caught the uptown express. But I got off at Ninety-Sixth.

I walked home and sat in the living room. I stared at the discolored rectangles on the wall and thought about Marie. Imagine that package arriving in Leopold's life and letting him have a night. The short forever.

I went into the bedroom and pressed a point on the wall at the back of the closet. A panel opened and I tapped a sequence into the number pad. There were three pistols in the gun locker. I took out the Walther PDP, the model they call the compact pro. Four-point-six-inch barrel and eighteen-round magazine. Three-dot sight. Polymer frame, twenty-six ounces fully loaded. I took it into the living room and laid a cloth on the coffee table and stripped it down. I oiled the pieces. When that was done, I loaded the magazine with the 124-grain Federal HST parabellum. Muzzle velocity 1,172 feet per second. Then I snapped everything back together. Handling a weapon, loading it with ammunition. It settles you. The smell of the oil, the beautiful precision of the parts and the singleness of purpose. But it didn't settle me. I thought of the smile Marie had let me see. That thin, cold smile when I'd kept her out of the vault. She'd smiled at Leopold, and then at me. A smile that said—I'll kill him when I like.

It was dark when I put on my running shorts and went outside and ran to the park. I went in through the gate at Ninety-Third Street and around the reservoir three times, keeping to the darkest part of the bridle path. I tried to empty my anger into the night, but the night wouldn't take it. Probably it was already full.

When I got back I texted my father that I was coming in the morning. I guess he called Annie, because five minutes later she messaged: "Pick you up at 6:00 A.M." A red dawn was licking at the fire escape when she came up the street in her banged-up F-150.

18

N ice boots," I said when I got in.

"Mmm," she said, smacked the stick into first, and gunned up onto Columbus. She looped over to Ninety-Third, took Amsterdam to Ninety-Sixth, gunned down the hill to make the yellow on Broadway, and straight down onto the Henry Hudson Parkway, showing me how well she could double-clutch, even in the cowboy boots. I'd bought them for her when she was fifteen, so they were usually a reliable opener for dad banter. Not today.

We went north up the river, got off at the Cross Bronx Expressway, fought our way through the morning crush of semis for a few miles until we peeled away for the Throgs Neck Bridge.

Long Island Sound glittered like a sheet of wrinkled foil. The early departures from LaGuardia flashed pink in the morning light as they banked to the north above the Connecticut shore. We reached the Long Island Expressway and settled in for the long haul east.

"OK," I said. "I can either check my email again or you can say what's on your mind."

"Yeah, I didn't actually think I needed permission to speak, Dad."

I let that go.

"But I do have something on my mind. This trip out to see Grampa, it's about diamonds, right?"

"It is."

"I hope you can be open to this, but doesn't it occur to you that he might be hurt by that?"

"Hurt by what?"

"That you just visit when you need something from him."

"No," I said. "That doesn't occur to me. I'm surprised it occurred to him."

"I didn't say he said it."

"Are you saying he *didn't* say it?"

She shot me an angry look. "Wow, is that ever you. You try to back me into a corner."

That fast. I let a mile go by.

"Listen, Annie. You know my relationship with him is problematic. We didn't have an easy time together when I was growing up. In my experience, he can be manipulative. So when you suggested he felt hurt by something I was responsible for, I assumed the idea came from him."

Voice of reasonable dad. Explain patiently. Take down temperature.

"And that's how you think of him—your own dad. A lonely old man sitting out at the end of Long Island. He reaches out to somebody, and suddenly he's manipulative."

Well, not suddenly.

I understood where this was coming from. The only child of divorced parents, Annie had a hunger for family. She'd formed a strong attachment to my father. I saw it happen and was helpless to stop it. When she looked at him, she didn't see a selfish bastard. She didn't understand our animosity. She saw my childhood in diamond exploration camps in Africa as one long storybook adventure, because those were the stories he told her. Nighttime bonfires crackling on the veldt.

Lane Turner knew more about the origin of diamonds than any man alive. He'd discovered a method for finding diamond deposits by locating a kind of garnet. By examining the chemistry of a garnet sample, he could tell the prospector who'd found them if he was on the right trail. Men had grown rich on his advice, but he'd never made a diamond discovery of his own, and the tent camps he pitched in the Kalahari, drilling duster after duster, were hellish places, brimming with his bitterness. His cruelty to my mother drove her into illness, and I blamed him for her death when I was twelve. I'd never shared that with Annie.

"You shouldn't worry about me and your grandfather," I said. "We had our life together. It wasn't much fun for either of us, and none of that is your responsibility."

"I'm your daughter! I *care* what's going on in your life. The violence, Dad—it isolates you. It wrecked your relationship with Mom. And what about Lily?"

Lily?

"What about her?"

"Can't you see she loves you?"

I tried not to look dumbfounded.

"I worked for *months* on that basket stich," Annie exclaimed. "For the diamond T-shirt. *Months!* It took a long time to get it exactly right, and I got to know Lily. And the way she talks about you. Like, you should be *living* with her."

I had no idea what Annie thought she'd learned about Lily and me, but if it had come from Lily, I guarantee it had been through the rinse cycle.

"Why don't you move in with her? Is it male pride? Wake up, Dad. It's a new world. It's OK for Lily to have more money than you. You don't have to stay in that dumb apartment."

Her face was red and her eyes bright, and her voice shook a little when she said, "I'm sorry I said that. It was really mean. It's just that, like, your hands and face are cut from whatever happened to you. I don't want you in that world. I wish you would just stay with Lily and be safe."

I reminded myself that Annie had grown up surrounded by money. Her mother was rich. Her mother's friends were rich. Minnie Ho was rich and so were her customers. I guess to Annie, not being rich was a choice. All I had to do was step through the door held open for me.

We passed Riverhead and took Route 25 out onto the North Fork. We were at Greenport when she spoke again.

"We don't communicate, Dad, and that's what hurts. I want you to know who I am."

"I'm sorry if you think I don't understand and admire you, Annie. I'm proud of you. You're very focused, and already making a career."

"But what about *me*? The real me that's underneath? I feel like you're not sure who I even am. I'm not some kid who sits around watching cat memes on TikTok. I'm a fully engaged adult woman. I have personhood. You know nothing about me because how could you? Too many dangerous things happen in your life. You don't have time to ask about me and who I am as a person. You don't even know what I want from life."

I didn't even know what a cat meme was.

We crossed the causeway and took the familiar streets through the village of Orient. We passed the white church and the old houses sleeping in the shade. On the edge of the village, we came to the gate. A sign warned of guard dogs and electronic surveillance. Both claims were false, but the gate and a camera mounted on a steel pole looked convincing. A lot of people sent diamonds to this isolated house. I'd been after him for years to put in security, and this was as far as he'd gone.

Annie got out and punched in the code. The gate swung open. A sandy lane wound through a grove of pines and came out at a gray-shingled bungalow with white trim. Banks of wild roses almost hid the windows on this side of the house. The front door opened and the round, red face of Mrs. Cutler, Lane Turner's longtime housekeeper, beamed at us in happy expectation. Her smile faded when she saw our faces—mine blank and Annie's still twisted by emotion. She stepped back in and closed the door. Annie and I sat there for a minute, patched up our expressions as well as we could, and went in.

19

He read us at a glance. He had a black belt in misery. He sat through breakfast with a delighted smile. Mrs. Cutler shuttled back and forth between the kitchen and the dining room, darting worried looks around the table as she brought in scrambled eggs and bacon. Annie thanked her with elaborate politeness.

"Lovely, Hannah," my father said blissfully. "And the good china too!" He took a nick out of my forehead with his smile. "She only does this for family," he confided, leaning toward Annie to savor her unhappiness. Then he sat back contentedly, surveying our frozen faces. "Isn't this as good as it gets? Annie, have some of that gooseberry jam on your toast. Hannah makes it especially for you." He took another slice at me with his sharp white teeth and settled down to a hearty breakfast. Nothing gave him an appetite like someone else's pain.

He wore his unvarying summer uniform—a spotless white shirt with the sleeves rolled up, khaki cotton pants fresh from Mrs. Cutler's iron. Blue canvas boat shoes. Thick white hair parted neatly on the left. Everything about him was tidy and ordered. Even his scorn.

"She's not a girl anymore," he said when we were through. Annie was helping Mrs. Cutler clear the table. "You should try to get to know her better. You've always thought you had all the answers. It was your failing as a child."

Annie disappeared outside with her coffee and iPad. I watched her drag a chair across the lawn to the seawall, slip on headphones, and stretch out. Beyond her, the course markers put out by the yacht club bobbed in a lively sea. I followed my father into his small lab.

It was a bright room. The windows faced the lawn and the pier where I'd kept my gaff-rigged dinghy moored when I was a kid. My mother had taught me how to sail. There was nothing tied there now.

We pulled out stools and sat at the immaculate work bench. Everything was in its place, the instruments arranged in perfect order. A scatter of loose diamonds glowed like chips of ice on a pad of clean white paper. The powerful Zeiss microscope with the binocular eyepiece stood beside them. He picked up tweezers and pushed a couple of stones in front of me. "Lab-grown," he said. "Take a look." I picked one up, laid it on the glass plate under the lens, and peered through the eyepiece.

I tweaked the focus and the stone jumped into view—an icy, jagged diamond of about two carats. One of the faces showed the growth marks of a diamond crystal called trigons—the raised outlines of perfect equilateral triangles. I turned the stone slightly, and a silvery streak, an inclusion shaped like a tiny needle, flashed into view.

"Looks like it's got a feather," I said.

"It does. From the flux. The feather is a small amount of metallic flux from the diamond press that got trapped in the crystal as it formed. It makes the stones magnetic. Some dealers use magnets as a quick way to screen for lab-grown mixed up with real diamonds. A metallic inclusion in a fake will pop it right out of a diamond sample. You can hear them tick against the magnet."

He glanced outside. A smile twitched at the corners of his mouth as he watched Annie. She'd got up from the chair and was standing at the seawall, watching the race that had just gotten underway. A fleet of yellow Lasers thrashed toward the first buoy on the racing course. The boats bumped against each other as they battled for position.

The bay sparkled in the sun. A mile away a trawler headed into the Peconic River on the way to unload its catch at Southold. Closer in, between the trawler and the yellow Lasers, an open boat threw up spray as it plowed through the chop. The tall fishing rods clamped into racks along the side whipped back and forth as the bow bucked through the waves. You could buy that idyllic scene on a hundred postcards: boats in pursuit of striped bass off the eastern end of Long Island.

"What about CVD?" I said.

"Chemical vapor deposition. That's how most of the lab-grown is made. It's much cheaper than buying a big diamond press, so it's easier to get into."

"It's a different process, right?"

"A CVD reactor is basically a microwave," he said. "They put in diamond seeds, just like in the big presses, but there's no flux. They flood the chamber with methane gas. Microwave radiation breaks the methane into carbon and hydrogen, and the carbon atoms settle on the seeds and build crystals. This is what they get."

He pulled out a drawer and rolled a few small diamonds onto the bench. I louped one.

"Nice."

"They're all Type IIa, which means there's no detectable nitrogen. So exceptionally pure. The quality is excellent."

"How would you distinguish it from a real diamond?"

He shot me an irritated look. It never took long. He was an impatient man anyway, and with me it had the special venom that only a father can feel for a son. It ate at him like acid. He got up and peered through the window.

"You'll destroy your relationship with her," he said, "just as you did with me." Annie had put her iPad on the grass to watch the race. A tangle of Lasers churned around the second marker. "Look at those morons," he hissed. He didn't mean the kids. The big powerboat with the fishing rods was wallowing in the chop on the far side of the course. "Nobody's ever caught a striper in that close."

"Can we just finish?"

He shot me a contemptuous glance. "You mean how can we be sure that a given diamond is a CVD and not a real stone?" He made an irritated gesture. "We'd be here all day if I explained all the tests. Grading labs have instruments designed to look for the differences between crystals produced in a lab and those created in nature. I don't do that. The diamonds people send me are rough diamonds from exploration sites. I examine the chemistry of the inclusions in the diamonds, so I don't need the kind of instruments a grading lab has. But I have this," he said, sitting down and tapping the tweezers on a boxy contraption hooked up to a screen. "It's a spectroscope. I beam infrared light at the diamond, and what the diamond does to that light gives me information about its structure."

"How about this one?" I dropped the five-carat oval I'd found on Leopold onto the counter. He plinked it onto a metal tray and slid the tray into a slot. The device made a low hum when he powered it on. A few seconds later a spiky, colored graph appeared on the screen.

"Well, there's no doubt about this one," he said. "It has an N3 center."

"What's that?"

He ticked the tweezers on the screen, indicating a part of the graph. "This absorption pattern here—that can only come from an N3 center. It's a point inside the crystal where three nitrogen atoms surround what's known as a vacancy—a place where the crystal is missing a carbon atom."

"And that means it's a real diamond?"

"Yes. You never get that in a lab-grown. Some lab-grown have missing atoms, but never like this, with the three nitrogen atoms packed around it. These N3 centers only occur in natural diamonds."

"So it would be impossible to make that happen in a lab? Shift the atoms around?"

He tossed the tweezers angrily on the counter. "Have you ever heard me say 'impossible' in your entire life? 'Impossible' is religion, not science. We never say impossible. We describe what we see and can establish by experiment. Nature can make an N3 center because it performs the same actions trillions and trillions of times. Diamonds form and dissolve back into nothing in the ocean of superheated magma a hundred miles beneath us. Nature has millions of years to form and unform crystals, so anything can happen. How many labs have that much time?"

I folded the five-carat into the paper and put it in my pocket. Lane Turner had defined the science of how diamonds form. He'd interrogated the crystal structure of diamonds until they yielded their secrets. The knowledge had made his reputation. And now he had identified a Chinese fake as a natural diamond. It hadn't taken millions of years to make a diamond with an N3 center. They had done it in a lab in a few weeks.

I was stunned. Maybe that's why I didn't really hear the bullhorn. It was there, but it didn't catch my attention. I was struggling to come to terms with the diamond that my father had got wrong, and what that meant, when he jumped to his feet beside me, sending his chair smashing into a cabinet. A shout from Annie made me look outside.

20

Annie stood at the seawall with her hands clutching her hair. The course marshal was standing in his boat, roaring through the bullhorn. The Lasers were crashing into each other in a panic. A wave rolled through them, and a chrome bow railing lifted above the little fleet and crashed down into a trough. The boat with the two fishermen was in the middle of the course. One of the men was leaning on the wheelhouse. At first I thought he was holding a rod. Then the Lasers got out of the way and I saw what it was. A rifle.

"Down!" I shouted, throwing myself at my father as a windowpane exploded. A storm of jagged glass swept the room. I lay beside him on the floor as a second shot blew out more glass. The hail of slivers rattled on the wall. I held him tightly in my arms. A warm, sticky fluid flowed down my neck. I scrambled to my knees. He had a long gash on the side of his head. His eyes were staring wildly and a thin sound came from his parted lips. I ripped off my shirt and wrapped it around the wound. Mrs. Cutler screamed.

I ran into the living room in a crouch, tripped on a footstool, and crashed into a table. A heavy Chinese lamp fell off and smashed to pieces on the floor. I crawled through the shards of broken pottery and reached the door to the lawn. I tried to open it but my hands were bleeding. I wiped them on the floor and got enough grip to open the door.

Annie had run to the tool shed and was huddled behind it with her hands pressed to her head. The shooter's boat had got sideways to the waves and was rolling dangerously. The waves and the inshore current were bringing the boat closer to the rocky shallows. The rifleman had one hand on the gunwale for balance while his accomplice struggled with the wheel. He got the boat around with the bow pointing out into the bay. He put a hand on the big chrome throttle and eased it forward. The bow rose up and smashed through the waves as the boat headed out into the bay.

I threw open the door and ran across the lawn and out onto the dock. I had the Walther out by the time I got to the end, but my hands were sticky with blood and the wind was making it hard to stand still. I threw myself flat on the dock and braced the pistol with my left hand. Easy targets—comletely exposed. The wheelhouse was nothing more than a hard canopy, open at the back. They were only about seventy yards away. But I could see yellow flashes on the water ahead of them—Lasers. Four or five of the little boats were scattered over the water beyond the target. The risk of hitting a kid was too great.

I dashed inside the house and grabbed my phone, punching straight through to operations. They picked up immediately.

"Turner," I said. "Take my coordinates from the phone. Attack by two shooters in a boat. Twin outboards, visible sports-fishing rods. On course now from my position toward the Peconic River. Require emergency medical at my position. Elderly male, multiple lacerations."

When I got back inside, Annie was kneeling beside Dad. He lay on his back. A red bubble ballooned from his mouth. Annie was gulping huge breaths and gasping, "No, Grampa. No." She kept placing her hands on the cuts in his neck where the blood was spurting, stopping one, finding another, frantically shifting her hand. "Please stop," she whimpered.

His face was gray. An ugly patch of damp was oozing into the top of his pants. Mrs. Cutler stumbled into the room with a towel. She pulled his shirt away and pressed the towel to the wound.

It felt like forever but was only fifteen minutes before the dry voice from operations said, "You should see it now." I spotted the black dot, low on the water, coming across the bay.

"Got it," I said.

"They want you to confirm location."

I went out and stood on the dock and waved my arms. A minute later the dark blue Sikorsky racketed across the seawall and landed on the grass. As soon as the skids touched, the door flew open and two EMTs jumped out. They ran in a crouch under the whirling rotors and followed me into the house.

21

Annie sat with her legs drawn up, her arms wrapped tightly around her knees. She hugged her legs against her, like a shield that would protect her from harm. But the harm had already been done. She bore its marks. Her hair was stiff with blood. Her clothes had hardened on her body. The room was thick with the coppery smell of blood.

A nurse came and sat beside her and whispered in her ear. Annie stared straight ahead with her jaw clenched. The nurse went away and returned with a set of scrubs. With infinite care she unlaced Annie's fingers and lifted her arms. She unbuttoned the shirt and pulled it away, like something made of cardboard.

A dark red, flaking smear covered Annie's stomach where she'd cradled my father's head. The harsh lights and the gleaming tiles emphasized her shocking pallor—as if a switch had been turned off inside her and everything that made her a young woman had drained away, leaving behind this staring, rigid, ashen-skinned survivor. The nurse slipped the pale green top over her arms. Annie raised her legs again and clasped her knees and stared at the doors that led into the operating room.

The last time they'd opened, someone in a bloody apron with red spatters on her crocs had rushed out, returning a minute later with plastic bags of blood. We sat in silence listening to the beep of monitors, the sound of instruments dropped into metal trays, sometimes a terse instruction. "Clamp." "Suture."

The same nurse who'd brought the scrubs came back and knelt in front of Annie with a basin and some towels, and washed her face. That was all she'd tolerate. She wouldn't let me near her. Or look at me. She let Tommy sit beside her, but she didn't talk to him or respond in any way when he spoke.

Three hours after they'd taken my father in, the doors opened and a short woman came out. She peeled off her cap and her nitrile gloves and dropped them in a bin. She pulled a white lab coat on over her blood-stained scrubs. I stood up and she walked over.

"Your dad?"

"Yes."

She looked tired. "He's stable, but he's very sick. There were all the surface lacerations and that deep wound in the lower abdomen. We had to remove his spleen. So although he's stable right at this moment, it's going to be touch and go. He's an old man and he lost a lot of blood."

I hadn't seen Annie get up, but now she was standing beside me. She put her hand against my chest and pushed me away from the doctor and stood in front of me. The doctor frowned and looked at me. I nodded that she should speak to Annie.

"So we're worried about two main things," she said then, directly to Annie. "One is infection. He was lacerated in dozens of places and there were particles of clothing in the wounds. I think we got them all, but they were small. We could have missed some. The other big worry is shock. We have him in the ICU." She tried to deliver a reassuring pat, but Annie pulled her hand away. The doctor looked startled, glanced at me.

"I understand you're upset," she said, turning back to Annie, "but we're the trauma center for eastern Long Island. He's in good hands here. The best thing you can do right now is go home and get some rest."

For a moment Annie just stared at her. Then she said, "He can come home now." Her voice came out in a mangled croak.

"Oh, no," the doctor said. She looked at me again. "He's much too sick."

"Annie," I said, and that's as far as I got.

The speed of her motion stunned me. She whirled and slapped me full in the face. She was strong, and the force of the blow froze me. Her expression didn't change. The same stranger stared out of an abyss of pain, then hit me again, a lightning strike with the flat of her hand. My face burned. My arms hung at my side like lead. Then the whole room moved at once. The doctor staggered backward. Lily, who'd arrived only minutes before, dashed in and tried to yank me away. Annie got another swing in, her fingers raking my eyes before Tommy smothered her in his massive arms and held her against his body.

"She doesn't hate you, Alex," Lily said as we watched the tail fins of Tommy's Eldorado disappear down the dimly lit street. He was taking her back to Orient. Annie had insisted on staying at the house to wait for her grandfather. *So there's somebody there when he comes home.* It was Tommy she'd said this to. She hadn't looked at me again. "It's not hatred," Lily said quietly. "It's fear." We made our way across the parking lot. "And not just for your father."

"Can you just shut up?" I snapped. "I'm not in the mood for your nickel-and-dime psychology, and I sure as hell don't need you to explain my daughter."

I wanted it to hurt. I don't think it did. She wouldn't show it anyway. The night gathered thickly around us. The lights in the parking lot made faint pools of luminescence in the damp sea air, like lanterns hung in the leaves.

"Did you get what I asked for?"

"It's in the car. I went to your apartment and packed the bag exactly as you said."

Maybe it was her calmness that made me so angry. When we reached the car, I said, "God help you, Lily, if I find out your partner did this."

Even for me it was a stupid thing to say. To Lily's credit she didn't pull out her little Glock and shoot me on the spot. Instead she took the key fob from her pocket and waited until I met her eyes. "This is what they want, Alex. Whoever is trying to kill you. They want you to lose your ability to understand. That is their objective. They will do anything, and I think it will get much worse. They could easily try to kill Annie. You should not have allowed her to return to your father's house."

She stabbed her fob at the door and the locks clicked open with a beep. We got in and sat in silence for a few minutes. An ambulance pulled in to the emergency entrance. The strobes splashed our faces blue and red. I thought about the house at Orient. It did look lonely. Even a satellite wouldn't find what we'd set up in the woods around the house and on the coast nearby. I didn't tell Lily that. The Porsche awoke with a roar and we shot out of the lot.

The streets were empty. She thrashed up through the gears, blowing two lights before we cleared the town. I watched the needle on the tach rise and fall as she ran the engine up to the red line at every shift. Cocooned by the howl of the engine and the primal scent of leather, we speared the night.

"Help me with the strategy," I finally said. "What do the Chinese want? Cornering the market in lab-grown is crap. That can't be their plan. Why corner a market that's failing? The price of lab-grown is in free fall."

"The obvious plan would be to stop the fall. Once China controls supply, they choke it back until demand forces the price back up."

"Sure. That's how the diamond cartel ran its business for a century. But that only works when the supply is finite in the first place. It doesn't work when you can just grow the product in a diamond reactor. Because as soon as the price recovers, somebody will set up another lab and start growing diamonds. That's the problem with the business right now. Customers finally figured out that something with an infinite supply is fundamentally worthless."

"Yes, I know it's nonsense!" Lily said, suddenly angry. "It's a measure of her desperation that Mei would even bother trying to get me to swallow it. Don't ask me why she has so suddenly embarked on this buying frenzy. I believe she has been ordered to by the generals who are her clients."

"You're her partner, Lily."

"In the mine, yes. Not in everything." She glanced at me. "I wish you would not pretend that you are ignorant of this, Alex. I find it annoying. You have the New York police outside my building, harassing my neighbors. You spy on me relentlessly." She waited to see if I would deny it. Her voice was cold when she continued. "I contracted to buy some of the product. Only the top goods. My plan is to make a few whimsical, high-end items, like the T-shirt, and see how they go. Buying up all those massive diamond plants: that's Mei's hedge fund. I have no share of it."

That sounded right. Lily didn't lie about things that were easy to check. Buying Chinese industrial diamond companies would take a lot of cash. It would leave a money trail impossible to conceal, and MAUREEN could track it. Would have already tracked it. Lily was right. Surveillance on her was basically 24/7 now.

"What you're really asking," Lily said, "is if I know why Mei's generals would want to kill you. Another way to put that is: What is it that they do not want you to discover about this sudden appetite for diamond manufacturers?"

"That's right. You're a professional criminal, so I value your opinion."

"You were a professional criminal, too, Alex. Less successful, but you don't need any lessons in deceit."

We were nearing the New York suburbs and hit some traffic. Lily dropped down a couple of gears and blitzed a line of semis. By the time she snapped the stick back into fifth, we were going a hundred and twenty. Oncoming headlights went by us like tracer. A strip mall in a floodlit plaza loomed in the darkness just ahead and then hurtled past. I had to say it helped, and when Lily hauled the car back down to ninety, I thought we both felt better.

"We have done terrible things," she said in a measured voice, "you as well as me. But let us not add stupidity to the list. Mei and I are not friends. I helped her in the struggle with her brother, a man your government wanted dead, and it was very nearly me who died. My reward was a share of the mine. There is no affection of any kind with Mei. She is a creature only of calculation. What I can tell you is I've never seen her less certain. Not panicked, because that's not in her nature. But anxious."

We were driving west toward the city. The hard edges of the night began to soften into predawn gray. It felt as if the present was rushing away from us at cosmic speed. Soon we would run out of time, and whatever was looming behind it would appear. So I just said, "Lou was dealing fakes. We don't know why he was murdered. If the Chinese were his suppliers, maybe they decided he knew too much."

She thought about it for a moment. "That doesn't make sense. Lou dealt high-end goods. With such stones, a fake would be picked up right away."

"Not these. They're undetectable."

This time she thought a little longer before she said, "You'll have to explain."

"I showed my father one of Lou's stones, a five-carat oval. D flawless. He put it through his spectroscope. He said it couldn't possibly be a fake. It had some anomaly that meant it couldn't be lab-grown."

"And you believe it was?"

"I know it was. It came from a Shanghai lab."

Lily frowned while she thought about it. "Did he say the anomaly was an N3 center?"

I looked at her. "How do you know that?"

"Don't be so suspicious. Just because you've never heard of something doesn't make it a secret."

"You won't mind answering my question, then."

She gave me a blistering look. "It's called research. Did you think I would jump into something new without any study?" She shook her head. "Lab-grown diamonds contain certain anomalies. That particular anomaly—never. Therefore, if a diamond had it, an expert would conclude the diamond was real."

The Southern State Parkway changed into the Belt Parkway. I logged into a private messaging service and thumbed in a short list of what I would need when I reached London.

Then Lily said, "If your father was right about the N3 center, and it came from a Shanghai lab, that changes everything. The falling price of lab-grown is of no concern if the product can be sold as real. The only problem for the seller would be provenance. Where do these diamonds come from?"

I finished my list, pressed Send, and put the phone away. I tried to put away my suspicion, too, but I didn't have a pocket big enough.

"Yeah, where do the diamonds come from?" I said. "That's a real head-scratcher until you remind yourself that the people interested in selling them, namely you and Mei, own a diamond mine and could easily feed the fakes into the mine's production."

"I have already said I am not part of Mei's plans."

"I know what you said."

We merged onto the JFK Expressway. The floodlit prairie of the airport came into view. We turned off at an exit with a sign that read: DEPARTMENT OF DEFENSE—AUTHORIZED ENTRY ONLY. At the security gate, a soldier came out of the guardhouse. I handed him my Treasury pass. He told us to wait, went inside, and picked up a phone.

Lily's face was tight. "I fear for you. I understand your desire for revenge. It will make you vulnerable."

The guard came out, handed back my pass, and raised the barrier. We drove through and parked at a low, gray building. I opened the door and grabbed the bag Lily had packed for me. I walked away without a word.

22

The dull gray air force plane waited on the apron. A fuel truck pulled away and a tug backed up and attached a hitch to the nose wheel. I went up the gangway and into the plane. An airman greeted me and checked my name off a short list.

A few rows of business class seats occupied the front of the cabin. A couple of generals, deep in conversation. They glanced at my bloody shirt and the cuts on my face from the flying glass. Not impressed. One of the first things generals learn is not to pay too close attention to people who look like they've been dragged through crap, because most of the time they are the guys who ordered it.

A narrow passage led down one side of the plane and ended at a gray door. The airman knocked, put my bag inside, and closed the door behind me when I went in.

The cabin took up most of the back half of the plane. It had the usual big important desk set up beside the windows so the people who used the cabin could have their pictures taken—the windows to show they're on a plane, desk to show how hard they work. On the wall behind: eagle clutching lightning bolts. Makes a nice snapshot for whichever senator needs home-state attention. The air force can grab that cabin from flat packs in the hold and bolt it into place in an hour.

Tabitha lay on a cream-colored leather sofa. She wore a cashmere sweater and a pair of old jeans, but she didn't look relaxed. She scooped up the heap of papers in her lap and dumped them on the floor, swung her bare feet to the carpet and plucked a red phone from the wall.

"We're ready now," she said, and hung up without waiting for a reply. "Boy, you look like hell. How's your dad?"

"Bad." I went to the little bar and inserted a capsule into the coffee machine and switched it on. It whirred through its cycle and dribbled a tarry stream into the cup. "He's old. He lost a lot of blood." Rummaging around until I found the cognac, I added a slug to the coffee. "It's only because he's a prick that he's still alive."

The seat belt sign came on with a *pong*. I sat in one of the leather chairs across from her as the plane began to move. The busy early-morning scene scrolled by outside. Airport vehicles and baggage trains raced around as the long-haul jets pulled up at their gates.

The pushback tug unhooked from the nose wheel and sped away. The aircraft engines rose to a higher pitch. We pivoted and taxied swiftly out toward the main runway. In the dawn light, the waters of Jamaica Bay took on a pearly luster. I watched the lights of the A train creep out onto the trestle as it made its way across the water to Far Rockaway.

"Tommy briefed me on the five-carat oval," Tabitha said, "and that you were taking it out for your dad to examine. What did he say?"

I told her exactly what he'd said—that lab-grown were easily identified by the machines that dealers and diamond labs used. Mostly machines developed by Van Kees, whose researchers worked ceaselessly to stay ahead of new developments in lab-grown technology. Then I told her what he'd said about the five-carat oval. When I was through, she grabbed a fistful of hair and twisted it into a rope. She clamped it in her mouth and sat there thinking. Then she took it out and untwined it slowly.

"You're saying that the Shanghai lab can put in one of the flaws?"

"Well, this one had it, so they put it there."

"Have you got it?" I dug the stone out of my jeans and handed it to her. She gazed at it with an unhappy expression. "OK," she said. "I have to keep this, Alex. There are some people who need to see it."

"What people?"

She twisted the hair into a braid again and stared out the window. A line of planes waited for takeoff. "People who will test it."

"It's been tested. By my father. Lane Turner. I just told you."

"Hey, we have a process, OK?" Her eyes flashed angrily. "I'm not, like, *concealing* something from you."

People only say that when they are.

"You haven't told anyone else about this, have you?" she said, rolling the stone in her fingers and frowning at it. I waited until she looked at me.

"You mean Lily."

Her eyes glanced away. "Why on earth would I mean Lily?"

She would mean Lily because the gate called her and would certainly have told her who was there. But fine. If that's how it had to be.

"No."

"No?"

"No, I didn't tell anyone."

Where lies are a currency, it's only prudent to create some of your own.

We turned onto a parallel taxiway and passed the waiting aircraft. They would be held until we cleared. As soon as we swung out onto the main runway, we went to full power. The sun came up and raked Long Island with a saffron light. We lifted off. The undercarriage folded up with a *clunk*. The glass towers of Manhattan ignited into blazing sheets. We turned over the Atlantic and flew into the breaking day.

When we reached cruising altitude, Tabitha unsnapped her seat belt and went to the desk. She put the diamond down and turned on the desk lamp, and I saw something new in her face. Tension. I didn't know if it was fear.

Tabitha came up fast. Instead of being posted to Langley after CIA training at Camp Peary, she'd been seconded to our small unit. It smelled from the start. She was too smart to be my assistant. Someone had put her there for a purpose. It turned out the purpose had been to spy on me while I investigated a presidential candidate involved in a diamond scam. The information Tabitha collected made its way through intermediaries to the candidate's running mate. That's who Tabitha was really working for. The running mate forced the candidate off the ticket, took his place, and won the election.

Tabitha went straight into the West Wing. That was where the first tiny lines were etched into her face. A few more appeared every year, tracking her phenomenal rise. When you get as far in Washington as she did, and as fast, the ascent is mapped onto your face by other people's malice.

A steward knocked and wheeled in a trolley. Unfolding a dining table from the bulkhead, he spread a white tablecloth, set two places with gleaming cutlery, and loaded the table with plates covered in metal domes.

"Serve you up, ma'am?" he said to Tabitha.

She shook her head. "I'll let you know if we need anything else." When he closed the door behind him, we sat there looking at each other. She touched her lips with her fingertips, then turned to the window. The morning light turned her hair to gold. "Alex," she said, but her voice broke.

"It doesn't matter," I said. It must have been two minutes before she spoke again.

"Your clothes," she said. She drew a deep breath and let it out. "I mean, if you want to change."

I picked up my bag and went into a bedroom the width of the plane. The king-size bed was unmade. Tabitha's pajamas lay tossed on the sheets. The room smelled of her skin and hair. I wondered where she'd been. She led a life of urgent flights, of nights spent hurrying to remote airports where cars waited on the runway.

In the bathroom I stripped off my clothes. I opened the glass door of the shower stall and turned on the water. I was just stepping in when I caught a glimpse of myself in the mirror above the sink. My neck was smeared with blood and my hair had stiffened into dark red clumps. Then the billowing steam erased the image.

I turned the water hot and bent my head under the powerful spray. In an instant the drain swirled with red. A rack held a bar of soap and bottles of shampoo. I scrubbed my body hard and worked the shampoo into my hair. Slowly the tension in my muscles eased.

I felt a cool draft as the door to the bathroom opened. Through the misted glass, her long body shimmered as she stepped from her clothes. We hit rough air just as she came in. She staggered against me and seized my hair in her hands and kissed me fiercely. Her breasts pressed against my chest. The plane hit another patch of turbulence and we crashed against the glass. She took my hand in a tight grip and pushed the door open. We'd been coming to this moment for a long time. Tabitha was a vortex. What waits inside a vortex is oblivion. I wanted it.

Later, her wet hair clung to the sheets in a fantastic arabesque. Her eyes softened and her skin was pink. She pulled my head across the pillow and brushed my face with her lips, inhaling me in a long, deep breath. We were like two people pulled from wreckage and, just for that moment, safe.

23

We were still in bed when Tabitha rolled up her sleeves and got back to work. She moved her head away a few inches on the pillow and blew a clump of hair from her eyes. "I was copied on your report about the meeting with Hassan."

"Uh-huh."

"It's kind of bugging me."

"Oh?"

"Well, those guys at the CIA are trashing me, and Hassan made a point of passing it on and you didn't tell me about it."

"I can imagine how hurt you must be."

She raised herself on an elbow and studied my face for a moment, then traced her fingertip along my nose. "You're a sarcastic bastard, aren't you, bruiser."

"Listen," I said, "I have an idea. Why don't we make believe that we're both professional espionage agents. That way you won't have to act surprised to learn that people are saying mean things about you, especially when they are people whose careers you could crush in a moment, but won't, because they are sliming you at your direction, whether they know it or not."

"You're such a cynic, Alex," she said, brushing my lips with her thumb. I could see her shuffling through the possibilities: tell him, don't tell him, lie, tell him a bit. I think she settled on the last one, but how would I know?

"It's true that I don't mind if Mei thinks my own people are unsure of me," she said. "The problem is it's true. When we removed the brother, we basically created Mei, because she got all the power, including that diamond mine."

"Yes, but you anticipated that when you pitched the operation. You pointed out that Mei would take over the hedge fund, and that since she was a much more stable person than her brother, she could be more dangerous."

She put her fingers in my hair. "They'll forget that. They'll hang this on me. I helped put Mei into diamonds, and that position has helped her get to this point, where she can use a whole industry against us."

Her face was very close to mine. A lock of hair lay on my cheek and her breath was warm. One of her legs slid over mine.

"Against us how?" I said. I thought for a moment she might tell me what was consuming her, but she put a finger on my lips to stop me. The plane hit more turbulence. The seat belt warning sounded, and a minute later the plane dropped into a downdraft and shuddered violently. The motion threw us together in a tangle of limbs. Our arms tightened around each other.

Tabitha showered first. She was dressed when I was through—dark suit with a pencil skirt, plain white shirt. Hair pulled back and fastened in a clip behind her neck.

We flew into the advancing night. As the light outside the cabin bled away, it seemed to take her spirit with it. She paced around the cabin.

"Where are you with that girl?" she said. "The one who shot Leopold Rose."

"Marie Hout? Nowhere."

"That won't be her name."

"No."

"If Mei is running an operation with the fakes, killing Leopold means she's mopping up. If she is, then something's frightening her. They killed Lou, and Leopold was next. Now they'll dial it up on you again." She stopped pacing and swung around to face me. Her face was pale. "They're not going to leave you on the board."

"So I keep hearing."

Her eyes flashed. "You don't seem to take this seriously."

"I'll tell you what I take seriously. I take seriously that you were way out in front of me on Mei's expansion into lab-grown, on the Chinese generals buying up industrial production, and on the Geneva white. You didn't advise me or consult me. Fine. You don't have to tell me what you know or think, whereas I'm just the dumb fuck getting his ass shot at and whose father's life hangs by a thread because of some plan that you understand and I don't."

"Alex."

"I'm not through. Not only have you kept me in the dark, but I'm supposed to buy your theory that what's happening is a Chinese plan to marshal their vast synthetic-diamond muscle into making fakes. Why? To gain an anonymous, universal currency for free and use it to corrupt the known world. And that's bullshit. For one thing, I don't see that a few hundred million in easy money for the Chinese is going to make your bosses too upset, when the real fight is a trillion-dollar struggle to the death for military superiority. And for another, if high-end fakes is what they're doing, we now know it, they know we know it, and sending assassins to New York is not a fix."

Tabitha sat down on the sofa. My outburst hadn't thrown her. It had calmed her. She folded her hands in her lap. Portrait of a lady.

"I didn't say it all makes perfect sense," she said. "We're not idiots." She smoothed her skirt while she thought about what to say. "But we have to put something on the file, don't we?"

Her face was grave as she watched for my reaction. She'd always been like that, from the first. She'd play a card and wait to see if you understood where she was going with it.

"You have a leak," I said. "You have a leak and you're planting a false lead."

"Put it like this: we're managing the need to know on a very tight basis."

So that was clear. She didn't believe that the Chinese motive was just extra cash any more than I did. It was something scarier, and so secret they feared I could unwittingly alert the target if I knew what the secret was.

The coast of Ireland twinkled against the black ocean. Twenty minutes later we started our descent to London. She sat on the sofa and stared out the window like someone watching the approach of a mortal enemy.

We crossed the Irish Sea. At one point I thought she wanted to say something more. She turned from the window, her hands clenched in her lap, and drew a deep breath. But she said nothing. By the time we were on final into London, she had herself firmly in control again.

Below, the dark serpentine of the Thames wound through the city. We were landing at Northolt, a Royal Air Force base. I was the only one leaving the plane in London. Tabitha and the generals were going on to a NATO meeting in Brussels. We landed in heavy rain.

"What will you get from Van Kees?" she said as we taxied in.

A gust rocked the plane as we turned off the main runway. The roar of powerful turboprops shook the air as a French air force transport taxied past. As the British capital's military airport, Northolt got a lot of NATO traffic. A Gulfstream with Turkish insignia pulled to a stop in front of the passenger terminal. We trundled past and headed for a distant corner of the field.

"Understanding how it might be possible to make the fakes—I guess that's still important or I wouldn't be here. Have I got that right?"

"Yes."

"Van Kees once ran the whole diamond business. They traded eighty percent of the world supply of rough at their London headquarters."

"And they make the machines that test for fakes."

"That's right."

We came to a stop in front of a dilapidated building barely visible in the driving rain. Every country has a back door for people like me. This was Britain's.

Tabitha watched as I put on my jacket. She bit a corner of her lower lip.

"They'll know about the Geneva white," I said.

"I understand. I wonder what they'll tell you."

I picked up my bag. "Lies. They'll tell me lies."

I went out the door and along the aisle to the front of the plane, down the gangway and into the rain. In the terminal, a tired-looking man glanced at my passport and nodded. I walked down a long hall and through some doors and back out into the rain. The pavement glimmered with a sickly yellow light. I climbed into a cab. The tail picked us up as soon as we came out the gate.

24

We took the A40 into Wembley, exited, and picked our way to Willesden. I directed the cabbie on a twisted route through northwest London until we found ourselves in Cricklewood. He'd figured out what was up long ago, and when I asked him to cut through Dollis Hill, he reached behind his head and slid back the Plexiglas panel.

"Just tell me where you want to end up, mate," he said, "and I guarantee there won't be anybody with us when we get there."

"West Hampstead tube," I said. With that we plunged into the maze of lanes and traffic circles and sudden squares that only a Londoner can love. Forty minutes later we arrived. I got out and paid him through the window and added two fifty-pound notes.

"Gray Volvo," he said. "I shook him off before Mill Lane."

I went inside and down to the platform and caught the southbound Jubilee Line train. At Baker Street I got off and ran upstairs and through the crowded hall. I grabbed a cab outside on Marylebone Road and got out at the top of Great Portland Street. Ten minutes later I entered a tiny bookstore on a sliver of a street near Tottenham Court Road.

"I believe you're holding a package for me," I told the frail old man who was standing on a two-step ladder, shelving books. He was the only one in the store. He'd always been the only one in the store. I'm not sure he ever sold a book. He climbed slowly down and peered at me over his glasses.

"Ah, yes. Mr. Ryder." He disappeared into the back of his shop and came out a few minutes later with a canvas bag. The shop on the little street where they don't ask questions. That's part of a spy's equipment too. Someone came by every month and paid him two hundred pounds in twenty-pound notes.

I hailed another cab and got out at Regent's Park. The rain had given way to that penetrating damp the British call Scotch mist. The leaves on the plane trees glistened like wet rubber. The lamps cast yellow smudges of light. The park was empty. I walked up through the zoo and across Prince Albert Road into Primrose Hill. Halfway up I stopped and watched the way I'd come. No one came out of the park.

London's skyline spread out to the south. The building called the Shard sliced the wet sky with its gleaming blade. I could just make out the dome of St. Paul's, and to the west, the tower of the House of Lords. The city came swimming to me through the soft night. I'd lived here for two years. London never hits you with a hammer. It sends out its coils and waits for you to step into them.

I left Primrose Hill by the gate into Ellsworthy Terrace. I walked through Belsize Park to a dilapidated hotel that had been cobbled together from three adjoining townhouses. You wouldn't find it on Tripadvisor. It housed a small population of bedraggled pensioners and the kind of repeat customers who arrived in the middle of the night and paid in cash.

"It's you, then, Mr. Ryder," Mrs. Goodwell said, appearing from her tiny office when I pinged the bell on the front desk. "How nice to see you again."

Nothing surprised Mrs. Goodwell. You could arrive on a dog sled in the middle of a blizzard and tramp in shaking snow from your parka—she'd say exactly the same thing.

"You'll be wanting your usual room, then. It's always the same with you, Mr. Ryder. Always," she repeated, her face glowing with approval.

She hauled out an ancient ledger, opened it, and ran a bony finger down a column. "There we are," she said. "Lovely. It's free." She beamed at the page. "So that's all fine, then. Top floor. Number 18." She closed the ledger with a dusty thud and fixed me with her faded blue eyes. "Private bath," she added in a low voice, as if such an extravagance was a secret we shared. She fished a key from the rack behind her and slid it across the desk. She nodded at my bags. "I'll let you manage on your own, then." She turned away before suddenly turning back and leaning across the desk. "Full English breakfast at seven," she whispered, confessing yet another folly. She disappeared into her shoebox office with a beatific smile.

In my room I locked the door and closed the curtains and moved the desk away from the window. You never know.

I sat down and positioned the flex lamp over the plain green blotter and opened the canvas bag from the bookshop. I transferred the contents to the desk—three small cardboard boxes sealed with duct tape, two phones wrapped in plastic, and a thick manila envelope. I put the bag on the floor and unpeeled the tape from the largest of the three boxes. I opened it, discarded the bubble wrap inside, and placed the pistol and the extra magazine on the blotter. Beretta 21A Bobcat. I picked up the gun and let it sit in the palm of my hand. Less than five inches long, it weighed twelve ounces. It was chambered for .25 ACP, which meant the magazine could take eight rounds.

The next box contained the silencer. Most silencers would double the length of the pistol, but this one was made of anodized aluminum to keep it light. It added less than three inches to the barrel. No silencer completely eliminates noise, but this one had an ingenious arrangement of baffles that crushed the sound to no more than a cough.

The last cardboard package was a single box of KelTec .25 ACP. Fifty rounds, full metal jacket. It's not a powerful ammunition, like 9mm, that can knock a man off his feet; but a fifty-grain bullet with a velocity of 760 feet per second will still make a hole in your head.

I loaded the magazines, snapped one into the pistol, and took out the phones. Both were burners—to be discarded after a single call. Taped to the outside of one phone was the lens I'd asked for. It looked like a pin with a drop of glass at the end. I opened the door and checked the hall. No one. I inserted the lens into the top of the doorframe, stepped back in, and locked the door. Next I opened my phone and paired the Bluetooth lens to the surveillance app. I checked the view. The tiny fisheye gave me clear sight lines both ways down the hall. I tapped an icon to add the motion sensor function, closed the app and turned out the lights.

As I lay on the bed I listened to the old hotel. It made a lot of noise. That was one reason I liked it. You could tell where people were. The squeak of the old boards tracked them up the stairs and along the corridors, like blips on radar screen.

I closed my eyes, slowed my breathing, and made myself relax. One by one I unpicked the knots from my muscles. The hotel wrapped me in its comforting smell of genteel mustiness. How is it that the sense of smell can transport you into the past in an instant? I remembered how I'd come the first time.

Hassan had got me out of a jam in Stockholm, getting the CIA station chief out of bed in the middle of the night for phony papers.

Hassan planned the route. From Sweden I went to Norway by bus, crossing the border north of Oslo and going on to Bergen. I took the ferry across the North Sea to Aberdeen. Another bus, this time to Edinburgh, where I caught the east coast night train south to London. My flight to Cape Town, where I was based, was booked for the following day. I needed a hotel. Hassan had sent me to Mrs. Goodwell's.

I was just drifting into sleep with this lullaby of memories playing in my head when I heard the squeak of a floorboard from the stairs and my phone made a tiny tick, like someone tapping a dime against the screen. The motion sensor outside had detected movement.

I grabbed the Beretta and eased myself off the bed. The surveillance-app icon pulsed on the screen. I tapped it, and there was Mrs. Goodwell. She had just come up the stairs with some folded towels. She glanced back down the stairs, and I saw a shadow appear on the wall, as if someone had stopped on the landing. Then Mrs. Goodwell came along the hall and tapped at my door.

"Yes?" I said.

"Oh, Mr. Ryder, you'll think me terribly forgetful," she said. "I'm afraid you'll find there are no towels. We weren't expecting you, and the maid didn't finish making up the room. I've brought them up."

That's how fast things can turn. I eased the bathroom door open. Sure enough, the towel rack was empty. Still, who was on the stairs?

"That's fine, Mrs. Goodwell. Just leave them in the hall."

"You must think me a terrible ninny, Mr. Ryder."

"No," I said. And I didn't.

She placed the towels on the carpet. "They're just here, at the door."

"Thanks."

"I'm sorry to disturb you."

"Not a problem."

She went back along the hall and disappeared down the stairs. Not the shadow, though. The shadow stayed. A full five minutes. Probably to see if I'd come out for the towels. Then the shadow disappeared too, and a minute later I heard a car door close outside. Softly, but I heard it. I stepped to the window and edged the curtain open. Gray Volvo at the end of the street. I let the curtain fall back into place and sat down heavily on the bed and thought: Mrs. Goodwell. Jesus.

The hotel creaked and moaned in the night. Once, I heard the clicking of high heels and the murmur of voices and got up to check. It was just a couple walking by. The two guys were still in the Volvo. I returned to the bed and stretched out again and thought about Hassan. Because that's who'd set me up. Hassan was the only link to Mrs. Goodwell. Other than Tommy, no other person would know where to find me. I was just about to call Tommy when my phone vibrated, and it was him.

"Alex, I'm sorry. Your dad didn't make it."

All the sounds of the hotel faded away. A thick silence settled around me. I didn't know what to say. There was already a dark hole inside me where a father was supposed to be. I don't know if the news of his death made it any deeper. When I didn't say anything, Tommy told me what had happened. My father had gone into shock again, and they hadn't been able to revive him.

"OK," I said.

Tommy let another silent space go by, then told me he'd called Pierrette. She was driving out to Orient to pick up Annie, or if Annie wouldn't leave, to stay with her there.

"OK," I said again.

Tommy waited for a moment, then said, "What's up, hermano?" So I told him. I included the tail from Northolt, how I'd shaken it off, and what had just happened with Mrs. Goodwell.

"She's the old lady who runs that shithole nobody knows you stay at except for whoever apparently intends to kill you with her help?"

"Yes," I said.

"I'll call operations."

"No. They'll use contractors. Whoever is running Mrs. Goodwell has contractors too. It's too risky. I can get out of here, Tommy."

I heard his chair squeak as he leaned forward. "I don't like it."

"It's my best shot."

The chair squeaked again as he got up. I heard him pacing around the room.

"What time are you going to go?"

"Five."

"If I don't hear from you by five thirty, I'm sending in the cavalry."

"Sure."

Then I made one more call.

25

At 5:00 A.M. I checked the Bobcat, sliding out the magazine and putting it back in. I screwed on the suppressor. Five o'clock was a good time to leave. It's not the middle of the night, when the guys outside would expect me to try. If I'm still here at five, maybe I bought the crap about the towels and was waiting for the full English breakfast of eggs, bacon, sausages, beans, and a .38 in the head.

I tried not to think about my father. Lots of men have dads who hate them. Some of those must die without saying they didn't mean it or giving their sons the chance to say the same. It's no good thinking about it.

Slipping the extra magazine, the box of ammunition, and the manila envelope into my jacket, I crossed to the window and checked the street. The Volvo was still there. The two guys were inside. I stepped away from the window, grabbed my wallet, and checked the surveillance app one last time. No one in the hall. No shadow from the stairs. I opened the door and stepped outside and stood with my back against the wall and listened. Then I headed down the hall away from the main stairs.

I kept to the side of the corridor, where the floorboards didn't squeak. When I came to a door marked STAFF ONLY, I eased it open and stepped into a steep, dimly lit staircase. There were three of these—servants' stairs from the days when the townhouses had been the separate homes of prosperous families. Mrs. Goodwell's housekeeping staff still used them. I knew where they were because I'd reconnoitered the hotel when I'd first stayed there.

I started down the staircase. At the second-floor landing I stopped and listened. A busy clatter came from the kitchen below as the staff arrived. I could hear them talking. While I couldn't hear what they were saying, it sounded like the casual banter of an ordinary day. Nobody was saying, "Don't forget to make noise so Mrs. Goodwell can sneak up behind that Ryder asshole." But they didn't have to. I was almost at the bottom of the stairs when a draft blew down and stroked the back of my neck, followed immediately by the sound of a shell being racked into the chamber of a pump-action shotgun.

"Dear me, Mr. Ryder," Mrs. Goodwell said, "isn't this a pickle."

"Yes," I said. I turned around. She had a twelve-gauge Mossberg riot gun.

"All this creeping about. Really, Mr. Ryder—what on earth is going on?"

"Early checkout."

"Are you going to drop that gun?"

We studied each other for a moment. She was as cold as ice. "Tell you what," I said. "How about if I disarm it?" She wasn't going to shoot me right there, where there were witnesses nearby, or I'd be dead already. I held the gun away from me, pulled out the magazine, and dropped it on the stairs. I pulled the trigger a few times to show the chamber was empty, and dropped the gun in my pocket.

"What's up, Mrs. Goodwell?"

"There's a red notice on you. Half the town's out looking for you. We didn't think you'd come here."

I stared at her. "Red notice?" A red notice was an Interpol alert to detain a fugitive. "Who is 'we,' Mrs. Goodwell? Hassan?"

She watched me carefully, the gun not wavering.

"Mr. Crawford has always looked out for you. That's what he's trying to do now. Protect you from people trying to harm you."

"I'm not so sure about that."

More banging came from the kitchen. She leaned her head forward slightly and darted a glance along the hall. I thought of grabbing the barrel. Maybe I telegraphed my intention with a slight movement, because she jerked her head back and the Mossberg stayed rock steady. "Please don't do anything foolish. I'm sure this is all a misunderstanding. We can talk better in the basement. There's a phone down there. We'll call Mr. Crawford."

"And until we reach Hassan, you'll keep a twelve-gauge shotgun aimed at me. It seems a lot for a misunderstanding."

"I'm only an old woman. I have to be careful. There are men posted outside waiting for you, but there's a door in the cellar you can use to get outside."

"Once we've had our chat with Hassan."

"Yes." Her eyes were like holes, and I thought: She's done this before. "Take the passage," she said, moving the barrel. "To the left of the kitchen."

The main part of the hotel, with the front desk, dining room, and kitchen, occupied the first of the row of three houses. The other two houses connected through a snakes-and-ladders maze of crooked halls covered in threadbare carpet. The route we took led past the kitchen, up a short staircase, then down again as it led into the next house. Whenever the hall doglegged, I could see her from the corner of my eye, keeping two paces back. We were in the third house when the hallway ended at a metal door.

"Wait," she said. "And please don't move. You'll hear me getting out the key. I can do that with one hand."

I heard the key unsnap from a ring, and she threw it on the carpet at my feet.

"Pick it up slowly. The lock is two turns counterclockwise."

I unlocked it. The door swung open to a steep flight of stairs that led down to the basement.

"Leave the key in the lock. When you get to the bottom of the stairs, wait."

I hesitated, and she nudged me with the muzzle.

That's when Frankie said softly, "Hey," and the barrel shifted as Mrs. Goodwell froze. I spun away and drove my elbow into her throat. I grabbed the Mossberg and clubbed her with the stock. I dragged her through the door and pushed her down the stairs. She lay in a heap at the bottom.

"I'll have to kill her," I said.

"I know, honey."

I went down and broke her neck. Frankie locked the door behind us. We moved carefully through the dark basement. A door at the back opened into a sunken area with steps leading up to a patch of lawn. We crossed the lawn to a hedge and through a gate onto King Henry Road.

"Catch you later," Frankie said, and disappeared into the shadows.

Ten minutes later I got out of a cab in Regent's Park and texted Tommy: "Out."

The rain had passed in the night and left the city crisp and shining. Big white clouds sailed through a blue sky. I got myself a coffee and sat on a bench and watched a man throw tennis balls for his border collie. The dog lay flat on the grass as if he'd been pasted there, his body quivering as he watched the ball soar into the air and bounce onto the lawn. At the word of command, he shot across the grass, snatched the ball, and tore straight back. He dropped the ball at his master's feet and immediately flattened himself to the ground again, as taut as a bowstring, waiting for the next toss.

I checked my phone for a message from Annie, but there wasn't one, so I called her. It went to voicemail. "Hey," I said, "it's Dad. I'm sorry."

The dog dashed back and forth across the wide expanse, never tiring. On the last throw, the man pocketed the ball when the dog retrieved it, clipped on the leash, and came along the path. When he reached the bench where I was sitting, his steps slowed and then he stopped.

"Excuse me," he said, "are you all right?"

"Yes," I said.

He had a kindly face and thin white hair. He dug in his pocket until he found a Kleenex and held it out to me. "I'm sorry, but you're crying."

When he was gone I waited a few minutes and left by the same gate. From the garden, I walked down to Marylebone Road. Twice I stopped and checked for a tail. Then I crossed the busy thoroughfare into Marylebone High Street and headed south. By now the watchers in the Volvo would have found Mrs. Goodwell. If Hassan could have me tailed from Northolt and arrange for a couple of hoods outside the hotel, someone was paying him real money. Also, he'd have contacts in friendly intelligence services. London bristled with cameras. It was one of the most surveilled cities in the world. With the right contacts, Hassan could turn the city into a single eye, one on the watch for me.

Two hours later I walked out of the John Lewis department store onto Oxford Street. I was wearing a dark blue suit, white shirt, conservative tie, new black shoes, and a dark green fedora with a narrow brim and a feather in the band. The hat made the blonde wig look more natural. I wore a reversible trench coat with the light side out. It was unbuttoned. I had thick black-framed glasses with plain lenses and carried a bright plaid garment bag.

I hopped a double-decker at Oxford Circus and rode up to Marble Arch, where I got off and went straight downstairs to the tube. I left the red plaid bag and the wig and the fedora on the bus and had the glasses in my pocket. The trench coat now had the blue side showing. That's a lot for the computer to sort out if, as I suspected, Hassan might be getting help from somebody inside the GCHQ—the Government Communications Headquarters, Britain's equivalent of the NSA. The computers are fast, but in the end an intelligence officer evaluating the data would have to make the call that the guy who came out of John Lewis was probably me, and then they'd have to sweat through masses of possible matches before concluding that the man who got off at Marble Arch was the one who boarded at Oxford Circus. Then they would spend a lot of time doing tube searches before they came back to Marble Arch and decided that I was the guy—this time without the trench coat, but glasses back on—who'd come straight back out of the tube station forty-five seconds after he'd gone in. Even then they'd have to track me through the dense crowd of shoppers on Oxford Street, where I took off my jacket and rolled up my shirtsleeves and ditched the glasses for good before I hopped in a cab. They would put it all together eventually, but all I needed was enough time to get through the meeting I'd come for and then get out of London.

26

The taxi came down Hatton Garden. The windows of diamond merchants blazed with jewels. At the bottom of the street, we jogged left onto High Holborn, then left again onto Charterhouse Street.

I watched number 15 come up on the left. Physically it looked the same as it had the last time I was here. Arrow-slit windows. Steel bollards on the sidewalk so you couldn't smash a truck through the wall and steal the diamonds. Once, there'd been a lot to steal. Most of the world's rough diamonds passed through that building. Today the bollards were like the battlements of an abandoned castle, protecting nothing but a memory. You wouldn't know it from the doorman though. Still magnificent in a blue swallowtail coat with a loop of braid at the shoulder and the monogram VK stitched in silver thread on the lapels.

I still had fifteen minutes before my appointment, so I had the driver make a U-turn and drop me off at Ely Place. At the end of the little cul-de-sac was St. Etheldreda's, an Anglo-Saxon chapel. I went inside and sat in a pew at the back. Men and women had been finding peace in that little church for nine hundred years. I sat there trying to find it too. I gazed at the stained-glass windows and inhaled the scent of incense and old wood. I didn't find the peace. Probably I needed more than fifteen minutes.

At noon on the dot, I came out of Ely Place and headed down Charterhouse Street. "Alex Turner," I said to the doorman in the swallowtail coat.

"Very good, sir," he said, opening the door with a white-gloved hand. "Just give your name in at the concierge, if you wouldn't mind. They're expecting you."

If they hadn't been expecting me, I wouldn't have got through the door. What was left of the Van Kees diamond-trading business had moved to the African countries where the diamonds came from. All that was left at the building in Charterhouse Street was burning resentment and the habits of a century, but maybe that was worth protecting too.

"Anything you'd like to leave with me, sir?" the concierge said. I handed him the Bobcat and the silencer. He received them with a face as blank as his starched white shirt, slipping them into a drawer and locking it with a silver key. He raised his chin at a young Black man sitting on a bench against the wall. He stood up and waited at the open elevator door. He was shorter than me, but he had the kind of build you'd get if your hobby was rowing oil tankers around. He had a busted nose and cauliflower ears and flat eyes. His shirt was tight across the chest. The door shut behind us and we rose slowly to the third floor. The car creaked and shuddered as it climbed. We studied each other the way guys who've taken punches sometimes do.

"Boxing?" I said.

"Rugby." He studied my face. "What's your excuse?"

"Bad judgment."

The elevator stopped with a lurch and the door rattled open. I followed him out into a green-carpeted lounge.

Van Kees sold its diamonds ten times a year at sales called sights. Dealers important enough to be invited were called sightholders. The lounge was where they used to wait to find out what Van Kees had decided to sell them that month. Some of the richest men in diamonds were made to sit in the lounge like fattened pigs until they were summoned into one of the small trading rooms and slaughtered.

"Not much going on these days," I said. He slid the flat eyes at me.

"Africa, mate."

We left the empty lounge, went down a short hall, and arrived at a door padded in red leather. He pushed a brass button on the wall. A loud click sounded. He pulled the door open and held it for me. I stepped through into a large, richly furnished room with Persian carpets and old, silk-shaded lamps and the simmering eyes of the deposed rulers of the diamond world.

"Teddy," I said. "Edwina."

"We're a bit pushed for time," Teddy rumbled. They were standing beside a long, polished table. The surface bristled with silver-framed photographs of elderly Dutch people glaring out at their posterity. Beside the photographs were crystal models of famous Van Kees stones, including some now in the British crown jewels. One was a piece of rough—a massive, craggy diamond shot with fault planes. At a glance I thought: three hundred carats. I could only think of one stone it could be. It was the diamond from the Transvaal pit that Sir Harry, Teddy's father, had tried to polish into a Lucifer cut.

Teddy drummed his fingers beside it.

"I must say, you look like hell, old chap," he said. He clenched his jaw and displayed a row of large teeth, a maneuver someone must have told him was a smile. "Someone catch you stealing diamonds?"

"Daddy," Little Teddy said, "we saw him in New York."

"Did he look like that?"

They both admired the damage before Little Teddy led the way to a pair of sofas that faced each other across a low table. As soon as we sat, a waiter in a white jacket glided in through a side door. He set down a tray laid with a silver coffeepot, china cups with the VK monogram, and a plate heaped with pastry.

"We don't need that," Teddy barked. "He's not staying."

The waiter didn't turn a hair. He picked up the tray and went. The Teddys were famous for tricks like that. I doubt there was even coffee in the pot.

"It's about Lou Fine," I said when the door closed behind the waiter.

"We don't know anything about Lou Fine," Little Teddy said coldly. She had a perfect oval face, like a figure in a Renaissance painting. Our Lady of Disdain. She crossed her bony legs and smoothed her dress and folded her hands against the deep-red woolen fabric. On the small finger of her right hand, she wore a gold ring with an old-fashioned mine-cut doorstopper of a stone.

"You knew him well enough to sell him diamonds for twenty years," I said.

"Hundreds of men fit that description. It doesn't mean we have special knowledge about why someone would, say, shoot him in the head."

Teddy made an elaborate show of looking at his watch.

"Who said he was shot in the head?" I asked.

She blushed furiously and glared at her hands.

"If he wasn't, then I suppose I assumed it."

"Sure," I said. "Listen, guys, this will go faster if we can all pretend I didn't just land from some distant planet. I don't need your help with the murder. We know who killed Lou. It's just a matter of time before we trace the killers to whoever paid them."

I let that sit for a minute.

"Here's what I want to talk about. You were Lou's main supplier. Most of his diamonds came in his regular Van Kees box. So tell me—how did a jeweler like Lou, dealing mostly Van Kees stones, end up selling an eleven-carat D flawless in Geneva for $1.4 million, a reasonable price if it was real, which it was not."

Now they were paying attention.

27

Teddy's clenched expression slid from his face like a load of old snow from a roof. I could almost hear it go *whump*. He sat there looking thoughtful. A wrinkle crept onto Little Teddy's face. She didn't look at her father.

"I see," Teddy said finally. "We were wondering why you'd come. We thought it must be important, but I suppose it's to be the usual rubbishing of someone's reputation. A dead man." He reached out and picked a crystal from the table. "And I thought he was your friend."

"He wasn't Mother Teresa, Teddy, and neither are we. Somebody murdered him. I think it had something to do with that Geneva white. You must have heard some murmur about it. Everyone else has."

Teddy revolved the stone in his fingers. "This kind of thing never happened in the single-seller days."

"Single-seller," I said. "You're the only people who ever called it that. You ran a cartel."

"Call it what you like," said Teddy, narrowing his eyes at the crystal. "We kept a firm hand on things. Everyone got a fair price for their goods."

"They got the price you dictated."

Suddenly Teddy gripped the diamond model tightly in his fist. "Of course we bloody dictated it," he snapped. "There would have been no diamond business if we hadn't!"

Little Teddy put her hand on his arm. "Daddy," she murmured.

He yanked his arm away. His voice was level but his eyes burned. "We invented the diamond business. Our family. Those first African discoveries. Tens of thousands of men flocking to the diamond fields. Jewels suddenly pouring into the world. The price collapsed!"

Little Teddy lowered her eyes as she listened to her father.

"We *welded* the mines into one," he said, raising his fist with the crystal glinting through his fingers. "We created a single mechanism. The price stabilized. We created the engagement ring. A *master* stroke!"

He sucked air through his teeth. The muscles of his face were tight. With an effort, he kept himself under control.

"They took it from us," he said. "The African countries. Not enough that we share the revenue and build their hospitals and schools and train their people. No. They must have the sales too. They must destroy the center of the diamond world. London," he breathed, "the great capital of diamonds."

He spoke the last words almost to himself, as if describing some vanished Xanadu that danced forever in his mind. I could taste his bitterness. He ran a powerful mining company and reaped large profits from his own share of what they mined. But for Teddy it was a pitiful remnant of what they'd had. Everything.

"You have something nobody else has, Teddy. GemCheck. It's the gold standard for checking for fakes. Why didn't it catch the Geneva white? Because according to the records, the auctioneer ran it."

"Impossible," said Little Teddy.

"And yet it happened."

"No no no no no," she said, wagging a finger at me. "The first thing you have to understand, Alex, is that there is no such thing as an undetectable fake." Our Lady of Explaining Things to the Dunce. "The lab-grown diamond that cannot be detected simply does not exist. It's a matter of science."

"Thanks, mom. But it leaves the question: How did they do it?"

She gave me a frosty smile. "You'd be surprised how often this happens. But if a lab-grown stone gets identified as real, it doesn't mean the fake was undetectable. It just means it wasn't detected. There are plausible explanations for that. Including fraud."

"Edwina," Teddy enunciated softly.

"No, Daddy. He should hear it."

What a pair. Alex must hear the horrible truth. I wanted to bang their heads together.

"The house collects a ten percent commission from the buyer and the seller each, for a total of twenty percent. If the stone sold for $1.4 million, the house made $280,000 and Lou made the difference between whatever he paid for a synthetic stone and sold as real."

"So it's a straight-out scam—that's what you're saying. It couldn't be a stone that beat the GemCheck."

"Not with a competent technician. It's a scientific instrument, not an oracle. It requires some basic gemological expertise from the operator."

"Maybe you could show me how it works," I said.

Her face hardened. "That would be inconvenient."

"How inconvenient can it be? It's in the basement. You moved the whole operation into this building a month ago."

Teddy looked surprised. "We never comment on confidential technical matters," he said. "I don't know where you heard this."

"Teddy, I don't want to argue. No one's accusing you of anything. I want to see how the latest models work. If you don't show me, I'm going to conclude you are hiding something and that Van Kees imports into the United States are not reliable."

Little Teddy twisted the big mine-cut on her finger. "Have you no self-respect at all?"

"Not on me."

The rugby guy was waiting at the elevator. "Third below ground, Nelson," Teddy said curtly. The doors rattled shut and the carriage began a shuddering descent. When it reached the bottom, it stopped with a slight bounce. The door shushed opened and we stepped out into a brightly lit room. Most of the space was taken up by a screening system like the ones at airports. Two guards in uniform manned the body scanner and the X-ray for bags.

Teddy motioned me through first. The scanner beeped. The guard waved his wand briskly over my clothes. It squealed at my belt buckle and my watch. He stood aside to let me pass. The Teddys also beeped as they walked through the frame, but the guard didn't check them with his wand. Teddy could have been carrying a twelve-gauge Mossberg riot gun. Probably not, though. He had Nelson.

We went down a short hall that ended at a door with a camera mounted on the wall beside it. Teddy pressed a button. A bell sounded on the other side and a red light glowed beside the lens. A voice said, "Yes, sir?"

Teddy looked blankly at the door. "Damn it," he said at last, turning to Little Teddy. "What's that bloody password again?"

"Firewatch," she snapped at the camera. The door buzzed open.

There must have been half an acre of polished concrete. The floor shone in the intense light. The light itself came from translucent panels on the ceiling. The panels diffused the light that fell on the ranks of metal tables.

The lab looked as if it was still being put together. Men and women in white coats sat on stools at the tables, assembling pieces of apparatus. Others uncrated equipment from boxes stacked along one wall and carried it piece by piece to the tables.

At the far end of the room, a line of offices with glass walls faced into the main room. A woman hurried from one as soon as she saw us in the room. She looked worried.

"Please show Mr. Turner how the GemCheck works," Teddy said.

"Yes, sir, the, um . . ."

"The new model," Little Teddy said sharply.

A few minutes later we were sitting at a desk in front of a black device with a curved lid. The woman opened it, placed a diamond in a slot, and closed the lid. She struck a few keys on a laptop and the image of a diamond popped into view on the screen. It was flooded with blue light.

"This is a natural diamond from one of our own mines," she said. "The instrument bombards it with ultraviolet light, causing the stone to fluoresce, saturating it with dark blue light." She brushed a finger on the touch pad. "As I rotate the diamond, you can see the dislocation network." She pointed at the screen. "All these fine lines. That tells you the growth history of the diamond, that it took millions of years to form, and during that time the turbulence and changing heat and pressure of the mantle created this unevenness in the interior of the crystal."

Next she put in a lab-grown diamond. The differences were obvious. The color was much lighter and the crystal showed flat, clean growth planes—the result of a controlled environment and a growth time of only weeks. The CVD diamond betrayed itself with a burst of orange fluorescence.

The Teddys hovered behind us, radiating impatience.

"But a dealer woudn't examine every stone like this."

"Oh, no," she said. "First it goes through a machine that just says 'pass' or 'refer.' Pass means it's fine. Refer means they would take a look as we've just done here."

"What about an N3 center?" I said.

"An N3 center," the tech repeated, seeming stunned by the question. Or scared. She glanced at Teddy.

"That's right," I said, "An N3 center. You know—a point inside a crystal where three nitrogen atoms surround a vacancy?" I could hear my father's exact words. "A place where the crystal is missing a carbon atom," I said. "Could you detect that with one of these?"

"That's enough," said Teddy, suddenly angry. "These people have work to do. Thank you," he said brusquely to the woman. She practically ran from the desk. "You asked to see it, and we've taken the time to show you," Teddy said. "We understood you were investigating the deplorable death of an old and valued friend. But now you are asking questions about our scientific research, which is a proprietary asset of this company."

"Are you researching N3 centers, Teddy? Is that something you know how to make? Wouldn't that be a breakthrough?"

He swallowed and waved his hand around. "I don't understand the half of what these people do. We really must ask you to let our staff get back to work. We'll show you out."

He lumbered across the room and yanked at the locked exit door until a guard dashed over and swiped a card through the reader. We went down the hall and through the security check and straight into the elevator. Teddy and Little Teddy looked like they'd seen a ghost. A smile twitched at Nelson's lips before he smothered it.

"Look, Alex, we're as worried by threats to the diamond business as you are," Teddy said when we reached the lobby. "All this new lab-grown, it's a tidal wave. We spend tens of millions of dollars a year on research to detect it. I have no idea what this N3 center business you're asking about is. We make devices to detect fake diamonds, and everyone benefits."

"Especially you."

Little Teddy actually put her hand on my arm. "And we give *every* diamond buyer in the world the security of knowing their stones are real." Our Lady of Being Mystified. "And yet if anything bad is going on in the diamond world, it's always us, isn't it? We created the diamond world, but for some inscrutable reason, we are the evil troll under the bridge." She grimaced as if in real pain. "I'm proud of my family. There are whole countries whose standard of living depends upon the jobs we provide. If someone is trying to corrupt the diamond trade, start looking at India." She tapped a finger on my chest. "They're the real power. They polish ninety percent of the world's diamonds. If anyone could smuggle fakes into the trade, they're the ones who could do it."

The elevator shuddered to a stop in the lobby. The door opened but I didn't get out.

"That model of the big rough upstairs," I said. "That was the Lucifer rough?"

Teddy's face froze. Little Teddy took his hand. Teddy cleared his throat.

"Are you taunting me? You know my father commissioned a Lucifer, and it ruined a very large diamond. He did that because, like all our family, he loved the history and lore of diamonds, and yes, their mystery. He loved them in a way you perhaps cannot understand. Edwina and I love them that way too. Now you are bringing up a personal unhappiness of our family, and that is very low."

"Ever thought of giving it a shot yourself?"

"Get out of here."

I stepped into the lobby, and the elevator doors slid shut. The concierge handed me my gun.

28

think they have an information leak at their lab," I said to Tommy, as soon as we were on scramble. I was in front of the Bank of England, heading across the square to Mansion House. It had taken twenty minutes to walk a crooked route from Charterhouse Street, checking for a tail. So far, so good.

"Never mind the information leak," Tommy said. "What happened at the hotel? We're picking up chatter. Did you kill that old lady?"

"Yes I killed the old lady! She had a twelve-gauge in my back. She was working for Hassan."

"Stop yelling. How do you know she was working for Hassan?"

"I asked."

"Did you manage to find out who Hassan was working for?"

"That must have slipped my mind while I was satisfying my blood lust."

"It has to be the Chinese. They have the money, and it keeps them at arm's length to use Hassan."

"The dream hire," I said. "An insider on a shitty pension."

"And ready to betray his country."

"Hassan is his own country."

"OK, so what about this leak from Van Kees. What's that about?"

I told Tommy about the stone I'd recovered from Leopold Rose's jacket—the five-carat oval that we'd seen in the Shanghai folder. I told him about the N3 center, and what that was.

"So this N3 thing," he said, "your dad said that only happens in real diamonds?"

"Yes."

"And the diamond he was looking at was one of the Shanghai stones?"

"That's right."

"So a top diamond expert thought he was looking at a real diamond when in fact he was looking at a lab-grown stone."

"Correct."

"And when you mentioned this N3 stuff in his research lab, Teddy Van Kees went all wonky and gave you the toss."

"Pretty much."

I cut down King William Street toward the river.

"You have to be thinking that if Teddy got thrown so much by you asking about this N3 defect, they already knew about it."

"Yes."

"So they understand that someone knows how to put this defect in a diamond, and Van Kees can't detect it."

"Worse. It means that even if they learned how to detect it, the presence of the flaw proves the diamond is real when in fact it isn't."

Thump, thump—feet on desk. *Creak*—leaning back in chair. "Basically that would mean the whole diamond business is fucked."

"Correct. Can we give it to MAUREEN? See what she can find out about this N3 flaw. Include China in the search terms."

We ended the call. I followed Monument Street to Lower Thames Street and walked up Tower Hill. In Trinity Square Gardens I found a bench and sat down. The gray stone battlements of the Tower of London loomed across the street. Downriver, the sun set fire to the glass-and-steel banking towers of Canary Wharf.

A cool breeze stole up the river. I felt desolate. I took out my phone and opened the contact for Lily. But what would I say? I need you?

I left the park and went down the stairs at Tower Hill station and caught the westbound Circle Line. At Westminster I changed to the District Line for Hammersmith. It was more habit than anything else. If the GCHQ was giving Hassan a hand, they'd get a hit from the computer pretty quick. On the London Underground, every car had a camera.

At Hammersmith, I got off and walked under the elevated expressway and made my way to the river. I loitered along the bank, mixing with the rowing fans who were watching a pair of rowing eights battle for position. The Thames has the toughest rowing water in the world. The boats were fighting not just each other but the current, the tide, and a sharp bend in the river.

The crowd jostled at the shore, shouting as the rival coxswains bellowed from the sterns and the rowers pulled furiously with their long blades. The river was thronged with race officials' boats, and the festive crowd cheered and raised their glasses as the boats stroked toward the finish.

I walked through the crowd and into the little park wedged between the expressway and the river. I stayed close to the bank, where the crowd was thickest. At the end of the park was a stone wall with a wooden gate set into it. I pushed through, walked across the tiny forecourt and straight into the Dove. Inside, I turned right and stepped into what the historical plaque called the smallest bar in London. Who could argue: there were only two stools. One of which was occupied.

Frankie drained her pint and signaled for the bill. She put down a ten-pound note and waved off the change.

29

followed her into the packed dining room. Every head was turned to a screen that showed the race. She pushed through a door at the end of the room and led the way down a flight of metal stairs that came out at the river.

Wooden houseboats were moored along the bank. Beyond them, an eight went stroking by, the coxswain bellowing the tempo through a bullhorn. We walked upriver. In a minute we came to a wooden pier. A dented aluminum skiff was tied up at the end with a length of rope. We climbed in and I cast off. Frankie gave the old ten-horse outboard a little choke. It started on the first pull. We puttered out into the current and threaded our way through the traffic at the finish line. Five minutes later we were alone on the river.

"Any surveillance we have to think about?" I said.

She shook her head. "Downstream, sure. London Bridge, Westminster. Not up here. This is an extraction route I've used before. We'll get out of London no problem." She adjusted the throttle. "So fill me in. Who was the old lady working for?"

"Hassan."

"Your rabbi. That's heavy."

"She said there was a red notice on me."

"Red notice my ass. A red notice doesn't end with an old lady dicking around with a Mossberg. It ends with fully tooled-up guys coming in the front and back at the same time."

The engine coughed. She turned on her seat and fiddled with the choke. When she faced forward again, her face was solemn. "So if Hassan is in it for money, whose money are we talking about?"

"Mei's hedge fund. The fakes Lou had were from a Shanghai lab. We assume they own it."

"OK. So the Chinese are running a long play to sell fakes. Why? I get that they make money, but how much?"

"That's my problem too. The diamond business is worth $100 billion a year. Let's say they're careful. They start with a trickle, then build it gradually until they get to—$2 billion? Still a lot of diamonds, and the problem is—where did they come from? Mei could be planning to disguise the fakes as production from the mine that she and Lily own. But that would take a long time to set up. The market knows what's in the pipeline."

"Maybe just use the stones as untraceable bribes."

"But then the person you're bribing has to unload it, and that's not easy. It's one thing for Lou Fine to sell a fake, and even then, the street sniffed it out."

"And that's not your biggest problem, anyway. Your biggest problem is Tabitha. Why is she on this so fast? She's on it because something is scaring the crap out of everybody. It can't be the money angle. If she's worried, that's not why."

She took a last drag and flicked the cigarette away in a high arc. It landed in the water with a hiss.

"Who are you, masked stranger?"

She winked. "Couldn't crack my file, could you?"

"You didn't learn to think like that at filing school."

"I was in the field. Then I got boss trouble. The kind that isn't over at five o'clock."

"You could have reported him."

"That's the problem. I did. It ruined his career."

We came to a low, three-arched bridge. The channel led under the middle span. Frankie steered the boat to the left until an old scow that had right of way cleared the bridge. Then we puttered through.

"And the boss had friends," I said.

"They waited six months, then dumped me onto a desk at Langley. They made it a promotion so I couldn't make a case that I was being punished."

"Then they pushed you even further out, into the Treasury."

"No, it wasn't a push. I applied for the job. I liked that little corner in the Treasury. Lots of operational action, and nobody knows we're even there. Plus, hey—New York."

She cut the engine and let the boat drift in. When it rubbed against the grassy slope, she hopped out. She looped the rope around a tree. We climbed up to a paved path and headed through some trees to a parking lot. When we got there, she thumbed the plastic fob on a set of keys. Headlights flashed halfway down a row. We got into a boxy gray Vauxhall and drove away.

30

n half an hour we reached the M25 motorway. Thick clouds moved in. By the time we cleared London, a light rain was falling. The traffic stacked up with semis heading for the channel. We crawled along until we left the expressway and plunged into the lanes of Kent. An hour later we drove into a village and parked behind a church. We pulled backpacks out of the trunk, stuck the keys on a magnet under the fender, and took a walking trail that climbed a wooded hill.

She led the way into a landscape of farms and ancient woods. The rain soaked us as we slogged along the muddy trail. The path wound its way past stone outbuildings and through pastures. We crossed fences and went through gaps in hedges. Finally we cut across a field to a small brick farmhouse. She found a key behind a bush and we went in.

There were sandwiches on the kitchen table and a thermos of tea. I got a fire going in an iron stove, and we dried out. Field agents have friends they help out. You do a favor, it goes into the bank. The little boat, the car, the farmhouse—Frankie was making some withdrawals.

Later, the clouds drifted away on a breeze from the south. A soft warm night settled on the countryside. We went out and sat on a wooden bench. She lit a cigarette and tilted back her head and blew a stream of smoke up at the pale moon.

She offered me the pack. I took one and she lit it with her Zippo. I sucked in gratefully and held the smoke before I let it drift from my mouth. The thing about smoking again—you can never remember why you stopped.

A sense of peace settled over us. Animals rustled in the hedges and an owl wondered who we were. The silhouettes of bats flashed past against the night. It was as if we'd passed through a wormhole into a different universe. A place without enemies. I don't know how long we sat like that before the crickets chirped and we drifted back through the wormhole.

"This Antwerp trip," she said. "The ticket's in your bag. You change at Brussels. But Alex. I don't like it."

"No."

"It's too easy to find you. If Hassan had people outside the hotel, then he has British help. Maybe contractors, but maybe not. A lot of people freelance."

"Yes."

"One last thing," she said. "You know I still have access to the department's internal traffic. Anything that goes through the secure server, including any message to you."

"Got another cigarette?" I said. I knew what she was going to say, and I wanted to have something to do while she said it. When I was smoking, she continued.

"So I know about your dad. I'm sorry."

"It's OK," I said.

She let that go. Her voice was gentle when she made her point. "If I were running you, I would cancel this op right now until we had time to understand what we were dealing with, and who."

"We know who."

"Not a hundred percent. If it's Hassan, we don't know what kind of help he can call on here. Probably some contacts in the GCHQ. But that's not the only reason I'd wait. There's you. This is your friend talking now. You look like hell. You're exhausted. You're hurt. This is not the time. People could be waiting for you in Brussels."

"They'll be waiting for me on the train."

She sighed and shook her head. "You planned this," she said. "When you asked me for an extraction route that would take you to the train. You knew someone would be after you."

"I want them to find me."

She stared at the night as she thought. "That's why you asked me to book it under Ryder, even though you have newer passports. If Hassan has a friend at GCHQ, the Ryder passport will trigger an alert."

The moon had moved behind some trees when Frankie went inside and came out with one of the bags. She took out a slim leather attaché case with metal corners. She showed me the catch that released the lock. When the lock clicked open, the whole side of the case dropped straight down revealing a SIG Sauer MPX Copperhead submachine gun and a spare mag. Held in with clips.

"What about the metal detectors?" I said.

"There's a new shielding material under the leather."

I practiced a couple of times. The SIG came out like a dream. The extendable stock had been removed, which reduced the length to twelve inches and the weight to four pounds. It had the thirty-round magazine.

"We'll wait here until seven," she said, checking her watch. "The train gets into Ashford at 8:25 A.M."

I went in and found the second bag and changed into a plain black cashmere turtleneck, faded Levis, and the brown suede boots I liked because you'd never guess they had a steel toe.

The sky was lightening in the east when I came out. Frankie opened the doors of an old stable and drove out in a white Ford van. I tossed the pack with my old clothes into the back, slid the door shut, and climbed into the passenger seat. A weak sun was breaking over the tree line when we went down the farm road and through the gate and headed east.

We took the A21 until it cut south, then followed a narrow, twisting series of roads that wound through eastern Kent until it came out at the gleaming steel-and-glass passenger terminal at Ashford, where the Eurostar stops before it dips into the tunnel that takes it under the English Channel to France.

We sat in the van for a while, watching cars and trucks line up for the shuttle that carried vehicles through the tunnel while the drivers rode in the passenger coaches. At 8:24 the yellow nose of the Eurostar came into view around a turn.

"Is this for your dad?" she said.

"No. It's for me. It's just time. They hit and they hit. Now it's my turn."

I took the attaché case and put it on my lap. A squall swept in and fired a fusillade of raindrops at the windshield and then blew off again. She put her hand on my arm. That's all. And I opened the door and got out, went up the steps and into the waiting room. The attendants opened the gate and I boarded the train, and five minutes later the Eurostar slipped into the tunnel and headed for France.

31

The first-class car was only a quarter full. The steward stood behind a small zinc bar, working the levers of a hissing espresso machine. I checked my ticket and made my way to an armchair in a corner. It had a table of its own, and a tiny lamp with an ivory-colored shade. I checked out the other passengers.

Mostly businessmen, including a couple of prosperous-looking Hasidim, probably diamond traders. This was not the Paris train, but the one to Antwerp by way of Brussels.

The lights of the tunnel flashed by outside the window. The carriage took on the feeling of a cozy restaurant, voices muffled by the thick upholstery and the broadloom. The clink of cutlery announced the arrival of the breakfast cart. With silver tongs, the waiter heaped smoked salmon onto plates and spooned a mound of caviar on top. The smell of fresh croissants mixed with the aroma of good coffee.

The first thing I did was log onto the secure server and send a text. I asked Tommy for a search by MAUREEN. I wanted to see if she could discover the reason for the NATO meeting Tabitha was attending. I hoped that would help me understand the real reason for her interest in the appearance of undetectable fakes. Because if money wasn't the issue, what was? MAUREEN couldn't hack secure government communications, but she could draw conclusions from the data she could amass so quickly. I suggested keywords: diamonds, China, defense, NATO, urgent.

It takes the Eurostar only twenty minutes to get through the tunnel, so we were already out and heading north through Normandy at 186 miles an hour by the time a guy in a pinstripe suit and pink-tinted John Lennon granny glasses barged into the car and started arguing with the conductor. After the ritual display of indifference that French train officials master after long study and tireless practice, pinstripe was finally allowed to pay an upgrade fee in cash. He made a show of uncertainty before taking the chair across the aisle from mine. He put his bag on the floor and gave me one of those embarrassed smiles that the English use to disguise the fact that they're not embarrassed.

"Awful mix-up," he said confidingly. "It's this online booking rigmarole. Never could get the hang of it."

He spent five minutes waving at the steward before the man listened to his order and went away.

"Can't stand Brussels myself," he said. "Go there often?"

"I live there," I said.

He frowned, then tried to change it to a smile.

"Awfully sorry. You're not Belgian, surely?"

"Italian," I said.

"Italian," he repeated. The smile was fighting a losing battle with something harder. "You've managed to lose your accent."

"American movies."

The steward appeared beside him and put down the coffee he'd asked for and a tiny round plate of stale-looking biscuits. They'd finished serving the salmon and caviar and were not going to bring it out again.

France didn't become a great nation by squandering its time on foreigners with the wrong ticket.

The man dipped one of the biscuits into the coffee. It dissolved into a sodden paste. He didn't seem to notice. He took a sip of the sludge, took out his phone and scowled at it. He lifted his round glasses and squinted at the screen while he surreptitiously snapped pictures of me. I could hear the whoosh sound as he sent them off to confirm that I was the guy he was looking for.

We hurtled across the plain. Inky clouds rolled in from the channel. The dark sky made the glass a perfect mirror. Pinstripe was using his foot to edge his bag closer.

The train started to slow. He shot covert glances at me and kept checking his phone. Finally it pinged. Somebody back in London, or maybe Beijing, had run the snaps and said: it's him. We entered the outskirts of Brussels.

Rain began to streak the window, first just a few stray drops, then a deluge. A crew working on a switch tossed their picks aside and headed for shelter. A shunter snorted black diesel fumes into the downpour as it pushed a line of dilapidated Belgian commuter cars onto a siding. Around us, passengers were stuffing away laptops. We arrived at Brussels Central.

The first-class car was at the front of the train. It emptied quickly as passengers rushed out to clear the platform before the horde from the second-class cars could fill it. The steward had disappeared. I wanted to stall until the platform filled. If pinstripe had accomplices waiting, I'd have a better chance in a crowd.

As soon as we were alone, I hit him with the attaché case. He saw the blow coming and ducked, but the metal corner of the case ripped a gash in his face and sent the granny glasses flying. He managed to land a kick at the side of my leg.

He fell into the aisle with the bag still in his hand and was pulling out a pistol when I hit him again. This time I smashed the case straight into his nose. He bellowed in pain and I stamped on his head, then got a good kick in with the steel toe and he went still.

I ripped off his pinstripe jacket, found the glasses on the floor, and put them on. I limped out of the car with the attaché case and headed up the platform.

The intercept team was waiting at the end—a couple of guys in Belgian National Railway jackets. They would be working from recognition images sent by pinstripe's handler, and I was betting that the ones for pinstripe would show him in the jacket and the glasses.

They were both short and had dark, slicked-back hair. They looked like matching weasels. I reminded myself that weasels are excellent killers and rested my thumb on the release switch. I hobbled up angrily to the closest one and hissed in his face, "Christ, where were you?"

He looked at me with steady dark brown eyes in which there was a seed of doubt.

"It is to be done here," he said in a heavy accent. "Upon the platform."

"Fuck," I said, putting as much outrage as I could into my expression. "I told them a hundred times—in the car! He's still there. I stunned him." I took a step away and then swung to face him again.

"He's not my job. He's yours!"

It could have been a great performance, if only I'd limped off up the platform instead of waving the attaché case, because my thumb moved a fraction of an inch and triggered the release. The side slid down and the weasels' eyes snapped to the MPX. I ripped it out and put a burst into the closest one. He catapulted back in a spray of blood. I swung the gun to the second man, but he'd had just enough reaction time. He darted sideways and stepped in. I saw the knife almost at the moment I felt the slash across my arm. The MPX clattered to the platform. I kicked at him as I fell back, but he dodged the boot and came in after me as balanced as a cat. His partner screamed and gargled at the edge of the platform, jets of blood spurting from a severed artery. A woman started screaming.

I slithered backward through the blood. The weasel tossed the blade from hand to hand as he advanced. He should have paid closer attention to his footing. He moved in for a slash and his shoe slipped in the blood. I grabbed his wrist and pulled him down on top of me. I smashed his hand against the platform but couldn't loosen his grip on the knife. With his free hand he punched me in the face.

An empty commuter train was pulled up on the side of the platform where we fought. Suddenly the couplings tightened with a series of loud bangs as the train started inching from the station. I heard a police whistle blow.

I had the attacker's knife hand by the wrist. With the other hand he landed another blow to my head. I yanked him close and we fell off the platform onto the crushed-stone ballast of the rail bed. A train wheel a yard in diameter went past my face, the axle squealing. Then came a gap between cars, followed by another wheel. The train was starting to pick up speed. As soon as the second wheel rolled by, I heaved myself over the rail and into the center of the track. The undercarriage brushed my hair.

My left arm was stretched back across the rail, grasping the knife hand. The weasel scrabbled in the ballast with his free hand, seized a jagged stone, and drove it into the back of my hand. It was all I could do to keep my grip on his wrist.

The next set of wheels was rolling toward us, the axle shrieking. With my free hand I grabbed a handful of denim jacket and dragged him onto the rail. His face was inches from mine, his eyes frantic. His body thrashed wildly as the wheel ground toward him. Our faces were touching and he tried to bite my throat. I arched away. He was staring at me, an animal sound emerging through his gritted teeth, when the wheel rolled through his waist.

The carriage scraped by above me. I waited for the next pair of wheels to pass, and threw myself off the track on the far side. I ran across two empty lines, climbed onto a deserted platform, and walked quickly into the main concourse. A squad of gendarmes was pushing its way down the Eurostar platform.

I limped toward an exit. My leg throbbed from pinstripe's kick and my arm bled from the knife wound. People stared at my bloodied clothes. I hurried out into the rain. A bullet-gray Alfa Romeo Giulia idled at the curb with the wipers going. I ripped open the passenger door and threw myself in.

"Jesus!" said Tabitha when she saw me. She banged the stick into first and popped the clutch.

32

The sky darkened and the rain came down harder. Tabitha hacked a path through the traffic. We went around the royal palace twice, leaving blaring horns behind us.

"Get up into Schaerbeek," I said, checking our tail in the right-side driving mirror.

"Somebody on the train?" she said.

"And two in the station."

"You killed them?"

"The two in the station. Not sure about the one on the train."

We drove quickly north out of the center of the Belgian capital and into the Muslim quarter. The storm swept off and the sun came out. Women in hijabs stopped and shook out their umbrellas. Young men in leather jackets sat on parked scooters and scowled at us as we drove by. Tabitha spotted a sidewalk market with racks of cheap clothes and shot to the curb.

"Stay here," she said, jumping out. She found a pair of black jeans, a plain blue shirt, and a cheap leather jacket. She added three T-shirts and paid with cash. In the shop next door, she bought a roll of paper towels and some water. "Do we need a doctor?" she said when she got back in.

I told her no and bandaged the cut on my arm with one of the T-shirts. While I slopped water onto the paper towels and scrubbed at my face, Tabitha punched a code into her phone. When she was done, a route popped up on the Alfa's navigation screen.

"New app from the company," she said. "You just ask it for an SDR and it gives you one. It doesn't matter where you are. It grabs your GPS coordinates and calculates the SDR in seconds."

The surveillance detection route took us on a tangled course that included one long, straight stretch along a canal. That was the point where a tail would be forced into the open. We covered the route three times—each time slowing when we reached the canal. Clear.

We took the A12 highway north out of the city.

"You heard about London?" I said.

"The old lady? Yes, I heard. And now two more at the station, and the one on the train if he's dead too. You're not exactly tiptoeing into Europe. I tapped the Belgian police radio while I was waiting for you. I mean, Christ"—she shook her head—"cutting people in half with train wheels."

"I'm trying to quit."

At Boom we got off the A12 and followed a zigzag course of secondary roads across the plain of Flanders until we came out at the River Scheldt. We pulled into a little park beside the river.

I got out and used a public restroom to change into the jeans and finish cleaning up. I unwrapped the blood-soaked T-shirt from my arm and shoved it into the garbage with my old pants. The cut was oozing, but not too bad. I tore one of the remaining T-shirts into strips and re-bandaged the wound and went back to the car.

A freighter stacked with containers came into view on its way down-river from Antwerp.

"Did you pick up anything at the NATO meeting?" I said.

"That news that I'm a Chinese double seems to be making the rounds."

"Who told you?"

"A British colonel. Listed as a military attaché at the Brussels embassy, but we have him tagged as MI6. According to him they dismissed the rumor, but he'd say that anyway. Especially if he thought it was true."

"Did he approach you?"

"We had dinner last night. We've stayed in regular touch since I moved to the DNI."

"That means he's their point person on you. They always watch to see who's moving up. They'll have been looking at you since you went to the White House. If you check, you'll find that his attendance at NATO meetings dates from the time you became an assistant deputy and started going to the meetings yourself."

The breeze from the river dragged a clump of hair across her face. She brushed it angrily away. "Really, Alex. I've had that charmer taped from the get-go."

I watched the river traffic. Ships had gone down that river for centuries. The trade had made Antwerp one of the richest prizes on the continent. Armies had plundered their way back and forth across Flanders since the Middle Ages. The wars never stopped. They just paused while everybody bought new equipment. Sometimes the weapons switched from guns to trade. A lot of the containers stacked on the ships had Chinese markings.

The sight seemed to push Tabitha further into a dark mood, as if the ships were carrying not only cargo but her own spirit down the river and out to sea.

33

don't know how long we sat there without speaking. Not more than
five minutes. I felt my body sinking into that mist of fatigue that
follows violence. The knife cut burned on my arm, and my left hand
throbbed where he'd smashed me with the stone. My right knee had ballooned. The phone vibrated. Message from Tommy attaching a summary
from MAUREEN. I tapped the icon. A bar crawled across the screen
as the file unzipped.

"You can't make this up as you go along, Tab," I said as I waited for the
file to finish opening. "You're going to have to tell me what's going on."

The subject heading from MAUREEN said: China, quantum, N3
center, NATO, DARPA. As soon as I saw the acronym for the Defense
Advanced Research Projects Agency, I glanced to see if Tabitha was
looking, but she was checking her own messages.

"What did you learn from Van Kees?" she said.

"Are you listening?" I said as I scanned the list of sources MAU-
REEN had vacuumed out of cyberspace. One was a DARPA report on
something called quantum computing and the role of diamonds in it.
"You need to level with me."

"What I *need*," she said, thumbing out a quick reply to one of her emails, "is for you to tell me what you found out from Teddy Van Kees."

At the top of the screen, MAUREEN had displayed a text from a Dutch researcher to an American scientist. They were part of a consortium working with DARPA on the use of subatomic flaws in diamonds as a way to establish a quantum-computing network. "See you in Brussels," said the text. "Chinese synthetic with N3!"

I put the phone facedown in my lap for a minute to think. The text was dated two days before: the day I'd arrived in London. Tabitha had the diamond with the N3 center and had said she was going to show it to "some people." The Dutch researcher must have been one of them. NATO headquarters was in Brussels, where he was meeting the American he'd texted.

"Teddy," prompted Tabitha, multitasking as she flew through her correspondence. "What you found out."

"They're running scared," I said. "They've pulled all their research into London and sealed it off behind a secure perimeter in the basement. They showed me how great they were at detecting fakes until I asked them about an N3 center. Then they threw me out. Maybe you can tell me why."

She frowned and looked up from her phone. The ebbing tide in the river had exposed mud flats. An old man and a boy were collecting bait fish from the puddles. She watched them, but I doubt she saw them.

"Did Teddy say they knew how to create an N3 center themselves?" she said.

"No. He claimed not to know what they even were."

She still had her eyes on the river. The recent rain had rinsed the sky into a limpid blue, swollen now with light. The old man and the boy looked like figures from an old Dutch painting, absorbed in a world of their own—a world incomprehensibly remote from the one Tabitha and I inhabited.

"What was the NATO meeting about?" I said.

"You know I can't tell you that."

"Let me put this another way. If the meeting had anything to do with quantum computing, that cat is out of the bag."

She closed her eyes and leaned forward and banged her head slowly on the steering wheel. "Fuck," she said. "Fuck, fuck, fuck." She sat up and looked at me. "MAUREEN?"

"One of the Dutch scientists forgot to encrypt," I said. "He sent a text about the N3 center and a meeting." I scrolled down the list of sources. "He was co-author on a paper linked to DARPA, so the meeting was probably the NATO one. Tell me when I'm wrong."

She rolled down the window and stuck her head out and turned her face to the sun. The down on her cheek caught the light. The smell of the river drenched the air.

"This isn't desk work, Tab. It's the field. It doesn't matter what they think of you in the West Wing. When people start shooting, they won't care who your friends are."

"You don't know much about Washington if you think I have friends, bruiser." She ran a hand through her hair, then leaned across and kissed me on the lips. She brushed her fingers over my face. "Now I have to make a call." She got out and stalked across the parking lot, already talking by the time she reached the path along the river. The person at the other end would be her boss, Noah Weitz, the director of National Intelligence.

I tapped the ear icon on my screen and settled back to listen. MAU-REEN always prepared a brief audio summary of a search. I liked her voice. It was like listening to your favorite grade school teacher reveal that she knew everything in the known universe.

❖

Quantum computing, she explained, harnessed the principles of quantum physics to solve problems too complex for even the most advanced super-computers now in existence. We had poured billions of dollars of secret funds into research teams spearheading the work, and so had China. Whoever got there first would have a calculator that took only moments to perform tasks that the most powerful computers in the world couldn't finish in a thousand years.

But there were problems. One was getting quantum computers to talk to each other. A computer needs to communicate, or it's like a genius sitting in a room who has a great thought but can't tell anyone about it. We had built the brain, but not the vocal cords. Theoretically, quantum computers should be able to share data without any physical movement of matter—a phenomenon called data teleportation. Like two people getting the same thought in their heads at the same time. In practice, no one had managed to accomplish that. Until a month ago.

Scientists at a California lab had manipulated a spinning electron in a subatomic space inside a diamond in such a way that the electron had "entangled" with another electron in an identical subatomic space inside another diamond in the lab. When electrons "entangle," it means they are behaving exactly the same. One electron, therefore, had communicated its state across space to another electron, with no physical connection. The achievement had stunned researchers. A true quantum network, they believed, was now at hand. And the empty space in an N3 defect had made it possible.

MAUREEN was just explaining why diamonds were used—atomic stability—when I saw Tabitha end her call.

"OK," she said when she got back, "I'll brief you as we go."

We went northeast from the river and picked up the Antwerp road. My arm started bleeding again. I tore apart the last T-shirt and tied on a clean bandage. Tabitha had her lower lip clamped in her teeth while she thought about what to say.

"Let me help," I said. "It'll be easier if you don't have to wonder what to lie about.

"You were watching Mei because you were afraid that her move into lab-grown meant China had discovered the place of diamonds in our quantum research. You caught the Shanghai shipment to Lou because you were surveilling the whole Chinese diamond industry. The stone you caught was the Geneva white. You had it checked and found the N3. You hoped it was a fluke, and now you know it wasn't."

She glanced at the fresh bandage. A dot of red had already appeared.

"I wanted to tell you. Noah said no."

"Of course he did. He wanted to see how hard they would come after me. How important the secret was to them."

"Yes. And now we know. But what exactly is the nature of the secret? We're still not sure they know what they have. If they did—why would they let the stones out of the country? I mean, if a five-carat oval has an N3 in it, how many N3s could there be in a stone the size of the Lucifer cut? Why would they ever let that go? It only makes sense if the main point is to sell them."

We came into Antwerp along a broad avenue. In the distance, the steeple of the cathedral rose above the rooftops. A string of white trolleys rattled out of a street and went down the center of the avenue. The traffic piled up behind them. We crept along in silence for ten minutes while Tabitha chewed her lip.

"Spit it out. What's the problem? Why DARPA? The Chinese aren't going apeshit with contractors because they want to be the first to solve *pi*."

She turned off the main road into a neighborhood of old mansions. We stopped in front of a gray-stone residence with a wrought-iron railing in front and a black garage door. A row of steel bollards set into the edge of the sidewalk guarded the garage.

She tapped a code into her phone. The bollards sank into the sidewalk. The door slid up and we drove down a ramp and into the garage. Fluorescent lights flickered on automatically. The door whirred down behind us. A camera with a winking red light panned over to record our arrival. We parked beside an elevator.

I pictured the bollards rising up outside, sealing the entrance from attack. The camera would be feeding the scene of our arrival to a screen in Washington. If the watchers didn't think we matched what they were expecting, we'd never get out of the garage.

I knew about these houses. The windows aren't even glass. They're made of optically transparent aluminum in a three-ply construction that can stop a .50-caliber machine-gun round without cracking. The windows, the bollards—it's all supposed to make the people who use such houses feel safe, although they are the same people who know there's no such thing.

"It's the speed," she said at last. "That's what everyone's afraid of. The Chinese as much as us. Quantum computers are terrifying. They'll be able to perform calculations and try out passwords at speeds we really can't conceive, because they're not subject to physical laws, but to quantum ones. I don't pretend to understand it, but our experts say that a quantum computer could hack every existing conventional computer in the world, almost instantly. The most closely guarded systems of the Department of Defense, including the nuclear codes, would be opened in seconds. If they get to that computer before we do, they could eliminate our defenses."

"And then we all die?"

"Well, not you and me. We have the bollards."

"There better be a bar in there," I said.

34

swallowed some Tylenol and finished washing off the blood and rebandaging the arm. When I was done I shoved the first aid kit back under the sink and checked out the walk-in closet. There were at least a dozen laundered shirts on an open shelf. I picked out a blue one, ripped off the cellophane, and tried it on. Bit loose, but OK. I tried on the pants from one of the suits arranged on hangers. No dice.

"Whose clothes?" I said when I went downstairs.

"SACEUR. Sometimes he has to meet people we don't want our friends to know about. This is where he comes."

SACEUR was Supreme Allied Commander Europe, an American four-star general based seventy-five miles away at Casteau. The first officer to hold that post was Dwight D. Eisenhower. If Tabitha had the use of a house reserved for SACEUR, Washington was not just chewing its fingernails, it was yanking its hair out in clumps.

Tabitha filled a glass from a frosted pitcher and handed it to me. "Shaken," she said in her best Sean Connery, "never shtirred."

We sat in a pair of easy chairs beside a window. The late-afternoon sun raked the lawn. She'd peeled off her stockings when I was upstairs, and now she angled her chair and parked her bare feet in my lap, crossing her ankles. Normally a woman's foot resting in my lap wouldn't send a wave of nausea through my body, so the knee was getting worse.

"Thinking back to Teddy Van Kees," Tabitha said. "Do you think he reacted so dramatically to your question about the N3 center because he can make one?"

Her feet were long and slender. The nails were painted a pearly color. The heel of the bottom foot was wedged between my legs. I lifted both feet from my lap and placed them on the table. She arched her eyebrows and tilted her head.

"When we landed in London you reminded me that Van Kees makes the machines that test for fakes. Now you want to know if I think Teddy can make an N3 center. There's something you're not telling me."

She picked up the pitcher and tipped it back and drained the rest of the martini. Some of it dribbled down her chin. She wiped it away with the back of her hand while she watched me. "You're sho shmart," she said, but neither of us was smiling. She turned her head. Outside, a long shadow crept onto the grass. When she spoke, her voice was hard. "I'm going to meet Teddy."

My leg was killing me, so I stood up and flexed it carefully, then took a few paces. It didn't help the leg but it gave me time to get rid of the dumbfounded expression and replace it with the blank look I keep for emergencies. It's a better look than the dumbfounded. Only just, but still.

"Why?"

"They know more about detecting fake diamonds than anyone else. The fact that the N3 diamonds evaded detection doesn't change the fact that Van Kees has the most sophisticated diamond lab anywhere."

"I'm not following you. Their machine didn't detect the Geneva white as a fake and we know it was. Mostly they catch a fake by examining the crystal structure. So it passed that test too. What do you want from Teddy Van Kees?"

"Collaboration. We want his lab to reverse-engineer an N3. If he can do that, we can make one."

"What's in it for Teddy?"

"We drop the antitrust investigation."

"What antitrust investigation?"

"The one we'll launch if he doesn't play ball."

"He doesn't have any operations in America."

"He sells most of his diamonds there."

A ping sounded from the staircase, where she'd left her bag. She glanced at it, then checked her watch.

The shadows swallowed the last sliver of sunlight on the grass. Some light current of air crept up from the floor and stirred Tabitha's hair. She blew it away with a puff, and I saw again the girl who'd showed up at my office in New York three years before.

The wild hair and stab-you-in-the-heart eyes. She drove her MINI Cooper around Manhattan in a mint-green blur. The shirts she got on sale at Saks billowed around her thin body like a magician's cape, and you were waiting for the trick she would perform. Except she was the trick herself. I knew because she'd played it on me. When she looked at me, her eyes were cold.

"You think I should have told you before."

The garden was invisible now. The darkness lapped at the window. Only the faint orange light of a streetlamp smudged the night.

"I'm sure you have everything firmly in hand."

Her phone pinged again and this time she leapt up and stamped across the room. I checked my phone too. Message from Tommy.

"For *fuck's* sake will you stop pinging me," Tabitha snarled. "I told you, if I don't answer, leave a message." She listened for a moment, then slid her eyes to me and held up her finger to let me know she'd only be a moment. I thumbed in my password and read Tommy's message.

MAUREEN had caught two CIA heavies boarding a company Citation at Joint Base Andrews. Flight plan: Antwerp. They'd left Washington an hour ago. That would put the departure at about the time Tabitha had been making her call by the river. I heard her say:

"OK. Tell him to call in five. Book it into the secure room upstairs and I'll take it there."

She ended the call and came back and sat on the windowsill, crossing her legs and clasping her knee and looking past me as she ordered her thoughts.

"Can you find out if any iffy stones have been coming into Antwerp? Anything out of the ordinary?"

"Iffy stones coming into Antwerp?" They'd be stumbling into each other in the street.

"It could be important. Can you get that done and be back here tonight?"

In time for the arrest team. "No problem."

The orange light from the streetlamp backlit her wild hair. Errant strands drifted around her head like fiery threads. She looked like a figure from Greek mythology—a goddess with human attributes. A being capable of fear and rage and sexual abandon. All that was missing was a human heart.

35

I stood in the shadows of the old town hall and watched the street I'd just come out of. I held the phone to my ear with one hand and massaged my knee with the other.

"We've stayed at that hotel before," I said to Lily.

"No one knows about it," she said. "Use the recognition protocol I gave you. I'll get the medicine you need and be there in an hour."

She ended the call. I watched the square for a minute, then limped into an alley and headed for the river. A dank breeze crept off the water. I zippered up the cheap leather jacket. When I reached the Scheldt, I went along the quay. In a couple of hundred yards, I came to a shabby hotel that faced the water. Faded green paint peeled from the stucco.

I pushed through a door into a dim interior that smelled of damp carpet and sausages. A cigarette was burning in an ashtray on the front desk. I pinged the bell and waited. Through the window I could see the dockside cranes across the river, lifting stacks of containers from moored ships. The floodlit scene cast a strong light through the dirty glass and into the lobby. I pinged the bell again.

A threadbare gray cardigan hung on a nail beside the row of empty mailboxes. The slap of slippers approached and a young woman in a dirty tank top appeared. She snatched the cardigan from the nail and pulled it on. She picked up the cigarette from the ashtray and took a drag, squinting at me through the smoke.

"Something quiet," I said, the recognition phrase Lily had given me. The woman sniffed and wiped her nose with the back of her hand. The smell from the kitchen was stronger. I recognized it now. Not sausages. They were *frikandellen*, a sort of hot dog made of minced meat. The smell was nauseating. She pulled a key from a pigeonhole and dropped it on the counter. She disappeared back inside. I dragged myself up the narrow stairs.

It was a dreary room. A threadbare bedspread might have once been white. On the tiny desk stood a yellowing card with the name *Hoge Raad voor Diamant*—Diamond High Council. The card listed phone numbers dealers could call to get the latest details of the London diamond sales. No dealer had stayed in that hotel for decades, and the London sales were a distant memory.

I lay on the bed and closed my eyes and woke up to Lily's fingers in my hair. The hair was stiff with the residue of dried blood. She examined my arm and ran her fingers lightly over my swollen knee. The jeans were already letting go along the seams. From a package on the dresser, she took a pair of scissors and cut them off. The knee looked like a rotten melon—dark and mottled and ready to burst.

She cleaned the cuts with antiseptic. When she was done, she unfolded a white cloth and placed two syringes on it. Lily had a Russian doctor in the city from when she'd lived here. He'd supply whatever she needed, for a price. One syringe looked like a horse needle.

"He's already filled these," she said, then swabbed a patch of skin beside the wound on my arm. "Antibiotic," she said, jabbing me with the shorter needle. She applied a small bandage, tilted her head at it with a satisfied expression, then turned to the knee.

She felt around the kneecap, identifying the insertion point, and marked it with a pen. She swabbed the spot again, picked up the horse needle and depressed the plunger to expel a drop of liquid from the tip.

"What's in that one," I said.

"Sodium pentothal," Lily said. "It's much easier than tying you up and beating the soles of your feet with a bamboo stick." She plunged the needle into the side of my knee. Five minutes later it was feeling better.

She slotted both needles into a hard-plastic box and put it away. Then she used a Q-tip to apply some topical medication to the cuts on my face.

"I'm sorry about your father."

"You know how we were," I said.

She put the Q-tips away and placed her fingertips against my mouth.

"Anger is not the same as hate, Alex. The man was your father. You will harm your spirit."

Lily was a Matryoshka doll. Previous Lilys nested inside the outer one, the one with the red leather jacket and the Glock. I had known her for years before she let me see the one in the cabin by the river, hiding out in the bone-snapping cold, sick, starving. After the plane crash that had killed her parents, she'd been thrown out of their apartment in Mirny by corrupt officials. With nowhere else to turn, she'd gravitated to a gang. She hadn't understood they charged for membership until they took a down payment on a filthy bed in a hovel—two of them holding her down.

She fled to the summer cabin her parents had built on a nearby river. The gang learned where she was. One of them came out to get her. Lily was skinning a muskrat when the ravens announced the approach. She saw him floundering through the snow, an AK slung at his shoulder. She dropped him at a hundred yards.

Lily had been in the cabin three months when one of her mother's friends learned where she was. The woman let out a cry of anguish when she saw Lily's face, covered in chilblains. Lily said nothing. Human speech had deserted her. She had become a forest animal. When the woman got Lily a job as a cleaner at Russgem's sorting facility, it was the forest animal who showed up. Now the plant would be her forest.

The rough flowed in. Hundreds of thousands of carats a week. Lily watched the stones as a forest animal watches the forest: looking for prey. She found it.

Russgem's scales rounded off the weight of diamond parcels to two decimal places. That meant the weights were accurate to hundredths of a carat. But that degree of exactitude was nothing more than a convenience. To make the weights come out to hundredths, Russgem had to effectively ignore the thousandths and the ten-thousandths that were also there. Those tiny weights did not cease to exist because they were tidied out of sight. They were hiding right there in the plant, in the thicket of numbers. You just had to know where to find them. By the time Lily had worked her way up to a job in the weighing department, she did know. And she went and got them.

It doesn't sound like much—stealing diamonds by the thousandths of a carat—but Russgem moved forty million carats a year through Mirny. It didn't take long for the thousandths of a carat to get to one whole carat—a size that Lily could pluck from the stream. Or for that single carat to grow to ten, and the ten to a hundred. From there it just kept growing.

"I checked on Dilip," she said. "He still goes out at the same time every day. Are you OK to walk?"

I got up and flexed the injured leg and took a few steps. It seemed OK. I changed into the clothes she'd brought. Dark blue jeans that weren't too tight, plain white shirt, black wool blazer. The last thing I took from the bag was a quick-release holster that fit in the small of my back. I unscrewed the silencer from the Bobcat and holstered it.

Lily sat there in her marble-statue state of self-possession. A forest animal interrogating the forest. The forest was Lou's murder, the attacks on me, my father's death. A military flight from JFK—she'd dropped me at the gate. Between then and now, more violence.

Mei was in the forest too. Lily would assume that. She didn't believe in coincidence any more than I did. The move into lab-grown—that would look like the launch pad for everything that followed. If Mei was in the forest, so was Tabitha. Besides, who had the chops to keep a military plane waiting at JFK for a Treasury agent?

Lily got up and went to the window. She watched the busy docks. I'd turned to her for help and she'd come. It wouldn't be free.

She stood framed against the window until she turned away and checked her watch and said, "It's time for you to go. I'll meet you after. You know where."

I opened the door and stood there for a moment, wanting to say something. Her face was bathed in the uneasy light from the window. I knew it better than any other face on earth. I'd spent whole nights examining it inch by inch. I'd turned my heart to cinders loving her. But I was a forest animal too. I closed the door and went downstairs and turned along the quay.

36

The glass dome of the railway station glowed against the plum-colored sky. Tourists packed the outdoor cafés along the broad boulevard of De Keyserlei. I cut over to Vestingstraat, walked to the end, and turned right onto Pelikaanstraat, the placid little Flemish thoroughfare that is the main street of the world diamond trade.

Only a few of the shops were still open. I stopped at one display and pretended to examine some larger stones laid out on a velvet cushion. A red Vespa pulled over in front of the diamond bourse. The rider pretended to check his phone. I knew he hadn't followed me from the hotel, but if someone wanted to find me in Antwerp it was a fair guess that Pelikaanstraat would be the place to wait.

I stopped at a plain black door with a brass plate that read GUPTA EUROPE S.A., and pressed a button beside the door. A pinhole of red light flashed for an instant as the camera on the wall snapped my picture. The buzzer sounded and the door made a loud click, and I pushed my way through into the Antwerp office of the largest diamond-polishing company in the world.

"I'm here for Dilip," I told the young woman at the reception desk.

She frowned at the appointment register in front of her. "Is he expecting you, sir?"

"No, but he'll be coming out of that elevator in about sixty seconds, so let's not bother him."

She looked at me suspiciously and picked up the phone, but I took it from her hand and hung it up. "We're old friends," I said.

Before she could think of what to do next, the elevator pinged and a short man in a dove-gray double-breasted suit emerged with his eyes on his phone. He glanced up, caught sight of me and stopped in his tracks.

"Alex," Dilip Gupta said. Plainly he wasn't glad to see me. A surprise visit from a US Treasury agent—never going to be a happy moment for a diamond dealer. But he recovered fast. "Come," he said, grabbing my arm and leading the way down a hall. We pushed through a door that opened into a narrow lane. A gleaming black Mercedes waited. The driver sprang out and opened the door, and I followed Dilip into the leather-upholstered back of the limousine. We slid into the evening traffic. He eyed me in the dim light. If he noticed anything about my appearance, he decided to ignore it.

"I hope this isn't about the Russian sanctions," he said.

"Let's hope it doesn't come to that." I wanted him in a cooperative mood. The Guptas bought millions of carats of Russian rough. Because India was a crucial Asian ally, Washington had left Russian diamonds that were polished in India off the list of US sanctions for the war in Ukraine. But now they were on, as Dilip knew.

"Damn it, Alex," he said. "We were allowed to buy that rough. We polished it in India and exported it legally to the United States. Suddenly you change the rules and we are stuck with millions of carats. Would you do that to the Israelis? Never! But the Indians are fair game. Your greatest democratic friend in Asia!"

"Knock it off, Dilip. You're one of Russia's biggest arms customers, and the second the war started in Ukraine, you were lined up to buy cheap Russian oil. You're whoever's friend you need to be. Tonight you're going to be mine, and I'm going to look the other way on how you unload all that Russian rough you think we haven't been counting."

He had a retort on the tip of his tongue, but bit it back. "So this isn't about sanctions," he said. When I made no comment, he relaxed.

We'd known each other for years, ever since he and his brother, Viraj, started running diamond parcels around Mumbai for their uncle, a small-time trader. Soon the brothers were trading on their own. Then they had a factory in Surat, north of Mumbai, with four hundred polishing wheels. Now they had thousands. Dilip's suits and shirts were handmade in London, and the paisley silk puff in his breast pocket matched the elegant tie. Still, you didn't want to turn your back.

The Mercedes left the packed streets and headed into a leafy quarter. Dilip let the window down and leaned back in his seat. I could almost hear him rifling through the possibilities that might have brought me there.

"Has this got anything to do with Lou Fine?" he finally said. When I didn't answer, he shook his head. "Really, Alex. A murder. We're not the mafia."

"Tell it to your customers."

Indian diamond polishing was controlled by powerful Jain families like the Guptas. Jainism is an ancient Indian religion whose followers try to attain a state of liberation and bliss through the "three jewels" of right belief, right knowledge, and right conduct. The bedrock principle is non-violence. They're supposed to be vegetarian. At the most observant end of the spectrum, Jains wear masks to prevent themselves from violating the life of some tiny insect by inhaling it. Dilip wasn't at that end of the spectrum. He was at the end where your family lives in a palace on the Malabar Hill with regiments of servants and a thousand feet of shoreline on the Arabian Sea. At that end, the insects can take care of themselves. You eat what you like, a diet that includes competitors.

"Get a load of this," he said, pressing a button on the partition that separated us from the driver. "The latest from Mercedes." A small door whirred open, revealing crystal glasses and a decanter. "Inventions like this, you wonder how the Germans lost the war."

"Anybody who thinks the Germans lost the war hasn't been paying attention."

Dilip poured us each a shot. "Single malt from the Isle of Skye," he said, handing me a glass. "Drink that. You look like hell."

He downed his whiskey and put the glass back on the tray. I did the same. He pressed the button again and the glasses and decanter disappeared into the partition.

"I knew him too," he said. He'd decided he was right, and the topic was Lou. "There was nobody like him. You remember when Gwyneth Paltrow won best actress for *Shakespeare in Love*? She was wearing a $300,000 necklace Lou made for her. Before the night was out, he had fourteen orders for that necklace." He gave me a foxy grin. "Lou knew how to hand out loaners. Whoopi Goldberg was host that year. She was wearing $41 million worth of Lou's diamonds. Geena Davis—he made her a diamond bobby pin." He poked my leg to underscore the sheer brilliance. "Millions of people watching on TV. A diamond bobby pin! That's why the rich beat a path to his door. So tell me. How does a man like that end up broke?"

"I think you probably know. You have more spies than Van Kees."

His cell phone chirped in his pocket. He snatched it out and listened for a moment, then delivered a torrent of Gujarati. The only word I recognized was *crore*. Indians still use an old counting system that has its own words for large numbers. Lakh means 100,000 and crore is 10 million. He used crore twice. He could have been talking about carats or he could have been talking about dollars. He placed the phone on an armrest.

"We'll save a lot of time, Alex, if you tell me what this is about."

We pulled up in front of a redbrick church that housed a famous Antwerp restaurant. So did the red Vespa that had been on our tail the whole way. The maître d' spotted Dilip and dove into the crowd at the door to take him by the elbow. I glanced over my shoulder, but the Vespa had disappeared.

The maître d' led us through the barrel-vaulted central room to a staircase in the corner. It curved up around a stone pillar and came out into the former organ loft on the second floor. A short man with a bald head and a waxed moustache stood behind a bar. The moustache made him look like Kaiser Wilhelm II. All he needed was one of those steel helmets with the spike on top. As soon as we sat down, he started serving us without a word.

"You won't need a menu," Dilip said. "Up here, the staff bring us what is best today. These are Zeeland oysters." He gazed lovingly at the small white plate in front of him with five oysters arranged on it. "They take six years to grow." He popped one in his mouth with a tiny fork. "The ones they serve in the Grote Markt are only three years old."

I shook my head. "And people actually eat them."

Dilip put another oyster in his mouth and closed his eyes. I speared three with my fork and gulped them down. I was famished. I speared the last two and forked them down as well. "Any bread?" I asked the Kaiser. He gave me a frozen look, then tore up a baguette and dumped it in a basket. I polished most of that off too. Dilip took a sip of the white wine and closed his eyes.

"Chassagne-Montrachet," he murmured. He opened his eyes and looked at the bartender. "2016?" The Kaiser awarded him a quarter smile. Dilip took another sip, pursed his lips, and drummed his delicate fingers on the bar. Then he seemed to make up his mind. He shook his head and blew out a breath. "It's that Geneva white, isn't it? That's why you're here. It turned out to be a fake."

37

To hide my surprise, I concentrated on the Montrachet—frowning at the glass, sniffing, swirling the wine around the way wine people do. Then I just tossed it back. I gave the Kaiser a thumbs-up. He snorted.

"Where did you see it?" I said to Dilip.

"Lou gave us a look at it before the auction. Very hush-hush. Vijay and I examined it."

"What makes you think it was a fake?"

"It was only eleven carats, but a perfect Carré. Perfect. Why have I not heard of it? Lou claims it is the property of a German princely family, and they have had it for two hundred years. But where is it in the reference books?"

"Did Lou say why he was handling it?"

"He said he could not resist such a perfect stone. He had re-polished a few angles to bring out the cut."

"And it had a certificate?"

Dilip dismissed the certificate with a flap of his hand. If he thought it was a fake, no certificate would change his mind.

"We put it through the GemCheck. Perfect. He even had a spectro-scopic analysis that identified some kind of atomic irregularity. I think there was a missing atom. He made a case that the defect was only found in natural diamonds. I ask you, when has someone ever mentioned such a thing? He was trying too hard. We didn't make an offer. I don't know who bought it. We tried to find out, but no one would say a word."

The Kaiser set out a platter of grilled squid and some pale green vegetable cut into thin strips, but Dilip's appetite seemed to have deserted him. "The cabbage is flash-fried in dashi," he said in a discour-aged tone. "Dashi is a kind of stock. Here they distill it from kelp and season it with sardines and dried shitake." He speared a piece of squid and chewed it dutifully. I sandwiched one with my last two pieces of baguette.

"You know," Dilip said, putting down his fork, "we were afraid this would happen. Vijay and I. We feared it."

"Feared what?"

He motioned with his finger and the Kaiser removed the plates and replaced the silver.

"The stone was too perfect." He picked up his wineglass and held it to the light. "It looked like something a computer would design. When I look at polished, I always look for some trace of the rough that produced it. In the Geneva stone, it wasn't there."

A waiter wheeled a cart behind the bar. With a flourish, the Kaiser whipped a silver dome from a serving dish. He placed clean plates in front of us. Wielding silver serving spoons, he prepared each plate with a bed of black lentils and some bright green leaves before tenderly adding two small lobsters. He whisked away our glasses and replaced them with smaller ones of a different shape. He plucked a bottle from an ice bucket, wiped it with a cloth, and showed Dilip the label. Dilip nodded and he poured the pale liquid into our glasses.

"This is Icelandic langoustine," Dilip said, poking a fork at the coral shape that glistened on his plate. "The black lentils are called beluga lentils. The greens are sorrel." He sniffed the wine. "The acidity of this Riesling will pair superbly with the sweetness of the langoustine."

"You bet," I said. The Kaiser looked at me with barely veiled contempt, as if he could see inside my head where the news about the sorrel and the lentils and the acidity of the Riesling was blundering around looking clueless. Maybe Shawna had called from the Dinosaur Bar-B-Que to warn him about me.

"It was only a matter of time before such stones appeared," Dilip said.

He cut off a small piece of the Icelandic langoustine, but I think it was just to show the Kaiser he was trying. He'd lost his appetite. Shawna would have put her hand on his shoulder and given him a squeeze, but the Kaiser snatched the plates away in a cold fury.

"This new production, Dilip. Is it Chinese?"

"Not here," he said, looking around. Like any good restaurant in Antwerp, it would be full of diamond dealers.

We made our way downstairs and through the crowd and out to the street. The limousine was waiting at the curb. We sank into the deep seats and the car pulled away. The red Vespa was waiting at the second cross street. Tucked in behind a parked car. Nice position. I wouldn't have spotted him in the dark street if he hadn't started the scooter as soon as he saw us. The ignition turned the headlight on.

Dilip stabbed the button on the front panel. The tray rotated out. This time he poured us each a shot of cognac. He didn't swirl it around and sniff it and tell me what year it was. He threw it back like a man who needed a drink.

"You heard about the Van Kees chef?" Dilip asked.

"Chef? Why would I have heard about a chef?"

"Six months ago one of their top scientists disappeared. They kept it very secret, but we have people." He made a vague gesture. "This man who left, he was the chef. That is what they call the one who develops recipes for growing diamonds in the lab. He was a little crazy, but brilliant. Because of him, Van Kees was always able to keep one step ahead of the growers. When you know the latest tricks for growing a diamond, you can make a machine to catch the trick."

The car glided through the leafy suburbs. I glanced out the back. Three cars back, the Vespa peeped out to take a quick look before it swerved back out of sight.

"But then," Dilip said, "he developed a diamond the machines could not catch."

"Even though it was their diamond, and they knew how he did it? The GemCheck couldn't catch it?"

"No."

The car turned into the lane beside the Gupta building and stopped.

"I haven't heard a whisper about this, Dilip."

"You can understand what would happen to the diamond trade if the news got out."

"Does Teddy know you're aware of it?"

"No, and now we will say nothing." By "now" he meant after Lou's murder. He put his hand on mine. "I ask you to keep my name out of this. For friendship."

"What did you mean when you said he was crazy?"

"Perhaps eccentric," Dilip said.

"I need the name."

"His name is Du Toit. Joos Du Toit."

◆

I walked north on Pelikaanstraat. The Vespa was waiting near the corner of De Keyserlei, but now the rider had to make a choice. I was walking toward him. He could assume I hadn't made him, wait for me to walk by, give it a few minutes, then follow. Or he could come down the street and pass me, then pick me up again on De Keyserlei, where I was headed. He took option number two.

The sound of the four-stroke rose as he eased into the street. I was walking on the same side that he'd been waiting on, and he drifted over to the other side. At first he went very slowly, but as he got nearer he accelerated, as if he wanted to get by me quickly. I waited until he was almost opposite, then dashed out into the street. I meant to drag him off the saddle or shove him into the parked cars, but he twisted away, and when I made a wild grab, it was his helmet I caught. The scooter wobbled. I got both hands on the helmet, but the rider, probably by accident, twisted the throttle. The scooter shot forward and reared up and the helmet came off in my hands. I staggered backward, clutching it, and sprawled across the hood of a parked car. The rider fell hard. His head smacked the pavement as the Vespa slid out from under him. I struggled off the hood and limped to where the rider lay. Blue eyes stared up at me without expression. The beautiful lips were parted. I knelt on the pavement.

"Hi, Marie."

I checked the back of her head. Sticky. She mumbled something I couldn't make out. A thread of blood trickled from her nose. I dug around for her ID. It was in the front pocket of her jeans. Passport, South African driver's license, address in Hout Bay. So Hout wasn't her surname: it was where she lived. Her real name was one I hadn't heard until Dilip had spoken it in his car. Du Toit.

Wedged in behind the ID was a folded paper—a diamond parcel. I could tell by the thickness that the stone inside was large, and I guess at that moment, with the girl lying bleeding in the street, I knew what it was.

Only a weak, yellowy light stained the pavement, but the Lucifer made a meal of it. The captured light lashed around inside the diamond like a frantic reptile. I sat on my heels and watched it drool a mustardy light onto the white paper. I tilted the paper and the stone convulsed. The color fled and the diamond sucked at the night. On a whim I snapped a picture with my phone and sent it to Teddy. Sometimes you just want to throw a rock into the middle of the pond and see what happens. Then I folded the jewel back into the paper and jammed it in my pocket.

I opened Marie's jacket and found her phone. I used it to call 100, the Belgian emergency number, and told the operator where to find her.

38

I paid off the taxi at the Grote Markt and went down the short street to the cathedral. A crowd of Asian tourists packed the little plaza, posing for selfies. It wasn't the church that brought them there. They didn't give it a glance. They were there for the marble carving of a boy and his dog.

The two lie side by side on the cobblestones, as if asleep, with a fold of pavement drawn over them like a blanket. But they aren't asleep. They're dead.

The carving commemorates a nineteenth-century story called *A Dog in Flanders*, in which a starving orphan freezes to death on Christmas Eve after sneaking into the cathedral with his dog to see a famous altarpiece. Virtually unknown in Flanders, the story had become a bestseller in Japan and Korea. Antwerp's city fathers knew a good thing when they saw it and gave permission for the memorial. Being Flemish, they managed not to pay for it. The Toyota car company did. They knew a good thing when they saw it too.

"*Onze-Lieve-Vrouwekathedraal*," a man beside me said in perfect Dutch. "The cathedral of Our Lady. She is Antwerp's patron saint."

He was a heavyset man with a bulbous purple nose. A network of broken veins printed the map of a hard-drinking life on his cheeks. He wore an ancient leather coat with a complicated arrangement of straps and buckles. He'd been slimmer when he bought it. Even with the belt cinched tight the buttons strained to hold the coat in place around his thick body.

A beautiful old Leica dangled on his chest. He raised it and snapped a shot of the façade.

"A chapel with a statue of the Virgin was a place of veneration in Antwerp from the twelfth century," he said. "Work began on the present cathedral in 1351 and stopped in 1521. Technically the church was never completed. The architects wanted two spires, not just one," he said, tilting his head and aiming the Leica upward for another snap. "It is more than four hundred feet high, making it the tallest spire in the Low Countries."

"You don't say."

"I'm sure you know all this," he said, snapping the lens cap on the Leica and fitting it into a hard leather case.

"Not me," I said. "I came for the kid and the dog."

"You don't recognize me, Alex."

It was the guy who'd been taking pictures of Grant's Tomb when I went to meet Hassan. I should have paid closer attention to him, but this time I got it.

"Kaliningrad," I said. The time the Russians set me up. I had to run for the Latvian border. He'd met me on a dirt road near the coast. "How are you, Mihails?"

He was a hood from Riga who'd done CIA contract work. Hassan had hired him and put him on standby in case I needed to run.

"This is for you," he said, pulling a manila envelope from his inside pocket. I shoved it in my jacket without opening it.

"From Hassan," I said.

"I can't tell you who it's from."

"It wasn't a question."

He nodded and cracked his knuckles and took a long, slow look around the square. Some habits never die. He turned his cold blue eyes back to me. Then he walked away.

I went into the cathedral and paid the six-euro entrance fee. I stood at the back and surveyed the cavernous space, then made my way toward the altar. Lily was sitting alone in a pew in front of a Rubens painting, *Descent from the Cross*. The picture is one of four Rubens masterpieces in the cathedral, and in *A Dog in Flanders*, the boy dies while gazing at it.

The cathedral was one of Lily's haunts when she'd lived here. She had a passionate but also businesslike relationship with God. Lily couldn't pass a bank of votive candles without stuffing cash in the slot and lighting every wick. In return for her devotion, and the large subsidies she paid to certain priests, she expected God to look the other way while she helped herself to illicit rough. I'm no theologian, but you'd have to say, so far so good. I slipped in beside her.

"What did Dilip have to say?" she asked.

"Have you heard of Joos Du Toit?"

"No."

"He was the Van Kees chef. I'm sure you know what that is."

Lily nodded.

"His main job was growing diamonds that could get past the detection machines. That's how Van Kees stayed ahead of the advances in lab-grown—they learned the best growing techniques before anybody else, and then tweaked their machines to catch it."

"I understand. What about him?"

"He disappeared six months ago. His sister was the one who killed Lou and Coco and Leopold Rose. She was following me tonight."

"Why?"

"I don't know, Lily," I snapped. "I guess to kill me. That seems to be a common default setting." And I told her some of what had happened. Mrs. Goodwell. The weasels. Now Marie.

"Is she dead?"

"Not when I left." My phone buzzed. I checked the screen. Tommy. "Here," I said, handing her Marie's phone. "See what you can do."

I got out of the pew and ducked across the aisle into an empty confessional. I shut the door. It was lined with a heavy velvet curtain that muffled the sound.

"Listen," Tommy said when I answered. "MAUREEN tracked that arrest team. They're in Antwerp now. I called Noah Weitz to ask what gives. It got heated, but here's the scoop. They've got a delicate op going. Bad news has been following you around, and they're afraid you're going to blow everything up and scare away the target. He said it's not an arrest."

"I don't have to tell you Weitz does not have guys like that, Tommy. If the DNI has that kind of operational need, the CIA performs it. The hoods will be from Langley, and they won't be here so we can all sit down and explore our points of view."

"They'll gut you and bone you and pack you in ice," Tommy said cheerfully. He was fond of violence. He missed it, and thought of my life as a kind of pro ball, except not as well paid.

"Tell me what's happening," he said.

So I told him about the operation as Tabitha had described it—to enlist Van Kees in an attempt to grow a diamond with an N3 center. Tommy already knew about the role of diamonds in the competition to develop a quantum computer: he'd sent me the report compiled by

MAUREEN. What he hadn't known was how alarming the discovery of the N3 center was—that it demonstrated an ability to manipulate diamonds far ahead of our own. Lastly I told him about my conversation with Dilip, what I'd learned about Joos Du Toit, and what had happened with Marie.

Tommy heard me through without interruption. I heard his chair squeak once and his feet thump as he took them off the desk, and I could picture him lumbering back and forth across the office as he absorbed what I was telling him. Tommy had a prosecutor's mind. He could pick his way along a twisted path, but he liked to stop from time to time to check his bearings.

"Let's lay this out," he said. "The strategic goal is the need to get to a quantum computer before the Chinese. Washington sees this as an existential challenge."

"Yes."

"We get there first or get fried."

"I know what existential means, Tommy."

"If China can put an N3 center in a diamond," he continued, "it means they're better at manipulating the atomic structure of a diamond than we are, and that will put them ahead in the quantum race. We now assume that if the Chinese have that ability, they got it from this Joos Du Toit."

"Correct."

"And Tabitha doesn't know that yet because you have not gone back to the house to tell her on account of the Langley knuckleheads."

"Right."

"So the immediate challenge is to get you out of there in some way that is not a CIA rendition flight."

"Yes."

"Any ideas?"

"It's all set."

"What's all set?"

"I already know how I'm leaving."

"Oh, no," he said. "Don't tell me. Not Lily. For Christ's sake, Alex, please say you have not got Lily involved in this."

"Tell you what. I'll tell her to beat it, and in return you send me a different diamond expert with her own plane, unlimited resources, a deep familiarity with the characters involved, and who's already performed clandestine work for the Treasury."

"She's a Russian criminal."

"She is the right hand of God."

A deep *whoosh* rushed through the church as the massive organ filled with air. The organist launched into a booming dirge. I stepped out of the confessional and caught Lily's eye. She tucked the phone she'd been hacking into her pocket and genuflected reverently to the altar. We went through the exit turnstile and pushed through the crowd buying postcards of the orphan and the dog. The sound of the organ followed us into the square.

"OK," said Tommy, who'd had time to think things out, "here's the memo. I'll write Weitz a formal letter saying this department fully understands and acknowledges the urgency of the blah blah blah. I have advised you of your duty to accord your lawful investigation with the aims and intentions of the Office of the DNI as and when you are apprised of such aims, and that failing such direct advice to you in person and in writing, you are authorized to take such measures as the Congress of the United States has empowered you to take in the relevant statutes, to wit, blah."

"You make me proud to be American."

"See if you can keep Lily from owning the world when we're through."

Lily and I crossed the square and sat on a bench. "Joos Du Toit," she said, "the chef. Marie is his sister. I got into the email. The document folders will take a little longer, but I can tell you one thing: they weren't living in Shanghai. They were living in South Africa."

"Hout Bay," I said.

"How did you know?"

"Her driver's license."

The purple night flowed through the streets. We heard singing from a café in the Grote Markt. Lily leaned her head against my shoulder. I slipped out a glossy eight by ten from the envelope Mihails had given me.

It was taken at night, but there was enough light to make out Tabitha standing on a rainy street. She had an umbrella and was bending down to speak through the rolled-down window of a limo. I couldn't really make out the features of the person inside, but I could see the Coke-bottle glasses and the blue hair clips. Brutus was there too. He had his mouth wide open, so at least I knew what one of them was saying.

"Meow."

"Sorry?" Lily said.

"Nothing. Is the plane all set?"

"We can leave tonight."

"Tommy wants to know what you're going to charge."

"Whatever I want."

39

Beneath the wing, the River Scheldt scrawled a black loop through the lights of the city. We climbed away from Antwerp and turned south.

"What does the flight plan say?"

"Monte Carlo," Lily muttered, immersed in Marie's phone.

"Let me guess. Just before we get there, the pilot will file a change for Casablanca, and as soon as we are over the Sahara, turn off the transponder."

"Stop fussing," Lily said, thumbing some instruction into the keypad. "No one will be able to track us."

The Dassault Falcon 7X gained altitude fast. Soon the lights of France were creeping by below. We flew south through the night at thirty thousand feet.

Lily put Marie's phone down on the coffee table. She'd been rifling the contents since I'd handed it to her outside the cathedral. Of course she'd cracked it. Russian teenagers in places like Mirny didn't have shopping malls to hang out in, Lily liked to say—they had the internet.

According to her theory, this explained why a country with an economy one-fourteenth the size of the United States had produced a generation of hackers able to pick the world's cybersecurity like a cheap lock. I didn't point out that a large supply of consumer goods hadn't stopped American kids from learning how to hack. I didn't want to get her going on the natural superiority of Russians. Chess. Ballet. Crime. It was a long list. Tolstoy. Vodka. Hard to argue. Plus it was her plane.

She looked up from the phone. "If Marie survives, she will alert her brother."

"She didn't make it. I called the hospital when you were talking to the pilot."

"Then the brother will know what happened to her."

"No," I said. "I told them I was from the South African embassy and we would notify the next of kin. Does the brother live in Hout Bay too?"

"It looks that way. He must fly to Shanghai when he needs to supervise work at the diamond lab."

"Maybe he just sent them instructions."

"Never. I toured some of the top manufacturers when Mei told me she wanted to get into lab-grown. I needed to see what they could produce, so I could decide what opportunities existed for me. The chefs make minute adjustments. They're tinkering all the time, getting the temperature and pressure mix just right, and monitoring the diamond growth. They need to be present."

"Did you visit a Shanghai lab?"

"There was no Shanghai lab on the list of properties Mei gave me. That does not mean she did not own one. Her hedge fund is opaque. It isn't subject to the same reporting requirements as American funds. Mei owns many diamond properties devoted exclusively to industrial diamonds. At least, that is what she told me."

"Maybe she left some out."

"I imagine it is inevitable."

The black night streamed by outside. On an impulse I dug out the Lucifer and handed it to Lily. She turned the parcel carefully in her fingers.

"Marie had it," I said.

"And killed Lou for it."

She revolved the parcel a few more times, then took it to a small desk at the back of the cabin. A powerful fluorescent light was mounted to the bulkhead. Switching on the light, she placed the parcel on a pad of clean white paper. She found a head loupe in a drawer and slipped it on. Then she plucked the parcel in her fingers and flicked it open. The diamond pricked her face with dots of light. I got up and stood behind her.

The slight vibration of the plane made the stone tremble. Ribbons of light licked around inside, as if the diamond's fire were trapped and wanted to break free.

"I don't understand," she said, picking it up and bringing it close to the loupe. "What has happened? It is not a real diamond cut—more a contest to create facets. As if there were no plan. That girdle—it takes over the whole stone."

"Thirty-nine facets on the girdle," I said. "The crown has thirty-four." She examined the top part of the stone, then turned it upside down to look at the bottom. "And the pavilion?"

"Sixteen facets."

She flipped the stone again and held it close to the fluorescent tube. When she was finished, she placed the diamond on the white pad and flicked it with her tweezers. The stone flared. She removed her head loupe.

"You are going to tell me it's a Lucifer cut." She slid a glance at me. "I have read the literature and heard the stories. For myself, I doubt that cut has ever existed."

"Yet here it is."

"This is not a diamond cut, Alex. It's an assault on order. A cutter polishes a diamond to reveal its light. There is an ideal form inside the diamond, the form put there by God, and the cutter searches for that form. But here the cutter has searched for nothing. He has imposed a fantasy on the diamond. He ignores what God created and seeks something of his own that will be better. The way the angel Lucifer attacked God. Lucifer was the most beautiful of all the angels and could not bear the authority of God. He waged war on heaven. But we don't challenge God when we cut a diamond. We reveal the splendor of God's order by honoring the structure of the diamond. The order imposed by the cutter is a hymn to God. The cutter does not challenge the order of the universe. He does not conquer a stone. He reveals it. This"—she prodded the diamond with distaste—"this is an insult to the light."

I picked up the diamond and the paper wrapping from her desk. The Lucifer spattered my fingers with dots of light as I placed it in the paper. I folded it back out of sight. I could feel Lily's cool gray eyes on me and her X-ray vision scratching around inside my head.

"Perhaps this is the time to unburden yourself, my darling," she said, brushing a curl from the tip of her ear. A smile toyed at her lips. "Now you must tell me the purpose of the stone. I understand the synthetic-diamond business very thoroughly. I would not have ventured into it otherwise. The same techniques that are used to make lab-grown diamonds for jewelry can also be used to make complex products for high-tech uses."

She turned off the fluorescent light and swung her chair away from the desk and waited for me to respond.

"Is that so," I said.

The smile stopped kidding around and went to full wattage.

"Dear Alex. You have been battered and bludgeoned and led around by the nose by that spotted girl, and now you will try to fool Lily. You must see how impossible it is. I do not believe and have never for a moment believed that the United States government gave a damn about fake diamonds. Yet plainly they give a damn about *something* to do with diamonds, and so do other people, or there would not be all this gunfighting at Bergdorf's and jetting off to NATO by Tabitha."

I tried to keep a blank face, but Lily wasn't buying it.

"You are wondering how I knew about the NATO meeting."

"The military gate at JFK. You took a guess."

"The military gate gave me Tabitha. My Antwerp people gave me NATO."

"You spy on NATO?"

"Russia spies on NATO. When I ran the Russgem operation in Antwerp, the GRU used it as cover to run agents against NATO. It was very convenient."

I'll say. A half-hour spin down the E19. The GRU was Russian military intelligence.

"I have kept some of the old contacts," Lily said. "I have always found it useful to know what governments are up to."

"You're not planning world domination, are you, Lily? I'm supposed to find out."

She stood up from the desk and opened a door at the very rear of the cabin. Sitting on the wheeled trolley she pulled out was a small gray machine. It looked like the one my father had used to examine the five-carat oval.

"Spectroscope," said Lily. "Identical to the one in your father's lab."

"You don't know that."

"I do. You forget it was your father who examined the mineral samples when Mei and I acquired the Arctic mine. I have been to his lab at Orient.

This is the same model of spectroscope as the one he uses. When I drove you to Kennedy," she said, plugging the device into a wall socket and turning it on, "you said he had examined the five-carat Shanghai oval with a spectroscope."

The machine hummed as it warmed up. The screen began to glow. She held out her hand. What the hell. I gave her the Lucifer. She put it on a metal tray and slid it into a slot in the machine. She pressed a button and the humming changed tone. A colored graph appeared on the screen—a spiky line with a row of three sharp peaks. Lily picked up her tweezers from the desk and tapped each peak in turn.

"N3 center, N3 center, N3 center."

"You've been reading up," I said.

She turned off the machine, pulled out the little tray, and handed back the Lucifer. She returned to the sofa, stretched out, and tucked a cushion behind her head.

"You'd better tell me everything."

40

'd been watching for them, and suddenly there they were—the mining ships of the Namibian diamond fleet spread out on the black ocean. Floodlights illuminated the tall derrick of the main drill ship. On the seabed, a massive crawler was smashing up the diamond gravels. Inside the ship, twenty-four hours a day, 365 days a year, a stream of crushed ore rumbled through the mill while diamonds plinked down a chute into a sealed sorting box in the bowels of the ship.

The lights of the fleet drifted behind. I pictured the radar screen in the control tower of the Van Kees airport at Oranjemund, their mining center in the Namib desert. Always suspicious of approaching aircraft, air controllers would be watching us as we left the fleet behind and came abreast of the diamond beach, marked by the bloom of light against the coast. The hundred-year-old beach mine was on its last legs, but there were still enough diamonds to keep the big bucketwheel excavators going through the night. We crossed the South African border. Half an hour later Cape Town flared into view like a torch held up to the dark ocean.

The best view of Cape Town is at night. The black mass of Table Mountain looms behind the sparkling city. Facing the brilliant spectacle across the water are the clubs and seaside restaurants of Bloubergstrand. It's an enchanting scene, until you remind yourself that Nelson Mandela looked at it every night for twenty-seven years from his prison cell on Robben Island.

We flew out to sea, looped back in, and crossed the Cape Peninsula. Ten minutes later a line of blue lights jumped out of a dark field and we landed at Henny Botha's private strip near Stellenbosch. He stood in front of his hangar with long-nosed flashlights, guiding the Dassault in. The jet whined to a stop beside Henny's Antonov. The door opened and the gangway folded down, and we stepped out into the scent of vineyards.

"Yank!" Henny boomed. "And you brought this lovely creature!" He swept Lily into a crushing hug. "Why are you wasting your time with this lousy Yank when you could have a real Cape buffalo," he growled in a stage whisper you could hear a mile away. Then he put his shaggy head back and roared with laughter. "Cape buffalo," he repeated, shaking his head and wiping a tear from his cheek with a battered knuckle. Henny liked any joke, but especially his own.

Henny flew where other pilots wouldn't. The single-engine Antonov biplane looked like a relic, but the Russians were still producing them into the twenty-first century. Powered by a massive, nine-cylinder radial engine, it could take off in six hundred yards and fly five hundred miles with a full load. In the days when I flew with Henny, the only load was me, my little Czech-made Skorpion machine pistol, and a few rolls of US cash. If I was buying in Botswana, we'd refuel just outside the border, wait for night, and fly into the Kalahari, where the three richest diamond mines in the world were located. The landing strip would be marked by flares. The thieves would light them when they heard us coming. The Antonov landed like a moth.

Henny tossed me a set of keys.

"It's that place in Green Point," he said.

"Signal Hill?"

He nodded. "I put in a few supplies. There's a good bottle of wine in there, but it's for you," he said to Lily. "This lousy Yank"—he clapped my shoulder with a spade-sized hand—"he can drink the beer."

He was still laughing when we pulled away in the beat-up Jetta.

We took the R304 north through the winelands, then picked up the N1 motorway west into the city. We got off the expressway at Newmarket Street, went by the seventeenth-century castle built by the Dutch, and kept straight up through the central part of the city.

The real power left Cape Town long ago, when gold was discovered on the Witwatersrand and tens of thousands of men from every corner of the world poured into the country. They headed straight for the gold. A few years later the same thing happened again, this time with diamonds. Johannesburg exploded into the continent's richest metropolis. Cape Town was left with the old castle, a view of the sea, and for consolation, the vineyards.

We were through downtown in minutes and climbed the slope of Signal Hill. The street we followed curled around the foot of the cliff and turned into High Level Road. We found the street we were looking for and drove to a large white-painted concrete house. It stood on the steep slope, its back pressed against the hillside. I thumbed the remote, and the garage door rumbled up. We parked beside a flight of stairs and grabbed our luggage from the back seat. I opened the trunk and took out the canvas bag Henny had put there for me.

At the top of the stairs, I swiped a plastic fob over a pad. The deadbolt shot free. We walked through into the living room and the eye-popping sight that cost Henny's customers on Airbnb two thousand dollars a night.

A wall of plate glass spanned the whole front of the house. The hillside plunged away. Far below, a line of headlights crawled along the seafront. The lighthouse at Mouille Point sent its beacon thirty miles out into the black ocean. The South Atlantic stretched unbroken to Antarctica.

I slid the glass door open and we went onto the balcony. A cold breeze drifted up the hill. Lily zipped her jacket up and tucked her chin into the collar. We stood there for a while until she shivered. "It's freezing," she said. "I'm going upstairs."

I put my hands on the railing and looked out at the city. I was always moved by Cape Town, especially at night. But I knew it for what it really was, behind the glitter. Only the tourists are here for fun. Everyone else is backed up to the cold shore, waiting to see how the story will end. Sir Francis Drake called the headland at the tip of Africa the "fairest cape in all the world." But Sir Francis was a pirate.

41

I n the morning I dressed and went down to the garage, unlocked a gray metal door, and switched on the light. On a bench along one wall were a drill press, a punch set, and a full set of gunsmithing files. There was even a spray can of finishing enamel called Cerama-Coat. Not everybody coughing up the two grand a night for Henny's house was there for the view. I grabbed a can of gun oil and some tiny wire brushes, stuffed a couple of rags in my pocket, and went back upstairs.

I made an espresso and climbed the narrow spiral staircase to the rooftop deck. In the clear light I could just glimpse a corner of the fairytale pink-and-white façade of the parliament building. Far below, the first tour buses were pulling into the parking lot at the castle. Miniature joggers ran along the seawall. The sun shone out of a cloudless sky. Flowering shrubs blazed among the houses that cascaded down the slope. The N1 expressway gushed a stream of cars into the city. A warm breeze came up the hill, carrying the smell of flowers and gasoline.

I spread one of the rags on the table, took the Skorpion apart, cleaned and oiled it, and snapped it back together. When I finished the espresso, I went inside, washed the gun oil from my hands, and came back out to check my email. Still nothing from Annie. I wrote a note saying I hoped she was OK and was sorry I couldn't be there. I knew I should have put in something about my father, but I couldn't. There was nothing inside me to put. Only a dull gray emptiness. Maybe that was better than anger.

Next I went through the elaborate protocol to access the secure server. That's where the surprise was waiting. A surveillance clip that only MAUREEN could have dug up. Tabitha. According to the time code, taped last night. I wondered if she'd even waited to see if I'd return to the house. Probably not. She'd only have had time to buzz in the Langley heavies, show them where the vodka was, and head straight out. She'd had a flight to catch.

She was in a small group boarding a chopper at the London heliport. The helicopter's destination was Biggin Hill, south of the city. Biggin Hill was a wartime RAF base that had been converted to a private jetport. MAUREEN had inhaled the output of every camera in the place, so I had a good view of the chopper coming in to land. It was a wide shot from a high angle, probably the tower. A red line appeared and drew a box around the people getting out of the helicopter. The landing pad was well lit, and the image-enhancing tool had magnified and sharpened the figures. I watched Tabitha, Teddy, and Little Teddy troop across the apron and up the gangway into a waiting Gulfstream. The image cut back to a wide shot and jumped ahead to takeoff. As the jet rose into the sky and the wheels went up, a line of text swiped onto the screen: *Destination: Elandskop.* They were on their way to Africa.

Lily appeared with a pot of coffee and sat down beside me. I ran the clip of Tabitha getting on the Gulfstream.

"What is she doing with the Teddys?" Lily said. "And what is Elandskop?"

"It's the Van Kees family's private game reserve in the Waterberg. I don't know why she's going there, but it has to have something to do with the N3 centers."

"But Teddy doesn't make them. The Shanghai lab does."

"It's Joos Du Toit who makes them, and he learned to do it working for Teddy. He can't have taken everything when he ran. There have to be some records at the Van Kees labs, something that documented his progress. That's what Tabitha will be after."

"And what does Teddy get in exchange?"

"From Tabitha? Silence. It would be enough to threaten him with revealing the truth: that a diamond grower knows how to make undetectable fakes and learned to do it while pulling down a Van Kees paycheck and working in a Van Kees lab. That's Teddy's private terror. Tabitha's is that Joos knows more about manipulating diamonds than anybody else on earth and is now sharing that information with China."

"And you want to kidnap him and bring him to the United States so your government can squeeze his brain like an orange."

"Well, first I'll club him senseless with a tire iron."

"It's not funny, Alex."

"It'll be a lot less funny if Hassan and Mei find him first."

"How do you know they haven't already?"

"If they did they wouldn't have to try so hard to kill me." I grabbed the Skorpion and stood up, and then it hit me. "Can you reach Mei? To find out where she is?"

"If she is coming to kidnap Joos, she is not going to tell me."

"Just message her with something she'll reply to. We can locate her position when she answers."

Lily thought for a minute, then thumbed out a quick message. When the text went chiming off, she crinkled her eyes. "I asked if she knew what an N3 center was."

"There goes her day."

"We must hope so," Lily said, and went inside to get her Glock.

42

We left the house and drove out to High Level Road and followed it around the flank of Signal Hill. Below us were the suburbs of Sea Point and Clifton, with the South Atlantic rolling breakers onto the rocky shore.

I picked my way down through the glass-and-steel houses blazing on the hillside, and took the road along the coast. Fifteen minutes later we drove through the village of Hout Bay and onto an unpaved road that ended at the street we were looking for.

A scrub-covered hillside dropped down to the ocean, about a quarter mile away, where a line of Monterey pines swayed in the onshore wind. I could just hear the boom of the surf.

Closer, orange surveyor posts caught my eye. They stood out here and there in the undergrowth, marking what looked like the grid of a planned development. So far there was only the single street where we'd pulled up, with three houses on it. Two were unfinished one-story concrete shells, but the third was complete—a large, modern, white-painted concrete house at the end of a drive that curved down the hillside. I pulled to the side of the road.

A chain-link fence topped with razor wire surrounded the house. There was a camera on the gate. A sign with a lightning-bolt logo warned that the fence was electrified.

Henny had left a pair of Zeiss binoculars in the glove compartment. I scanned the property. That's when I saw the heavy power line. It came in along the side of the hill on poles, then dropped down to a metal transformer box with the logo of Eskom, the South African power company. Something that needed a lot of juice was running in the house.

I fished out the Bobcat from under the seat and holstered it at the small of my back. Lily took off her jacket and slipped on the custom-made shoulder rig. She checked the six-round clip on her Glock subcompact, smacked it back into place, put the pistol in the holster.

I drove slowly down the hill and stopped at the gate. A call box was mounted on a post. I studied the house.

On the side we faced, the only windows were the frosted sidelights that flanked the entrance, and a narrow window at the top of the garage door. A dark blue Subaru was parked in front. As we studied the building I felt a kind of throbbing in the air.

"Can you hear that?" I said.

"The ocean?" She tilted her head. "I can hear the surf."

"No. Steadier."

She listened. "Like a hum."

"Yes, and look at the roof. The air at the back is shimmering."

She squinted at the house. "Like something is burning behind it."

I opened the door and stepped to the call box, but before I could press the button, Lily said in a low, tight voice, "Alex, don't." She pointed to the gate. The opened padlock dangled from the latch.

I stepped quietly to the car, opened the back door, and slid the Skorpion from the canvas bag. Lily got out with equal care. We left the car doors open, pulled the gate ajar, slipped through. The noise from behind the house rose to a high-pitched hiss, clearly audible against the booming of the sea.

The Subaru was the only vehicle parked out front. I snicked the safety off on the Skorpion and approached the garage. I took a quick look through the window. Rows of boxes ranged along two walls. No other vehicle. I looked at Lily and shook my head. I pointed to the Subaru.

Lily nodded, tapped her chest, and jerked her head at the front door. She drew her gun, walked quickly to the door, and flattened herself against the wall. I checked the Subaru.

A thick coat of red dust clung to the windows. I didn't think the car had been anywhere in a long while. I cleared a patch on the passenger-side window and peered in. The seat was covered in folders and stacks of paper. I tried the door. Unlocked. I opened it silently and pulled out a labelled folder. *Geometric modeling of homoepitaxial CVD diamond growth.*

"It's Joos's car," I said when I reached Lily. "I think he's here, and alone."

The hum from the back of the house was making the glass in the sidelights tremble. I could feel the vibrations in my feet. "I didn't notice an alarm box, but I doubt anyone would hear it." But the second I turned the knob, a furious barking erupted deep inside the house. It quickly got louder, until the outline of a shaggy head pressed itself against the frosted glass and snarled at my ankles.

Lily bent down to squint through the glass at the gnashing teeth. "I don't see anyone coming."

I edged the door open slightly, sending the dog into a frenzy. He thrust his muzzle into the gap, baring his teeth.

"It's a wire-haired dachshund," Lily said. The dog melted at the sound of her voice, and the barking changed to a desperate whine. She put her hand down and he licked it madly. He didn't seem to mind that it held a Glock.

"For heaven's sake, Alex, let him out. It's the only way he'll calm down." I opened the door and he shot into Lily's legs, wrapping himself around them in ecstasy.

The humming sound was stronger now. Tremors shook the air. I stepped into the vestibule. No one came to see what had aroused the dog. I cleared the kitchen, an office, and two bedrooms. No one.

The main room took up most of the floor. Large windows looked out at the South Atlantic. The hill plunged away steeply to the shore, about four hundred yards away. Huge green rollers with a thousand miles of open sea behind them smashed to pieces on the rocks. Fountains of spray shot up like geysers. And above the tumult of the ocean, the steady noise droned on. Now I could see where it was coming from—a windowless cube of concrete, painted the same white as the house.

Lily joined me at the window. She'd managed to quiet the dog. He stuck to her like a burr. I jerked my chin at the view.

A flight of concrete steps led from the basement level of the house down the slope to the second building. A gray steel door was wedged open, and the space inside glimmered with a fierce light. Exhaust poured from stainless steel vents on the roof, curling through the air like an eddy roiling water.

"There's a reactor in there," Lily said.

"Yes. That's what the heavy power line is for."

We watched the light shimmer through the door.

"His test kitchen," Lily said.

"I guess so. Grow diamonds here, get the formula just right, take the recipe to Shanghai, run it there where they can scale production."

Lily's phone buzzed. She dug it out, read the message, and showed me the screen. Text from Mei: "Important we talk," she'd written. "Where are you?"

"Shut your phone down so she can't track you," I said. I texted Tommy with Lily's sat phone number and the time of Mei's message, and asked him to pinpoint Mei's location. When I was through, we went down to the lower level. A door opened to the flight of steps that led down to the second building.

Lily told the dog to stay. He sank to the floor and put his head on his paws and looked at her reproachfully. I shut the door behind us.

The noise from the building grew to a roar. It drowned out the wind and the crashing seas. Lily held the Glock along her leg as we approached the open door. I switched the Skorpion to semi and stepped through.

The reactor was mounted on a steel frame four feet high. A perforated screen of shiny metal enclosed the chamber. A red firestorm howled inside. The heat struck me in the face.

A young man in a blue lab coat sat at a desk with his back to the reactor. His head was propped in his hands and his elbows rested on the desk as he gazed at two screens. One screen displayed a large grid filled with numbers and symbols in different colors. Except for the advancing numbers on a timecode in a corner of the screen, the figures did not change. The other screen, too, was crammed with numbers, but these formed a dense, ever-shifting cloud of digits, winking on and off and changing color constantly. As he watched, the combination N3 appeared in red in the seething mass on the second screen. The N3 pulsed slowly three times, darkened into black, and stayed where it was. The man pulled a keyboard closer and quickly typed an entry. A line of numbers and symbols appeared at the top of the static screen. He pushed back his chair and stood up with a look of satisfaction. He ran a hand through a wild clump of blonde hair that stuck out from his head, turned, and caught sight of me.

He staggered in astonishment. I held the machine pistol away from my body, put it on the floor, and spread my hands to reassure him. Lily holstered her Glock as she followed me in. The man stepped back and gaped.

"You must not be here," he said, his voice barely audible above the roar of the reactor. "It is not permitted."

"I'm sorry to come in like this," I said. "The gate was unlocked."

He took another step back and looked anxiously from me to Lily. "The gate," he said, as if he had no idea what I was talking about. "But why are you here?"

"You're Joos Du Toit?" I said.

"Of course," he replied, as if his identity were an observable fact, like the color of his eyes—a remarkably candid blue. He was the spitting image of Marie. Only his expression differed. Marie had a calculating look. Joos looked out at the world from a face as innocent as a child's.

"We wanted to talk about your work," I said.

"But Marie is not here."

"No," I said, "but it's you we wanted to talk to."

"That is not possible," he said. "Only Marie may speak to people. Joos must not. Joos is not permitted."

"She said it would be fine," said Lily.

"She did?" He gave his hair a tug. "But where is she?"

"You're growing a diamond now?" I said.

His expression cleared immediately. "Of course." He stepped to the reactor. "You see it there, positioned on the substrate."

"That flat thing."

"Certainly. The carbon accretes to a wafer placed on the substrate." He turned to Lily. "Joos has also grown the wafer."

"Please tell us about it," she said.

"I must not."

"Except this time it is permitted," Lily said, leaning close to him so he could read the depth of sincerity in her eyes.

"It is never permitted," Joos said. "Only if Marie is here."

"That is why she made us promise never to reveal what you tell us," Lily said, placing her fingers on his wrist.

Joos stared at Lily's fingers. She gave him a little pat. "Temperature at substrate," he blurted, "four thousand degrees Fahrenheit. Temperature of plasma, eight thousand degrees. Plasma destroys everything that is not diamond. What it does not destroy *becomes* the diamond." He gazed at Lily. "Marie said yes?"

"She insisted," Lily said.

"But where is she? Joos must not be alone."

Lily gave him an encouraging smile and touched his sleeve. "I am interested in the plasma," she said. His face flooded with relief.

"Only one percent of the carbon present in the plasma becomes diamond," he said. "The rest does not survive. It is consumed. This makes the growing of a diamond very wasteful. That is why so much energy is required."

"Can you improve this process?" Lily said.

"No."

"But perhaps in time?"

"Never," Joos said.

"But you have made very large diamonds," Lily said.

"Of course."

"And some of them are indistinguishable from natural diamonds."

"Certainly."

"And how do you do it when no one else can do it?" Lily said.

I saw the glimmer of an emotion on his face. Not gloating. Not even pride. Something quieter. Satisfaction.

"I change the atomic structure."

43

He led the way to an adjoining room. A diamond press was bolted to the concrete floor, its jaws spread open. He stopped at another door, pressed two fingers to a pad. The door unlocked and we went through into a small, windowless office with a long table. Two screens took up most of the space on the table. The screens appeared to mirror those in the reactor room. A second N3 had appeared among the cloud of digits. It pulsed, settled, and hardened into black.

Joos bent to the keyboard and rattled in an entry. A second line of type appeared on the static screen.

"You see?" he said, spreading a hand in front of the screen with the orderly grid. "Here are the data parameters, and *here*"—he moved his hand to the swarming cloud of digits—"is the plasma." He whirled around and fixed his eyes on Lily. "Input," he said, gesturing at the first screen, "and output." He pointed to the second.

"And the N3s," I said. "You can make those?"

"Of course," said Joos, still looking at Lily. "The N3 signifies a vacancy with three carbon atoms arranged around it."

Lily nodded, brushing a lock of hair from the tips of her ears. Joos blushed.

"I would love to know about vacancies," Lily said.

Joos seized the tuft of hair on his head and yanked so hard a few strands of blonde hair came out in his fist. He flushed deeply again and nodded. He found a stylus with a plastic tip and stepped to a third screen, this one mounted on the wall. With a few deft strokes he sketched a crystal shape. The lines glowed to life on the black screen. Next he drew a series of lines through the crystal. "Growth planes," he said. Lastly he added tiny circles along the lines. "Atoms," he stated. "Most are carbon, but in CVD stones, some will be nitrogen." He looked at Lily. "You understand CVD?"

"Chemical vapor deposition," she said.

Joos gave her a look that pledged his devotion to the end of time. He dragged his eyes back to the screen and quickly labeled a dozen circles with Ns and Cs.

"The presence of nitrogen gives CVD stones a brown color," he said. "To make the stones clearer, growers must purge the nitrogen atoms from the crystal."

"Fascinating," Lily said.

"To expel the nitrogen," Joos explained, "they treat the stones with high heat. At temperatures above three thousand degrees Fahrenheit, the atoms move. *And*," he added, tapping the screen with the stylus, "not *only* the atoms."

"The vacancies," Lily murmured.

He raised himself on his toes and tipped his chin at her, turned back to the screen, and pressed a button on the side. The drawing vanished and Joos sketched in another crystal. He labelled most of the atoms with a C for carbon, then lettered a pair of side-by-side atomic spaces with N and V.

"Sometimes when the atoms move, a nitrogen atom will come to rest beside a vacancy. We call this an NV center."

"Is it very hard to make?" I said.

He waved his hand dismissively. "Anyone can make this. They are abundant."

"But you are not making those."

"Oh, no," Joos said. He shook his head. "No no no." He sketched in another diamond lattice. This time, clustered tightly around the vacancy, he put in three Ns. He stepped back and stared at the screen. "N3 center," he said to Lily. "One vacancy, three nitrogen."

"I suppose they must be very hard to make?" she said.

"Oh, yes. Very hard."

"Yet you can do it," Lily purred.

"Oh, no. No one can do it. Generative artificial intelligence algorithm. Algorithm can manage one hundred trillion data parameters. Algorithm feeds directly to reactor from position behind chamber."

"But where does it get the data if you don't put it in?" I said.

"Alex," Lily murmured, "it's AI. It generates the data by itself."

A movement on one of the monitors caught Joos's eye. In the cloud of digits that monitored activity inside the reactor, numbers were seething around the two Vs and a swarm of Ns. At the same time, the grid of static data blinked several times, each time repopulating the grid with a new set of numbers.

"Algorithm is changing inputs," Joos said, and hurried into the reactor room. Behind the perforated screen, the fire hissed and roared. Spheres of intense white light appeared in the midst of the orange storm. As we watched, one of the balls of light faded away into the orange of the inferno. When I checked the cloud on the monitor, one V had disappeared. But the other V was changing. From the boil of digits around, three Ns emerged.

"N3 center," Joos said.

I looked for the box he'd mentioned, where the inputs came from. A cable ran from the reactor to a point high on the wall behind it, where a thick layer of what looked like thermal shielding enclosed something cube-shaped, presumably the box that held the device.

"Joos," I said. "Does the Chinese lab get data directly from here, or does it have its own AI?"

The still blue eyes remained fixed on the cloud of digits, his mind transfixed by the orderly arrangement of the atoms in the firestorm of the reactor. Then he turned his gaze to Lily.

"Chinese?"

"He means your lab in Shanghai," she said.

He stared at her, plainly baffled. "Here is lab."

"Yes." Lily smiled. "But we're asking about the one that grew the large stones sold in America—the Shanghai lab."

He wrinkled his forehead. "No lab in Shanghai," he said. His gaze returned to the cluster of Ns around the single V. A faint smile appeared on his lips. His mind had returned to the crystal.

"Joos," I said over the roar of the plasma. "Who gets the diamonds you make here?"

He squinted at the screen. He had returned to his own world. He scribbled a notation on a Post-it note before he answered. "Teddy."

And the shape that had been there all along stepped out of the boiling digits and showed me its teeth. Its eyes were yellow and hard.

"You still work for Teddy," I said.

"Of course."

There was a stylus here too, and he used it to tick two boxes in the grid. Work he had started in London and continued here. Joos hadn't fled. He wasn't hiding from Teddy. He was working for him.

I turned to Lily, but she was staring at Joos. I pulled her into the reactor room.

"Do you think he even knows who he's working for?" I said.

"I was wondering the same thing."

"Marie was running the operation. She could have been running it for the Chinese, and just told Joos it was for Teddy to get his cooperation."

Lily gazed at the orange tempest. "Possibly, but I don't think so. Because if it's Teddy, that answers an important question: Why were the stones ever sent to Lou? Mei had no motive to do that, and every reason not to. The secret was too important to risk just for money."

"And Teddy had every reason."

"Yes," she said. "It restored his power over diamonds. It didn't matter that no one else knew it. Teddy would know it."

I looked back into the room where Joos was watching a diamond form. He was just starting to make new notations when my phone pinged. I took it out and checked the screen. Tommy. I tapped in my password and read the message. MAUREEN had found Mei. I showed the screen to Lily and watched her face freeze as she read where Mei had texted from. Elandskop.

44

J oos was still watching the screens when we left, his face enraptured by the swirling numbers. The orange cloud of plasma howled above the growing diamond. Eight-thousand-degree heat devoured everything but the carbon. Atom by atom, the carbon that survived descended through the tempest, and the diamond grew.

In a few weeks it would weigh ten carats. In a matter of months, a hundred. Then Joos would clean off the black coating of graphite. He would expel the nitrogen atoms from the crystal, keeping only three. Three would stay inside the crystal, tightly clustered around a vacancy—around a part of the atom that was, literally, nothing. The most valuable zero on the planet.

I grabbed the Skorpion from the floor. We left. The sound of the reactor dwindled. A fresh breeze blew uphill from the sea. The razor wire twinkled in the sun.

"If Joos is working for the Teddys," Lily said, "how did Mei learn about the fakes?"

"I don't know. I guess Teddy told her."

"And now they're all at Elandskop for what—some kind of auction?"

"Unless they share a common passion for giraffes, then that would be my guess. Some kind of sale."

"And nothing came out of Shanghai."

"I think we're going to find it was a shipping blind to disguise where the lab was. Send the stones from here to Shanghai, and from there to Lou."

"Then who killed Lou?"

"It's still the Chinese. It takes money and documents and backup to get assassins into place, hide them, arm them, kill Lou, put a hit on me. It's part of Teddy's price for the N3 formula."

"And Hassan runs it."

"Are you kidding? He's the star. Hassan's the MVP. I don't know how Mei found him, but he'd know right away that I was the spoiler. And what to do about it."

"But what about the N3? How does Mei even know about that? You only know because your father identified it. For that matter, what does Teddy know? He knows that the presence of an N3 center is supposed to mean a diamond is real. Does he know what it might mean to quantum computing?"

"Lily—I think we just have to accept he's doped it out. The most powerful woman in Asia just flew in to his game lodge in the Waterberg. Let's see what we can find in the office before I call Tommy. This is going to go very fast now." I should have added: "and you can quote me."

We headed up the flight of steps to the house. As soon as we got near the top, the dog began to whimper and scratch wildly at the door.

"There's my brave boy," Lily cooed when we went in. She scooped him up in her arms and kissed his head, fondling his ears while he slobbered at her chin.

We went upstairs and crossed the living room to the hall that led to the office. Suddenly the dog stopped licking and began to growl.

"What's eating him?" I said as I opened the door and stepped into a block of cement shaped like a human fist.

45

I came to, sitting in a chair, my hands cuffed behind me. The plastic zip ties dug into my wrists. One side of my face felt as if it had been put there with a nail gun. All I could see was a hazy shape. The haze cleared and the shape turned into Lily.

She was sitting too, holding the dog in her lap and staring bullets at a mountainous white guy who looked like a nose tackle for the Chicago Bears. He had a head like a pineapple and hands the size of catchers' mitts. Also a Vektor R4 South African assault rifle. His hip was propped on the windowsill. The barrel of the gun was aimed at Lily but his eyes were on me.

On a desk against the wall sat a fit-looking Black man with a benign expression. He had a diamond stud in his ear and was wearing one of those braided bracelets that show you support some cool charity, like caring about animals. Maybe they were here to check on the dog and it was all a misunderstanding.

"Who the shit are you, man?" the Black guy said. *Who the sheet are you, men?* He flipped through a leather ID folder that I recognized as mine. "Start talking."

That was going to be hard. I had the cognitive agility that came with a punch to the head. I glanced at Lily. She flicked her eyes around the room. Ear stud was still examining my papers. Nose tackle was measuring me up for another clout. Lily mouthed a word at me. I couldn't make it out.

"I'm waiting," the Black guy said. He held the folder out toward me and frowned at the picture on my ID, the way border police do when they're checking if it's really you. I glanced at Lily. She mouthed the word again. This time I got it. Scream.

I leaned back and bellowed at the top of my lungs. Nose tackle moved to stand up, and as he did, the rifle shifted slightly away from Lily. Not much. But enough. She grabbed the barrel and yanked hard enough to make him stumble, and in that fraction of a second the Glock was out and jammed under his chin.

"Nine-millimeter hollow-point," she said. "Your call."

"Fuck," he hissed through his clenched teeth as he let the R4 clatter to the floor. "Fuck fuck fuck."

"Virgil, you arsehole!" his partner yelled. "You didn't fucking pat her down?" He jumped to his feet. The dog launched himself from Lily's lap like a torpedo. "Shit," the Black guy said, dancing around while the dog attacked his ankles.

Lily leapt from the chair. Now she had both of them covered. "You at the window, stay where you are. And you"—she jerked her chin at the Black guy—"put the dog outside and close the door. If you reach for that pistol, I'll shoot you."

He managed to grab the dachshund around the waist, push him out, and close the door. While the dog alternately whined and growled on the other side of the door, Lily told the Black guy to discard his pistol and cut my cuffs. A few minutes later we had them both zip-tied and sitting on the floor. I rubbed the circulation back into my hands.

The Black guy's name was Bhekizizwe. "Zulu name," said Virgil. "He a Zulu warrior, man. Name means 'take care of the nation.' He take care of you and leave you in the bush in pieces."

"Just call me Ziz," he said. "Don't pay attention to this asshole." *Esshole.*

"So, guys," I said, "what's the story?"

"We just security guards, man," Ziz said.

"Fuck him," Virgil snarled. "Don't tell him anything."

"Ach, man, would you relax? We shooting baboons and chasing kids. It's not a state secret." *Stight sikret.*

"And you need an R4 for that line of work?" I said.

Virgil made a sucking sound through his teeth and shook his head in disgust. "It just for practice, man," he said. "Otherwise we going crazy out here."

They worked for the developer. Mostly that involved trying to clean out a troop of baboons and keeping the local kids from pulling out the survey stakes. But they kept an eye on Joos too.

"Somebody paying you to do that?"

"Nah," Ziz said. "We got nothing else to do. That guy could not tie his own shoes. He kind of crazy."

"They were in there an hour and a half, man," Virgil growled. "They know he's crazy."

I thought about them for a minute. Virgil had a tattoo on his forearm—a stylized star. It was the logo of the South African Special Forces, an elite reconnaissance and sniper unit known as the Recces. Apex predators. They weren't hoods, or the scream trick would have got me a bullet in the knee. They were vets. South Africa was full of men just like them—highly trained combat soldiers who'd served out their hitches, maybe hired on as mercenaries until younger men replaced them. I'd seen Virgil wince when he'd got down on the floor. An overweight rhino with a hip issue. Ziz—better shape, but like his partner, out of the medals long ago. Still, their former lives had depended on close observation of human targets. They had time on their hands and not enough to do. My guess: they knew exactly what Joos was doing.

"Does he have many visitors?" I said.

"We could remember better without these," Virgil said, holding up his wrists.

"Would you remember any better if I came over there and sucker-punched you in the face?" I said.

Virgil grinned. "You were carrying a Skorpion, man."

"Talk to me."

Virgil shifted himself. The leg was hurting. He glanced at Ziz, then me, and said: "You know about the sister?"

"Uh-huh."

"She not the only one who comes."

"Who else?"

Virgil looked at his watch. "The other one who comes will be driving up your ass in half an hour."

"Who?"

He shook his head and raised his wrists again. He had hard gray eyes. His hands were impregnated with dirt and gun oil. Maybe he wasn't in tip-top shape, but he wasn't washed up either. We studied each other for a minute. Lily had the Glock on her lap and I had the Skorpion again, so what the hell. I took out my penknife and sliced off the ties. They rubbed their wrists.

"Every two weeks the sister leaves at 9:00 A.M. on the dot and drives to Cape Town airport," Virgil said. "If she's been away, she comes back the night before to be ready. Always leaves the house at the same time, always picks up the same guy, always comes straight back here. Today is the day. That's why we here. See what happens. Log it."

"What time?"

"Ten thirty. Never later."

"OK," I said, checking my watch. Half an hour. "Except the sister's not here."

"No. So we not sure the man will come. But he's never missed before. Maybe they're coming together." Virgil had a glint in his eye, but I thought that had more to do with the fact that his hands were free than Marie's driving arrangements. I caught his eye and shook my head. I tapped the safety with my finger so he could see that it was off. He gave me a glimpse of broken teeth.

"Where do you watch the house from?"

"Nah," Ziz said, "we not giving it away, man. We got an excellent OP." Observation post. They sat there watching me intently, like I was having trouble finding my place in the script and they were directing brain waves in my direction to help me locate it.

"But you'd be happy to share the OP with me," I said, "in exchange for some token of my gratitude."

"That's very decent, man," Ziz said. "Cash for example." *Kesh for ixemple.*

"Tell you what," I said. "I'll give you ten thousand rand right now. You take us to the OP. If the guy shows up, you get another ten."

Twenty thousand rand was twelve hundred dollars. Real money for a couple of guys so far down on their luck they were pulling baboon duty in Hout Bay. Ziz glanced at Virgil. He nodded. Lily counted out the ten grand, handed it over. Ziz shoved it in his pocket. Virgil glanced at the Skorpion, then nodded at the R4 on the floor.

"Since we friends now?"

I shook my head. "Not on the first date."

The dog gave Lily a stricken look. She promised she'd be back. He didn't look like he was buying it. We shut the gate behind us and left the padlock dangling in the latch. I stood to one side with the Skorpion while Lily put Ziz's pistol and the R4 in the trunk and tossed in the combat knives we'd found when we frisked them. The Recces had left their vehicle out of sight at one of the unfinished houses. Lily drove the Jetta up and I followed on foot, the two South Africans in front of me.

When we got to the house, I gave Lily the Skorpion and searched their Jeep. Vektor 9mm pistol clipped under the dash, and in the back, a huge rifle in a canvas bag. I unzipped the bag for a look.

"Jesus Christ," I said. "Is that a Denel?"

"NTW-20," Ziz said.

Bolt-action anti-personnel gun developed by the Denel Mechem company of South Africa. It could take out a target a mile away, and not just a person. Using special ammunition, the NTW could transform a tank into bits of metal. They have a round that can set a refinery on fire.

I put the pistol and the big Denel in the trunk with the other weapons. Lily parked the Jetta behind the house. We climbed into the back of the Recces' Jeep. Twenty minutes to go.

46

We drove down a steep, narrow track toward the ocean. The road followed a cleft that had washed out into a series of gigantic potholes. Boulders blocked parts of the road, forcing us into the scrub. The Jeep lurched and bounced. The booming of the surf got louder, and sometimes a tower of spray shot up in front of us. The house appeared on our left, then vanished again as the wheels slipped in the loose soil and we juddered into a trough. Lily fell against her door and I had to grab the back of Virgil's seat to keep from tumbling into her. I had the Bobcat in my hand.

We came out at a grassy plateau about a hundred yards above the rocky shore. Black-backed Cape gulls rose up in alarm and wheeled around us, crying.

The OP was set up in a dense grove of pines. The wind had tortured them into crazy shapes. The constant thrashing of the trees would make it impossible to see us from the house.

They'd made themselves comfortable, with a rough table and a bench. Virgil set up a tripod at one end of the table and screwed on a spotting scope. I sat down beside him and braced my elbows on the table and twisted the Zeiss binoculars into focus. I was just scanning the exterior when fluorescent ceiling lights flickered on in the office.

"He getting things ready," Virgil murmured beside me, his eye to the scope. Joos opened a cupboard and took out a tray. He set it down on a high desk with a microscope, and pulled over a stool. He picked up a pair of tweezers from the desk and transferred an object from the tray to the plate below the lens of the microscope.

"CVD diamond," Virgil said.

"Been doing your homework," I said.

"We know what he's making, man. Worth more than twenty grand to find out everything we know."

Joos bent his eye to the instrument, switched on a powerful beam, and adjusted the focus as he examined the object.

"Incoming," Ziz said. "Right on time."

I panned up to the road. A plume of dust trailed through the scrub. The uphill angle kept the car hidden. The dust disappeared behind the house.

"He'll be coming down the driveway now," Ziz said. I turned the binoculars back to Joos. His head stayed bent to the microscope for about thirty seconds, then he sat up, slipped from the stool, and left the room. I kept my glasses on the office, and about a minute later Joos reappeared. Two men followed him in.

"No sister this time," Virgil said. "The little guy, he the one who always comes. I don't recognize the other guy. He look like a pro, man. Take a look," he said to Ziz.

Ziz bent down and adjusted the focus. "Ach, the big one? That bastard is a pro for sure."

They were right about that. They were both pros. Mihails must have been hot. He was still wearing that beat-up leather coat with all the buckles. He hauled out a handkerchief and mopped his forehead. The smaller man looked much more comfortable. He wore a crisply pressed safari suit. But that's what you'd expect. Hassan knew how to dress for the Cape. He grew up here.

"Joos looking not too happy," Ziz said.

"Probably asking where his sister is," I said.

Joos waved a hand wildly in the direction of the lab. He paced around the office, stopped in front of Hassan, and wrung his hands as he spoke. Hassan patted him on the shoulder and said a few words and gestured at the microscope. Joos took up the tweezers again, removed the diamond he'd been looking at, and replaced it with a larger one. Hassan sat on the stool and put his eye to the microscope. When he was through, he got off the stool and spoke for a moment while Joos stared miserably at the floor. At last Joos nodded, and he and Mihails left the room.

As soon as they were gone, Hassan unplugged the computer and carried it from the room. He returned a minute later, opened one of the cupboards, and took out a canvas bag. He collected all the diamonds from the tray, wrapped them hastily in bubble wrap, and stuffed them in the bag. As he was doing that, Mihails and Joos appeared around the corner of the house, went down the steps, and disappeared into the lab.

"I don't like it," I said. "I'm going up for a closer look."

I slipped into the bush and started to pick my way uphill. Thorn trees and the sandy soil made the going tough. The ocean breeze didn't penetrate the dense tangle of the scrub. Soon my shirt was plastered to my body and sweat ran into my eyes. Short, stiff branches raked my face as I pushed my way through the brittle undergrowth.

I reached a narrow slot that had been hacked through the bush. Orange stakes marked the cut line. A blue plastic tag with the power company logo warned against digging. This was where the underground power cable ran into the lab. I stopped and listened. The wind rushed through the tops of the taller trees, but even with that background noise I could make out the hum of the reactor.

The scrub thinned. Ahead lay the cleared perimeter around the fence. I had almost reached it when Mihails came out of the lab with a laptop under his arm. I flattened myself against the ground. He stopped outside the door, looked back inside, then turned and scrutinized the bush. I was close to the open strip in front of the fence and he was fifty yards beyond. Virgil would have him in the crosshairs of his scope. I rolled slightly on my side and tugged the Bobcat from my belt. I watched Mihails studying the bush. I brought the pistol around and braced my elbows and put the barrel sight on his chest. His eyes scanned past me, then stopped and came back. He raised his hand to shield his eyes from the sun. He hadn't seen me, but his eye had registered something, maybe a denser patch of shadow where I lay. I snicked the safety off. Just then a small, dark shape rushed snarling from the house and cannoned down the steps.

Mihails whirled around and faced the dog. It launched itself at his legs. He planted his left foot and with his right delivered a savage kick that catapulted the little body into the air. The dog squealed, twisted horribly, and landed in a broken heap.

Mihails shot a last glance into the lab, then hurried up the steps and disappeared. I looked up at the office to see if Hassan was still there, but this close to the house the angle was too steep. I couldn't see inside. I didn't know where he was until I heard car doors slam and an engine start and the sound of tires crunching up the gravel drive.

I scrambled out of the bush and into the cleared perimeter. The wind whipped the trees and moaned through the razor wire and whirled the loose sand into my eyes. It took me five minutes to get up the slope and reach the gate. I ran across the parking lot, through the house and down the stairs to the side door.

As I approached the lab, the glimmering light through the open door seemed stronger than before. Orange patterns swarmed the walls and floor. I gripped the Bobcat tightly. I don't know what I was defending myself against. Even as I held the gun, I knew I didn't need it. There wouldn't be anybody to shoot. There would just be Joos.

The door of the reactor gaped wide open. The plasma stormed inside the chamber. A raging eight-thousand-degree inferno designed to devour everything but the growing jewel in its midst. Joos lay on the floor beside it, his arms flung out to the side and his blue lab coat spread like a cape, as if he had tried to take off and fly, and the experiment had failed. The exotic bird that was Joos had crashed to the ground. It would never fly again. Nothing remained of his head but a charred stump.

47

Virgil came into the office with thunder in his face. "If I find those bastards," he growled, "I'll kill them with my bare hands."

I was tapping out a message to Tommy. I needed to bring him up to date so he could get hold of Tabitha's boss, Noah Weitz. It wouldn't be Weitz who was running Tabitha in the field. She'd have a CIA case officer. Whoever that was, he had to understand the danger she was in. I put it in point form:

1. The fakes didn't come from Shanghai. Joos had made them in Hout Bay, and made them for Teddy, not the Chinese.
2. Joos could create N3 centers at will. They weren't flukes.
3. Hassan and Mihails had murdered Joos and grabbed computers and CVD diamonds. Hassan worked for Teddy, and maybe also Mei.
4. Teddy, Mei, and Tabitha now at Elandskop. Urgent to advise Tabitha of developments.

Virgil thumped a large clump of wires and stainless steel onto the desk.

"The brains," he said.

It was the AI "black box" from the wall behind the reactor. I'd told him where to find it. Our relationship with the Recces had evolved. Lily paid the original twenty grand and added twenty thousand more for a rundown on what they knew. A lot.

They had surveillance data, not only on Hassan's regular visits, when Marie picked him up and returned him to the airport, but on other visitors too. Teddy and Little Teddy. High-res head shots taken with a telephoto lens. Ziz had copies on his phone. He airdropped them to me and I sent them on to Tommy.

Naturally the Recces' plan was to rob Joos. That part had got bogged down in the baffling complexity of the stones. Most of Joos's rough diamonds were rectangular and heavily graphitized. A Van Kees cutter came down from London every few months, cleaned off the graphite, and polished them into polyhedrons before they left for Shanghai on the first leg of their journey.

"It's just a bunch of black chips!" Virgil exclaimed in disgust. *Blek chips.*

"I can imagine your outrage."

Lily was on the floor in a heap of the offending chips as we spoke, examining them with a loupe. The dog whimpered from the hall and she rushed out to comfort him. Ziz had found a sheet of plywood in the basement and used it to carry the dog into the house and upstairs. It bit him twice. Ziz paid no attention. "Ach, he in pain, man. He just defending himself."

Ziz was now in the kitchen with some painkillers he'd found in the medicine cabinet. He placed a pill on the counter, laid the flat of a butcher's knife on top, and with a hard slap of his hand produced a smudge of powder. Using a smaller knife, he separated out a small amount and put it in a glass. He filled the glass with water and stirred the powder until it dissolved. He handed the glass and a spoon to Lily.

"Don't give too much," he said. "He weighs maybe eight pounds. The pill is for a human who weighs twenty times as much."

I found some shipping records and started to sort through them. "Don't bother with those," said Virgil, leaning over to see what I had. "Got a file with all that information—dates the diamonds were picked up," he said, waving the screwdriver, "where they were taken for shipping, destination."

I found a canvas shipping bag. Virgil wrapped the black box in bubble wrap. I put it in the bag along with the diamonds and the files. The Recces carried the dog outside on the sheet of plywood and loaded him carefully into the back of the Jeep. Lily came out with his food- and water-bowls and a twenty-five-pound bag of kibble. She went back in and got his dog bed and placed it beside him. "For security," she said. She climbed in and sat cross-legged on the bed, holding a paw. Ziz drove slowly out the gate and up to the street. He pulled over at the unfinished house. I picked up the Jetta and followed them into town. Ziz and Lily were carrying the plywood with the dog into the vet's when I pulled in behind them.

"Poor little fellow," the vet said, injecting him with a sedative while Lily held his head and told him, for the hundredth time, what a brave boy he was. Ninety minutes later we carted him back outside and put him in the Jetta, sliding the plywood onto the back seat and wedging it into place with the canvas bag. The dog was out cold. Two stainless steel pins held the fractured ribs together. The vet loaded Lily up with a supply of dog painkillers and sedatives. I exchanged contact details with Virgil. The details included bank transfer codes for an account that Virgil and Ziz had in Liechtenstein. Mercenaries understand banking, and our business wasn't finished.

Lily and I went back to the house on Merriman Road. I thumbed the remote as we approached. The garage door rattled up and we drove in. Henny had come through again. A white Beemer 300 series was parked beside the stairs.

We unloaded the dog and carried him upstairs and put him on the terrace. He was groggy but awake. I came back down for his bowls, the kibble and bed, and the bag with the drives and diamonds. I got a couple of beers from the fridge and we stretched out on the chaises and watched the ocean turn into a million miles of hammered copper. The lights came on in Bloubergstrand. The dog whimpered and raised his head. He had one of those plastic cones around his neck to keep him from biting his bandages.

He sniffed at his bed, tried to get to his feet, gave up, and lay back down. Lily got the bottle of dog painkillers, added half a tab of sedative, and wrapped it in a piece of bacon. The dog gulped it down. His head thudded onto the plywood and he started to snore.

"I'll have to see Hassan," I said.

"What makes you think he's still here?" Lily said.

"I used my superior spy powers and checked my email."

"He wrote you?"

"Don't sound so surprised. He knows we're here. There was a camera on the gate at Hout Bay. Besides, he sent Mihails to contact me in Antwerp, so he knew I was there. It was only a matter of time before I'd hear that Joos had gone missing from Van Kees. Next thing, Marie turns up dead, so he concludes that now I know where to find Joos."

"But why contact you?"

"He has to settle with me. This is where he'd pick. He was a Cape Town hood before he was a spy. This is where he learned to kill. It's a great town for it."

The night pulsed with light. Elegant apartment buildings wrapped in glass flowed down the hillside to the sea. People drifted onto balconies and inhaled the night. The scent of jasmine drenched the air. Streams of headlights wound down the slopes. On the far side of Table Bay, Bloubergstrand strung a necklace of lights along the black ocean. The running lights of ships marked the passage around the Cape of Good Hope, to India, to the Malabar Strait, to the empire that drew them to its shores today as it had for centuries—China.

48

I n the morning I got up, shaved, and took a long, hot shower. I let it run cold for a full minute at the end. Then I put on a clean white shirt, fresh jeans, and my desert boots with the steel toes. Always the pessimist.

"Woof," the dog said when I came into the kitchen. He followed that with a little whimper. It sounded tentative, like he was trying it out for a painkiller.

"Forget it," I said. "I'm not your dealer."

I made a double shot of espresso and took it out onto the terrace. A Cape sugarbird landed on a pink protea, cocked a beady eye at me, then got to work spearing the florets with its long, black beak. The dog woofed again and put a little more pathos into the whimper that followed, so I knew Lily was up. A few minutes later she came out with a coffee, slumped into a chair beside me, and took a sip.

"What time are you meeting him?"

"Ten," I said.

"And the cable car runs every fifteen minutes?"

"Yes."

"I don't like it."

"We've been over this." I got up and collected the Bobcat and holstered it at the small of my back.

"You're taking the Jetta?"

"Yes. The keys for the Beemer are on the counter."

"Make sure you're at the cable car ahead of him."

"It's Table Mountain, Lily. You can see people coming a mile away up there. There's a hundred tourists standing around taking pictures. It's not a great place for an ambush."

Talk about famous last words.

I drove out to High Level Road, made a right, and followed the road around Signal Hill until it became Strand Street. Where Strand plunged down the hill into the city, I turned off and headed for Kloof Nek Road. Kloof Nek was a low saddle in the hills between Table Mountain and Lion's Head. Instead of following the road through the pass, I cut left for the mountain.

I made one call on the way. "Blue Cortina. Driveway on the left when I came out onto High Level."

Now the mountain loomed to my right, the sheer cliff rising above me. Suddenly I was wrapped in a dense fog. It streamed across the road like thick gray smoke. In Cape Town they call it "the tablecloth." It can drop from a clear blue sky. It had today, cloaking the mountain in fog that poured down the cliff like a waterfall. If I still lived here, I'd have planned for that. So that was a mistake.

I parked the Jetta behind a vanload of people with cameras and wide-brimmed safari hats, and followed them to the entry. They exclaimed in delight at the torrent of fog flowing down the cliff. They wouldn't be so happy when they got to the top and went looking for the view.

I waited behind some tour buses and watched the first cable car vanish into the mist at 8:00 A.M. Fifteen minutes later it reappeared, gliding out of the fog just as the second car left the station and went climbing past it. Each gondola held sixty-five passengers, and the big rush for tickets was first thing in the morning, so there weren't many people in the waiting area when Hassan Ubered up, bought his ticket, and boarded the gondola. At 9:30 sharp he disappeared up the mountain. I let two more cars go while I watched for Mihails. When he didn't show, I bought my ticket and went up.

The Table Mountain gondolas rotate a full three hundred sixty degrees as they make the climb, giving everyone a view of both the mountain and the city. Often the city view was unaffected by the tablecloth, and the condensation hugged the cliff as it spilled over the top. Today it was thicker. I caught a few glimpses of Table Bay glistening in the sun before the fog snapped the curtain shut.

At the top, even sounds seemed muffled by the layer of cloud that moved across the flat surface of the mountain. The chink and whir of the cable car faded quickly as I left the upper station and struck out on a path. It led to a boardwalk that traversed a marshy area. Lights along the way carved little caves of luminescence from the fog. Sometimes a puff of wind twitched the blanket aside for a moment and the bright blue sky appeared. Then the mist closed in again.

Hassan was waiting on a worn bench just off the boardwalk. It was where we'd often met in the early days, when he'd just recruited me and I was still operating from the Cape. On a good day, the view was great. Today, the mist stripped the world of its dimensions. We were nowhere, isolated in the otherworld of impenetrable mist. His shoulders were hunched and the collar of his jacket turned up.

"We're both armed, Alex, so don't be foolish."

"You killed my father. That's never going away."

"It was Teddy who ordered that."

"No. That's what he had you for."

"I tried to warn you to stay away."

"You don't *warn* me, Hassan. I don't come to you for advice. I met you that day to see if you had anything other than that garbage on Tabitha your friends have been feeding you."

A smile crept onto his face. "You're trying to see if I know that they were not actually working against Tabitha: they were working for her. Langley wanted me to spread the rumors, and they wanted me to say where they came from, so the Chinese would pick them up and think Tabitha was vulnerable." The smile faded from his face. "Really, Alex. I've been watching that play develop for years. Tabitha's handlers want the Chinese to believe she's vulnerable, so maybe they try to turn her, and you have a double in place."

The fog curled thickly around us. Hassan shivered and shrugged deeper into his jacket.

"You have no idea what the CIA is up to, Hassan, because you're not on the inside. You're just the guy who sold out his friends."

He turned a twisted face to me. "*Friends?* When did I ever have friends in the company? I've spent my whole life working for Langley. I killed for them." He was so angry he slammed a fist on the bench. "I went into some of the most vicious places on earth for those bastards, and what did I get for it? Nothing! I was just the hero's bastard kid. He never even registered me as his son. No citizenship. Pathetic pension." He waved his hand at the side of the mountain.

"My mother still lives down there on Mitchells Plain, in the cheap one-bedroom house he bought her. My dad—the handsome American. She was seventeen when they met. She's still down there, not so pretty now, living on what I send her. In the picture beside her bed, my father wears dress whites. I grew up with that phony god."

"Spare me, Hassan. I know all about the shitty dad club. You were a gangster before you were ten, so I'm not sure how much your dad had to do with it. One thing I'm curious about. Why kill Joos? Isn't he worth more to Teddy alive?"

He gave me a pitying look. "You've met the man. He can't tell a lie." The fog swirled around us. "Joos was just good housekeeping. The whole fake-diamonds thing got away from Teddy. He was terrified he'd be discovered. We'd have taken Marie out, too, but you got there ahead of us."

"It surprised me you were working for Teddy. I'd thought Mei."

The smile returned. "You still haven't got there." He savored his moment, but he was in a hurry. He stole a glance at his watch. "Teddy was going to be a straight shakedown. That was my plan for Teddy. A friend from the old days saw the heavy power going in at Hout Bay and kept an eye on it. Then the big diamond press arrived, and the CVD reactor. It didn't take long to find out who Joos was and that he was cooking fakes. Then I discovered they were making it look like the stones were coming from Shanghai, and I thought of Mei."

"Did she know about the N3 centers?"

"I told her."

"But how did you understand what the N3 centers were?"

He glared at me. "This was always your abiding sin. You had to put everything in its tiny slot before you were satisfied." He shook his head. "I didn't understand. Not at first. But Mei was in diamonds, and China was making lab-grown, and whatever Joos was doing had to be important or Teddy wouldn't have hidden it."

"And now you're going to deliver Joos's notes and the computers. That's why she's at Elandskop."

"Come on, Alex. You're almost there. That's not all she's getting."

And of course I saw it then. It had been there all along, in plain sight, like some origami bird folded this way and that, its true shape hidden until its creator tugged it open.

"Tabitha," I said.

Hassan stood up and I heard the creak of the leather coat, and Mihails stepped out of the fog with a Makarov. Hassan gave me a last glance and shrugged and held his hands palms up. Then he walked away.

"You came up last night," I said to Mihails.

"We knew you'd arrive at the lower station early to make sure he was alone."

"You don't have to do this, Mihails."

"It's a job, Alex. You take the money, you do the job. It's nothing personal. Hassan is a rat. I'm sorry it's you." The barrel of the Makarov was pointed at my head.

"He killed my father," I said. I was looking for something to say, just to gain a moment, maybe try a kick. That's what the desert boots were for. Anyway, I didn't. Mihails paused, and I concentrated on making sure my eyes didn't flick behind him, where the mist had drifted aside. There was not so much as the sound of a brushed leaf, and then his eyes popped wide open and he stuck his tongue out at me. A long, silver, pointed tongue. The tongue twisted and Mihails made a gargling sound and blood gushed from his mouth. He fell face forward on the boardwalk, the hilt of the dagger sticking from the back of his neck. Lily bent down and pulled it out and wiped it on his pants.

49

The Cortina was still there when we got back, parked on High Level Road. Police swarmed around it, but I caught a glimpse as we went past. Blood splash on the windows. Hassan had guessed that Lily would follow me out as backup. The guys in the Cortina were there for her. But I had friends in Cape Town too.

"You didn't go after him?" said Tommy when I told him what had happened.

"Hassan knows more ways off that mountain than the fog."

"Did you really just say that?"

"Listen, Tommy. If Hassan thinks I'm dead, so do Mei and Teddy. If they were worried about me, now they're not. That makes it urgent that Tabitha understand the danger she's in. Did her case officer alert her?"

"I just talked to Weitz. He said her CIA case officer didn't even know she'd got on the Van Kees plane until we told him. He hasn't been able to reach her since London. She's out of contact."

"Imagine that," I said. "In the middle of a private wilderness owned by a rich and powerful man who's complicit in a string of murders, and her phone's not working. Langley must be dumbfounded."

"It's hands-off, Alex. I've been instructed to pass that on. The South Africa station chief is aware of the situation. They especially don't want you endangering her by barging into the middle of their operation."

"There is no operation. There's a sale. Teddy Van Kees is selling an assistant deputy director of National Intelligence to China. He'll sweeten the deal with Joos Du Toit's computers. Hassan will deliver them. So the Chinese get that too. Has the station chief reached out to the South Africans?"

Lily came in from the terrace and started opening and closing cupboard doors and ransacking the fridge. She did this with a minimum of noise so she could eavesdrop on my conversation.

"The feeling is that the South Africans are in China's pocket," Tommy said. "They owe China billions of dollars in loans. They conduct naval exercises together. They're strategic partners. Now we have an agent inside their country whose operational target is the most powerful woman in China, with close ties to the Chinese leadership."

Lily removed two slices of bread from a loaf and returned it to the fridge. She found a jar of peanut butter. She placed these on a tray, added a knife from the cutlery drawer, and carried them to the dining table, which was right beside me. I edged away into a corner of the room. I could practically see her ears swivel.

"There's no extraction plan, is there," I said. "They're just going to leave her there."

"It's delicate. Any scrap of information we can get about where the Chinese are on the quantum research is worth the risk. Tabitha's smart. Since we can't reach her, we can't judge the situation on the ground."

"Excuse me? Sure we can fucking judge the situation on the ground. They'll just take her. We can't complain because she's not supposed to be there. She's a foreign agent operating without any treaty protection in what is effectively a Chinese client state. Remember what we did to

Mei's brother? We kidnapped him and flew him to a military base and pumped pentothal into him until we'd drained every secret from his brain. And when he was a wrung-out zombie, that's when we returned him."

Lily spread the peanut butter onto the bread, then cut each slice into smaller squares.

"The judgment in DC," Tommy said, "is that the risk in harming her would be too great for the Chinese. Tabitha's a high-ranking officer with close ties to the White House. They know we'd respond."

"Respond to what? They're not going to drag her out and hook her up to the truth serum while we watch on the satellite feed. They'll fly her out to China. And I doubt they're afraid of retribution. What they're afraid of is us getting to a quantum computer before they do and that suddenly somebody in the United States is cracking all their codes and giving phony orders to their subs and aiming their missiles somewhere they weren't aimed before."

"Duh," said Lily, no longer even pretending not to listen.

"She's out there, Tommy," I said, "and nobody is running her. She's alone. And when it all goes wrong and Langley's watching it on live TV, they are going to see everybody get in planes and fly away. You know what they'll do then, don't you? Nothing. They won't send some terminator to take out a big-time Chinese spook in retaliation. They'll bury the file. Somebody will go out to the Kowalski farm in Minnesota and give Tabitha's parents a medal in a velvet box. They'll spew a load of crap about operational exigencies and make sure everybody understands not to make any noise. Then they will wait and hope for a chance to trade a Chinese agent for what's left of her."

"Bastards," Lily snarled, snatching up the tray and stalking out onto the terrace.

"Sorry?" said Tommy.

"You know people, Tommy. Reach out. Do your fucking job."

"I know this is personal for you, Alex. It's a dirty business. Weitz has put out some feelers through the British to see if they can help with the South Africans. He's not optimistic."

"He doesn't know the right South Africans," I said, and ended the call.

"I have a bad feeling about this," Lily said when I came out onto the terrace. She was kneeling beside the dog, checking his bandage while he concentrated on the little squares of bread and peanut butter.

"You heard," I said. "She's out of contact."

Lily nodded. She slipped a bandage off and replaced it with a fresh one while the dog was busy with the food. "Tabitha put herself there through her own stupidity," she said. "The woman is an imbecile."

"Other than that, though."

When the dog was finished, she picked up the plate and put it on a table, then came and stood beside me. "Not everything is your responsibility."

"I'm not going to leave her there, Lily."

Her knuckles were white as she clenched the bloody bandage.

"I know. It makes me very angry, because you will be the only one who understands the danger. She cannot conceive that anyone would dare to harm her. That is the problem with her rank and youth. It's not a reason for you to blunder out there like a cretin."

I was getting off lightly. Lily had as many words for idiot as the Inuit have for snow. She leaned on the railing, the bandage clutched tightly in her hand.

"It will be Teddy," she said. "That is who will be the greatest danger. Not Mei."

"I agree. Teddy would be ruined if the news about the fakes gets out. Mei couldn't care less about it. She wants the technology. If she can grab Tabitha, she might. But she will assess the risk."

"And she would negotiate if she had to. We do not know what Teddy would do."

"For Teddy it's exactly the reverse of Mei. He'll do anything to keep the news about the fakes from getting out, and selling the N3 formula is now part of that. Both sides would pay a fortune for the N3 data, but who's the best bet for keeping their mouth shut about the fakes? An oppressive police state with vast surveillance and totalitarian control over every aspect of life, or the country that brought you Edward Snowden?"

Lily dug the Lucifer diamond from her jeans and held it in her hands. The dog's bloodstained dressing trailed away in the breeze, as if the stone itself were a just-unbandaged wound.

"I called Billy Louw," she said. The cutter who tried a Lucifer cut for Teddy's father.

"I didn't know he was still alive."

"He's an old man now. He says it wasn't his fault the stone blew up, and not Sir Harry's. They wanted to stop with what they had. The stone was too flawed to go further. But Teddy wouldn't hear of it. He went into a rage, demanding a polished diamond that would outmatch the descriptions in the literature."

"So Teddy was responsible for destroying the diamond."

"And I checked the date," said Lily. "That was around the time that the African countries where Van Kees operates began to take more control."

"Good-bye empire."

She handed me the diamond. "If Teddy was obsessed then, how does he feel now? He must have asked Lou Fine to polish it into a Lucifer. He would possess a mythic jewel."

It didn't take an advanced degree in psychology to see what the Lucifer would mean to Teddy. In his imagination it would wind the clock back to his family's days as masters of the diamond universe. Even better that it was a fake. If he could pass it off, he would triumph over those he saw as stealing his family's diamonds. The Lucifer would be the greatest diamond in the world, and the Van Kees family would have created it. Without the usual help from God.

I put the diamond in my pocket, went inside, and made a call. That took an hour. There was a lot of detail to get straight. Lily would handle the banking.

In the morning we loaded everything into the Beemer. I carried the dog down last. He growled all the way. I placed the bed carefully in the back seat. Lily shoved me aside and spent ten minutes yanking clothes from her bag and wadding them around him so the bed wouldn't slide on the seat. She kissed him and stroked his nose while he regarded me with hatred. Next time he could have the damn pills.

We took the same route to Table Mountain. This time I turned off for the pass at Kloof Nek and went through the hills and straight down into Hout Bay. From the village, I took the road that snaked up Chapman's Peak. By the time we crested the summit and went down the other side, I knew there was no one following. I took the turn for Fish Hoek and came out on the coast of False Bay. The road stuck to the shore past Muizenberg and Mitchells Plain, then cut away from the sea and ran straight up to Stellenbosch.

The Dassault waited on the apron, running up its engines, the gangway down and the co-pilot making his last checks around the under-carriage. Lily grabbed her bag from the car. I gave her the case with the

AI black box and she took that up the gangway too. I carried the bed plus dog. The smell of aviation gas and the whine of the jets seemed to worry him. He forgot to growl.

Lily settled him in the cabin and followed me back out. She looked away across the airfield before turning back to me. Her eyes glistened, and that made her even angrier than she already was. "It troubles me that you put your life in danger for her."

"I can't leave her there."

She clamped her arms ferociously around my neck. "I know," she whispered. "I know, my darling, but I fear for you. If they kill you"—her voice was hoarse—"I will track them down and cut their throats."

She ran up the gangway. The steps folded up behind her. The Dassault pointed its nose down the runway and soon it was a dwindling speck in the brilliant sky. Henny shook his head as he watched it go. He thought I was crazy too.

He finished gassing up the Antonov. I heaved in my bag. We took off and flew northeast over the vineyards. Cape Dutch farmhouses nestled in the shade of giant camphor trees. Then the roads grew farther apart and dwindled into tracks, and the villages grew smaller and sparser until there was nothing beneath the wings but the desert of the Great Karoo.

Just south of the Botswana border, we turned east. Henny brought the Antonov down to a few thousand feet. Soon the hills and valleys of the Waterberg appeared, and the treed savannahs that South Africans call bushveld. Zebra dashed away from the sound of the approaching plane and herds of panicked impala sprang through the high grass as they fled for cover. Elandskop's landing strip appeared. Two jets were parked in the shade of the open-sided shed at the end of the runway. We flew past, then the big biplane banked hard and came around, lined up on the strip, and landed like a butterfly.

Henny kept the engine turning over. He looked through the slowly revolving blades of the propeller at the parked aircraft. "The Gulfstream is Teddy's," he said. "The other plane is the new Global 8000 from Bombardier. It cruises at just below the speed of sound. The registration"—he jerked his chin at the tail—"that's Chinese."

So were the guards. Two of them in gray fatigues. They were standing at ease under the wings, watching us impassively. They could afford to be cool. They had People's Liberation Army submachine guns, the Type 05 that came with the built-in suppressor. Henny blew out his cheeks and shook his head. I grabbed my bag and climbed out into the African sun. Henny turned the Antonov down the runway. Five minutes later the plane was a tiny dot, and I turned to watch a dust plume thread its way toward me through the bush.

50

The Land Rover slid to a stop. Nelson climbed out of the driver's seat. He still had cauliflower ears and his shoulders hadn't gotten any smaller, but he'd ditched the jacket and tie for a black polo shirt. Aviator glasses.

"Mate." He shook his head and watched the Antonov disappear. "I don't think I have your name on my arrivals list."

"Just call Teddy. Tell him I'm here and that I have it."

"Have what?"

"He'll know."

"Mr. Van Kees is viewing game with guests." He looked away and waved an arm, as if to show me where the game was being viewed. The landing strip was on a flat-topped ridge. The ground fell away on three sides. Some kudu grazed in the distance. The aviator glasses panned back to me.

"I'll have to check that bag."

I shook my head. "Just personal effects."

He squared on me. "I check all luggage for weapons. If you have a gun, I'll lock it up until you leave." He laid a little stress on "leave."

"But you make an exception for Chinese Type 05s," I said, jerking my head at the guards. He threw an angry glance in their direction. He didn't like them any more than I did. "Just so you understand where I'm coming from," I said, "I'm a United States Treasury agent."

"I know who you bloody are."

"Fine. You've got a radio." I nodded at the Land Rover. "Call Teddy and give him the message."

Nelson put his hands on his hips. It had to be a hundred degrees out there on the strip. I could smell the gun oil from the Bobcat I had inside my shirt, and the Skorpion and the Vektor pistol in the bag. If I could smell it, so could he. The aviator shades stayed aimed at my face. He was probably inspecting the bruise that Virgil had put there, and thinking of adding one of his own.

"Ah, fuck it," he said, and grabbed a radio handset from the Land Rover. "Base to mobile," he said. "Do you read me?" A few seconds later, the set crackled and Teddy's voice came through.

"Mobile to base. What is it, Nelson?"

"We have an unscheduled visitor, sir. A plane dropped him at the strip and took off before I could intervene." The dark lenses stayed on me. "Mr. Turner. He said to tell you that he has it."

After a few seconds of silence Teddy said, "Put him in Number Three. Don't shoot him just yet, there's a good chap. Ha-ha."

"Roger that. Guest in Number Three. Do not shoot. Base out."

The first sign we'd reached the lodge was the electrified game fence. Nelson pressed a button, and a gate swung slowly inward. We drove through, waiting on the other side until the gate clicked shut behind us.

We took a sandy road that curved around a hill. The main house came slowly into view—a long, low building of dusty brick, awash in a sea of bougainvillea. As we drove by, I saw that the house had two wings, separated by an open breezeway shaded with vines. The architect had planned the approach for maximum effect, because it wasn't until that last moment, when we rolled to a stop at the breezeway, that the panorama of the valley came into view.

I jumped down with my bag. The wings of the main house stretched to the left and right. Ahead was a wide lawn that ended at an infinity pool. Beyond the pool were the roofs of the guesthouses, on a lower level than the lawn, all of them facing down the valley. Every feature of the complex had been designed to attract the eye to that vista, a broad plain dotted with thorn trees.

A movement caught the corner of my eye, and I glanced to my left. At the far end of that wing—another Chinese guard with a Type 05. Nelson was looking at him too.

"Wait here," he said, stalking back to the Land Rover and driving away. A few minutes later he reappeared in a golf cart. We rolled away and took a crushed-stone path that circled the lawn and went down to the guesthouses. He stopped behind the third one, led the way to the front and onto a veranda. He unlocked the door and handed me the key.

"Just to be clear," he said, "my job is to protect the Van Kees family. Maybe I don't like what's going on, but that's still my job."

In front of the veranda was a thin screen of trees, and a movement beyond them caught my eye. A pair of elephants lumbered into view, fanning the air with their ears. The rest of the small herd appeared behind—half a dozen adults and some calves. We watched them plod into a shallow concrete waterhole and start to drink.

"I'm taking Tabitha out of here," I said.

"How do you plan to do that?"

"There's a Delta Force extraction team on the Botswana border. Two stealth Black Hawks. I call—they're here in forty minutes."

He actually laughed out loud.

"Please," he said, grinning. "Delta Force. Right. And the way they start their op is by sending in some guy in a biplane, alerting the targets that something's up and you can kiss the element of surprise good-bye."

A family of warthogs trotted out of the grass and stared at the elephants. A young bull trumpeted and spread his ears and went thrashing out of the water. The pigs retreated, but not far. They were thirsty too.

The grin faded from Nelson's face. "Stealth choppers—that's a night op. Everybody strapped up with night vision goggles. They land a mile away and come in and start cutting throats." He shook his head. "There's no Delta Force."

"You learned all that playing rugby?"

"SAS. Iraq. I know how it works."

SAS was Special Air Service. British commandos. A radio crackled from the golf cart. He frowned. "They're coming back."

"How many Chinese guards at the house?"

"I don't know. I've seen two. There might be more. That's not counting the ones at the plane."

"OK. For the record, I'm not here to hurt Teddy or Edwina. Teddy's been playing with bad people, and I think it got away on him. The fact that I'm alive will tell him that the US government knows he has Tabitha. I'm going to make the case that he should let us leave."

"And if he won't?"

"Let's hope it doesn't come to that."

He gave me a long look, then went back to the golf cart and drove back up the crushed-stone road. I slid open the door and stepped into a large bedroom. It had a king bed and a pair of easy chairs. Cathedral ceiling. Fans suspended from the rafters stirred the air. I put my bag on the bed and checked out the adjoining dressing room. It had closets along one side, an elaborate vanity, and a marble bathroom through an arch.

I put my jacket in a closet, stripped off my shirt, and sat on the veranda in the shade. I pulled over a metal table, broke down the Skorpion, and cleaned it. Henny had found two empty clips and some ammunition. I reassembled the gun, loaded the clips, slapped them in and out a few times. Then I had a look at the Vektor I'd got from Virgil.

The model CP1 was a beautiful pistol. I hefted it. It fit like a glove. No sharp edges. Streamlined to prevent snagging when you drew it. It was designed as a concealed-carry weapon. Virgil had given me a simplified shoulder rig to go with the gun, and I slipped it on and practiced drawing a few times. It came out like a dream. It had a twelve-round box magazine of 9mm parabellum, plus one in the chamber. I had an extra clip for the Vektor too.

When I was through I took out a roll of duct tape and looked for a place to hide the Skorpion. I couldn't very well take it with me when I went to meet Teddy, and Nelson would search my cabin when I left.

The electrified fence was about thirty feet in front of the veranda. A viewing hide for observing the waterhole had been built among the trees, just inside the fence.

I followed a flagstone walkway to the hide. It was open at the back. At the front was a narrow observation slot cut horizontally. A ledge below the opening gave watchers a place to rest their elbows while they aimed cameras or binoculars through the slot. The room had a sloped roof braced with crossbeams. I taped the Skorpion and two magazines to the top of a beam and returned to the veranda.

I'd kept the Zeiss binoculars and now took a longer look at the valley. A hundred yards beyond the waterhole, impalas grazed among acacia trees. Every now and then one of them would leap straight up into the air with its back arched, a display called pronking. I raised the glasses. A mile away, a slowly moving shadow in tall grass turned out to be a herd of wildebeest. I was scanning the edges of the valley when a safari vehicle appeared at the far end. It crept out of the trees onto the open veld. It was the usual design for a game-viewing truck: a tier of benches built into the open back, each bench slightly higher than the one in front. I adjusted the focus.

Teddy sat in front beside the driver, his face shaded by the brim of a huge safari hat. Behind him sat Little Teddy, and at the very back, their heads pressed together as they talked, Tabitha and Mei.

The vehicle rocked across the valley, then took a track that wound through thorn trees and would bring them to the compound's gate. They were about three miles away. At the speed they were going, it would take them half an hour to reach the compound.

I went inside and stripped. I scrubbed off the dust and washed my hair, turned the shower to full cold, and stood there for a minute. When I came out I toweled dry on the veranda, pulled on my jeans, and laced up the desert boots with the steel toes.

I dug out my old bush shirt. It had special pockets for clips and was made to be worn untucked. I checked sideways in the mirror. The drape hid the ammo and the Vektor. And it hid the Lucifer. I took that too. I grabbed some zip ties. You never know. Last, I shoved the Bobcat into a quick-draw holster at the small of my back. I called Virgil on the sat phone.

"Where are you now?"

"Two hundred yards from Elandskop main gate. In the bush. Ziz went forward for a recce."

"What about comms?"

"No cell coverage here, and they not having sat phones in the guard-house, man. Radios. Don't worry. They won't see us coming. Wait one." I heard Ziz mutter a question and Virgil answer. "We through in five," he said when he came back on.

"How far then?"

"I make it five miles to the house, but the road was washed out in three places between Vaalwater and the gate. Could be worse past the gate. What's the intel?"

"The Chinese came heavy. Maybe five guys with submachine guns."

"OK, we going to hit the guardhouse now." He ended the call.

Teddy's safari truck lumbered out of the trees beyond the watering hole and turned toward the gate. They'd be here in minutes. I put the sat phone back in my bag and left the house. A flight of stone steps led up past the infinity pool to the lawn.

A servant in a white cutaway jacket waited in the breezeway by a sideboard lined with frosted bottles and buckets of ice. In a minute I heard the rumble of the engine, and the massive dark-green vehicle appeared around the back of the house and rolled to a stop.

"Alex!" Teddy boomed as he hauled himself out. His face was scarlet from the heat. Sweat ran down his cheeks and into his collar. He crushed my hand in his fist. The attendant handed him a glass. He released my hand and tossed back the drink. He kept his tawny eyes on me.

Tabitha fanned herself with a large straw hat. Strands of hair clumped to her cheek, and her cotton dress was plastered to her body like Saran Wrap. Expression cool as ice. She said, "You've missed the lions."

"Let's hope so," I said.

"Did you bring the confirmation from Noah?"

You have to hand it to her. Outplayed. Middle of the bush. Chinese with submachine guns ready to load her into the hurry-up wagon, and she gives it the all-part-of-a-plan shot.

"He's not happy," I said.

Teddy's eyes darted back and forth between us. He'd know who Noah Weitz was. Did he really believe that I'd arrived with a message from the cavalry? Probably not, but the problem was, he didn't know how to handicap it. He was like a player from the minors who suddenly finds himself in Yankee Stadium and hasn't learned to read the signals. Hassan would have reported me dead. The simple fact of my appearance now put everything Hassan had said in doubt. If he'd got that wrong, what else had he misreported?

"What nonsense is this?" Teddy said, grabbing my arm and leading me onto the grass.

"Check with your office," I said in a low voice. "There's a message from Washington."

"That's not true. I'd have heard immediately."

"They're probably trying to get you now. I spoke to Noah Weitz before I landed. We have the N3 data, Teddy. Joos showed us the program."

We were standing a little apart from the rest of the company. He turned and looked at Mei. Then Nelson appeared on the drive behind the breezeway. He had a Benelli SuperNova—a twelve-gauge pump-action tactical shotgun. Another thing you don't learn about in rugby.

"What do you want, then?" Teddy growled. He'd seen Nelson too.

"I'm taking her out of here. You can finish your business with Mei. Sell her the drives. But not Tabitha. She leaves with me. Pin Joos's murder on Hassan. You'll probably get away with it. The United States government doesn't care about the fakes. That's what Weitz will tell you. So your business survives. But we're leaving. Plus, you can have this." And I fished out the Lucifer.

It sucked the light in like a vampire. When I twisted it, brilliant, molten shapes swarmed down my arm and fled across the grass. At the sight of the diamond, Mei broke away from the others. It must have looked to her as if Teddy and I were sealing some agreement, one that would snatch away the N3 data before she could secure it. Little Teddy rushed after Mei. And that pretty much cooked it.

Things might have worked out differently if I'd had another moment alone with Teddy. I think he swallowed the Weitz bullshit. We already had the AI black box. Teddy might not have even known about it. Hassan would have assumed he'd taken everything important when he grabbed the computers, and that's what he'd have reported to Teddy. Teddy would wonder what information we thought we had on the N3, but in the end, that's not what he cared most about.

I think I could have talked us out to the air strip. Teddy gets his stone. No need to murder Americans—always going to cause a problem. Maybe he'd have even found a way to get rid of the snake. Anyway, it didn't work out like that. Mei came rushing over. Her agitation alerted a guard at the corner of the house, and once that trigger had been pulled, everything bad that could happen did.

"Please explain what you are doing," Mei demanded.

The guard picked up on the tension. He had a radio clipped to his belt. He used it now, making a short call. When he finished, he unslung the submachine gun.

"Tell that guy to stay where he is, Mei," I said, dropping the Lucifer back into my pocket.

Her face twitched, giving me a nanosecond glimpse of malice before she erased the expression. "Do not make a fatal error," she said.

The guard took a few slow paces across the lawn. At the same time, Teddy shifted his weight. I thought he might try to grab me, which would put Mei out of reach and give the guard an opportunity to shoot. I punched Teddy in the face. He staggered and fell heavily. I ripped out the Vektor, hooked my arm around Mei's neck, and put the barrel against her temple.

"Stop fucking around," I said.

She rattled a command in Chinese and the guard froze. But he didn't drop the gun. The safety switch on the Type 05 doubles as the rate-of-fire selector. It's just above the trigger, and he inched a finger toward it. I tightened my grip on Mei's neck. "I'm not going to say it again," I told her, and this time when she shouted, the guard put down his gun.

"Tab, Bobcat at the small of my back. Go get the Chinese gun." She grabbed the Bobcat and advanced across the lawn, waving the pistol at the guard to back him away from the submachine gun. She snatched the weapon from the grass and pointed it at him as she backed away.

"You're gangsters!" Little Teddy blurted.

Mei's face was red from the chokehold, and one of her lapis lazuli barrettes had fallen off. A lock of black hair fell across her face.

"You won't make it out of here, Alex," Teddy said, holding a hand to his face. His eyes were streaming and a string of snot dangled from his nose.

Nelson came through the breezeway and onto the grass with the Benelli at the port. I shook my head at him and tapped the pistol on Mei's head. He stopped. Tabitha and I backed across the grass, past the infinity pool and down the steps to the lane at the bottom.

"My place," Tabitha said, and we hustled Mei onto the veranda and inside.

51

I gave Mei a quick pat-down.

"I am not a hoodlum." Her voice trembled with rage. I had never seen so much as a hairline crack in that porcelain composure, and now I had seen it twice in as many minutes. She was mad. She didn't even call me pumpkin.

I bound her wrists with zip ties, moved an easy chair away from the door, and told her to sit down. Tabitha put down the Chinese submachine gun, fetched her suitcase from the dressing room, and tossed it on the bed. She ripped off her pink sundress.

"Hang on a sec," I said. "I have to go next door. Cover me." She picked up the Type 05 and followed me outside.

"I'm going to get the sat phone and another gun," I said in a low voice. "I have people coming, but it's not going to be pretty."

"I'm not leaving here without the N3 data," she said.

"There's a good chance you won't leave here at all, Tab, so can you forget the fucking N3 data while we try to not get killed?"

She looked at me and bit her lip. She nodded. With her lean body and her freckled skin, she looked like a leopard. She pressed her back to the wall and peered around the corner of the house. She had a clear view of the steps that led down from the lawn. I dashed next door and grabbed the sat phone, then headed for the blind. I tore off the tape, grabbed the Skorpion, and pocketed the clips.

"I tried to get a message to you," I said when I got back.

"They confiscated my phone," Tabitha said as we went inside, unsnapping the suitcase and flinging open the lid. "What was the message?"

"Teddy had already decided to sell the N3 data to Mei. The real reason for Mei's trip to Elandskop was to buy something else."

Tabitha pulled some pale green chinos from the suitcase, and a pair of Converse sneakers.

"I know," she said. "I was part of the deal. I'd kind of got there on my own."

"He is lying," Mei said. "I would not betray you. We have a long history of mutual benefit. I value you as a trusted associate. I would never harm you."

"Gosh," Tabitha said, cocking her head at Mei. "That's so sweet." As she spoke she reached into the suitcase to rummage for a shirt. She wasn't looking where she put her hand, and I didn't see the coiled shape until I heard the distinct, warning *puff*.

"Tab!" I shouted. "Stop!" And in that instant the adder struck.

"Oh!" Tabitha said. She sat down hard. Now her head was level with the snake. She stared at it in horror. The puff adder's fangs glistened in the gaping pink mouth. It hissed as it drew back its flat, triangular head and readied for another strike. I emptied the Skorpion into the suitcase in a single burst. The snake's thick body thrashed. A violent spasm flung it onto the bed, and it sank its fangs into the covers.

Mei struggled to her feet, made a choking sound, and rushed out onto the veranda.

I dropped the gun and grabbed Tabitha and dragged her away from the bed. Her skin felt cold already. A blue tint was spreading around two red puncture marks on her forearm.

"She might survive," Teddy said behind me, and I whirled to find him standing in the door. He had an old Luger in his hand. I stood up slowly.

"You bastard, Teddy. You put it there."

One of his eyes had swollen shut. The remaining eye was bloodshot. He glanced at Tabitha and then at the puff adder, twitching in its death throes. I kept my eyes on Teddy. The barrel of the Luger followed his gaze as he stared at the snake. He was about ten feet from me. I shifted toward him. The gun snapped back to me.

"Don't," he said. "I'll shoot you right here." With his free hand he wiped the snot from his nose. The Luger stayed pointed at my stomach. "Give me the diamond," he said. "We have antivenom. She has a good chance. She's young. I want the diamond."

He could have shot me right then and just taken it. He didn't, because it's not so easy if you've never done it. So I had that on my side, and Tabitha. Teddy kept shooting glances at her as she sat there turning blue. She made a mangled sound. I think she was trying to say my name, but she was already losing the ability to speak.

"Call for the antivenom, Teddy." Each guesthouse had a phone that connected to the other buildings. "Or tell me the number and I'll call. You can cover me."

"The diamond," he said hoarsely.

I pulled it out and held it in my fingers. The light cannoned around inside the jewel.

Teddy drew in a ragged breath. "Put it on the bed," he gasped. He was afraid I'd grab his hand if he reached for it.

I held the Lucifer in my outstretched hand. Dots of light seethed on the terrazzo. Perspiration poured down Teddy's forehead into his bright red eye. He dashed it away with a fist.

"She can have the antivenom. Put it down."

"Maybe there's a fault plane," I said. He knew the risk if I dropped it. A large diamond can shatter if there's any weakness in the crystal. He tried for a smile, but it crumbled away. "I'll save the girl. You have my word as a gentleman." He licked his lips. "Put the diamond on the bed."

"Here," I said, and flicked it at him. He lunged to grab it before it hit the floor. I shot him in the chest.

The round punched Teddy backward onto the veranda. He landed on his back with the Luger still clutched in his hand. I ran out and kicked it away and saw Nelson coming along the side of the house with the SuperNova. Little Teddy, her face chalk white, clung to his arm. I covered him with the Vektor.

"I won't hesitate," I said.

Nelson held the gun away from his body, gripping it by the barrel in one hand. "I can put it down," he said, "but there's two more Chinese guards up there now. The ones from the plane. So that's three, and they're scoping you from the lawn. From the way they look, they'll be happy to kill all of us."

52

OK, come ahead," I said. "Put the Benelli on the veranda."

"Shit," he said when he stepped around the corner and saw Teddy. A red bubble had grown from his open mouth and a pink patch was spreading on his chest. Then Little Teddy saw him too.

"Daddy," she whispered. "No." She staggered up the steps and knelt beside him. The Lucifer lay nearby, lapping up the color of the blood. I stuffed it in my pocket. "No, Daddy," Little Teddy whispered again, frantically tidying his hair. She brushed the red bubble from his lips, then sat back on her heels and cupped her face in her bloody hands as a high, keening sound emerged from her parted lips.

"Where's the antivenom?" I said to Nelson.

"Jesus Christ," he said, catching sight of Tabitha. The blue patch was spreading through her skin. Her breath sounded like a saw.

"Teddy put a snake in her suitcase."

"The antivenom's at the house. We'll never get to it." Just then I saw a patch of gray camouflage moving through the trees.

"Move a pace to the left," I said to Nelson. "There's a Chinese guard coming along the fence." I picked up the Benelli.

THE LUCIFER CUT

"There's one in the chamber and the safety's off," Nelson said, and I stepped to the front of the veranda and fired. The buckshot tore a hole in the vegetation and flung the man back into the fence. The wires sparked when he hit them, and at the same time a submachine gun opened up and the windows that faced the lawn blew in, spraying the room with glass.

"Bring Edwina," I said to Nelson. I ran inside and gathered Tabitha in my arms and carried her into the bathroom. I grabbed some towels and threw them into the tub and laid her carefully in, where she was safe from splinters. Her eyes were open. I don't think she saw me. Her lips were blue.

Nelson led in Little Teddy. She was making a sound like hiccups. I lifted her and placed her inside the tub beside Tabitha.

"Edwina," I said firmly. The hiccups stopped and she stared at me. "You need to stay here. It's safe. Tell me you understand." She squeezed her eyes shut as she nodded.

"Hold Tabitha and keep her warm," I said. "She'll die if you don't."

Nelson and I hurried back to the main room.

"You OK with the Type 05?" I said.

"I can manage." He picked up the Chinese gun, checked it out, and flipped the fire-selector to semiauto. "Probably best to conserve ammunition," he said.

"Take the Benelli too. I've got the Skorpion and the pistols." I grabbed the sat phone and thumbed in Tommy's number. There was a loud *pong* as he came on.

"I called Weitz again," he said. "He thinks it's a very long shot they will do anything that will offend the Chinese."

"Here's what you need to tell Weitz, Tommy. His deputy has been bitten by a venomous snake hidden in her luggage by Teddy Van Kees while he got ready to sell the future of the world to the People's Republic of China. Tabitha is lying near death while hoods brought here by Mei

267

come for us with submachine guns. Tell him to explain to the South Africans what the United States can and will do if Tabitha dies while they refuse to help. And if he thinks that's beyond him, remind him that it was the president who put Tabitha where she is."

"I think I know who to call," Tommy said, "and it isn't Weitz."

An ear-splitting boom from the veranda announced that Nelson had sent a load of military-grade buckshot up at the attackers.

"Now would be a good time, Tommy." I ended the call and shoved a fresh clip into the Skorpion.

"They're bracketing!" Nelson shouted as two guns opened up at once. The Benelli boomed twice in quick succession.

I ran out with the Skorpion and took the other end of the veranda. I lay flat on the boards and poked my head around the corner. A storm of dirt and stones erupted on the path as a shooter emptied a clip at me. He was up by the pool. When the firing stopped, I leaned out and fired a burst. He dropped out of sight, but I didn't think I'd hit him.

We were pinned down. Guys with submachine guns had the high ground. We had limited ammunition. The way they were shooting, they had plenty. They had a clear field of fire. They could change position without being seen. The fence was close behind us: we couldn't retreat. I called the Recces.

Virgil gasped into the phone, "Just got in position, man. Fucking gun."

The Denel weighed seventy pounds. Two guys a long way past their sell-by date, lugging it through the bush. Plus ammunition, bipod, sighting scope.

"Anybody you see in gray fatigues with a bullpup submachine gun, kill their ass."

The Benelli boomed again and Nelson shouted, "Fence!"

I whirled around. A gun chattered from the trees twenty yards away. The steps beside me exploded into chips. The Benelli crashed out again and blew the shooter off his feet. It was the last round of shotgun ammunition. Nelson grabbed the Chinese gun.

"The guy on the fence made four," I said.

He met my eye. He was thinking the same thing I was. They had more men than we'd thought. The Chinese guns had fifty-round box magazines. They had as many guns as they had men, plus extra mags. We had just one Chinese gun with a single magazine, the Skorpion with two twenty-round clips, and a couple of pistols.

The shooters on the lawn opened up again, raking the house with a coordinated fire. The windows in the bedroom dissolved into shards. I heard the tinkle of falling glass from the bathroom. I dashed in. Tabitha was entwined in Little Teddy's arms. Their hair glittered with glass. I put my hand on Little Teddy's shoulder.

"Just hold on," I said. I was running back to the veranda when an earth-shaking *whump* shuddered through the floor, followed a split second later by the report of a heavy gun.

I peeked out the bathroom window. A Chinese guard was standing up by the infinity pool, staring at a hole in the bank. A cloud of dirt was still settling through the air around him. I don't know what he was thinking, but it wasn't what it should have been. What it should have been was: ranging shot. Because the next round obliterated the embankment below the infinity pool, and of course, the guard. A head with a gray camo cap came bobbing down in the torrent. Nelson came into the bathroom and looked out the window beside me. "Friends?" he said.

"Recces," I said. "Denel NTW-20."

I was watching a guy on the road running like hell. But really, what good was that going to do? A twenty-millimeter anti-materiel round traveling at twenty-four hundred feet per second is more like a rocket than a bullet. He vanished in a cloud of dirt.

The sat phone beeped.

"They leaving in a safari truck," Ziz said.

"All of them?"

"Looks like it."

"Is one of them a woman?"

"Confirm."

"They're going to the jet strip," I said. "Can you cover that?"

"Not from here. Have to reposition."

"Go," I said. "Put a round in the plane, if you have to. Do not let it take off."

"Might not make it in time, man."

"Try."

It was only when I bent to lift Tabitha from the tub that I saw the blood pooling under her and the shard of glass sticking from her leg. Her skin was cold and clammy. The blood was flowing freely from the wound. I pulled out the glass, grabbed a towel and wrapped it tight. When I got outside, Little Teddy was crouched at the edge of the veranda, vomiting. Nelson grabbed her arm and they followed me up to the main house.

I put Tabitha on a couch. The towel bandaging her leg was soaked with blood. Her forearm was darkening into an ugly bluish black around the puncture wound. I made sure her arm hung over the edge of the couch to keep the wound below the level of her heart. Her breath sounded like something tearing inside her. Nelson came in with the medical kit.

"Have you got a pressure bandage in there?" I said.

"No." He handed me a roll of plain gauze bandage. I tore off a long strip and cinched it as tightly as I could around the towel.

"I don't know which one is the antivenom," Nelson said as he rummaged through the contents of the kit.

"I do," Little Teddy said. She stumbled to her knees beside Tabitha. She wiped her hands clean with alcohol, found a green ampoule, and broke it open. She drew the contents into a syringe. Her face was smeared with her father's blood. "Wipe her arm with alcohol," she said. Then she injected the antivenom.

"Will you stay with her?" I said.

A single sob racked her body. "Yes," she whispered.

Nelson and I ran behind the house to the Land Rover. We had the Skorpion with one remaining clip, and the Benelli. Nelson handed me a box of shells and I loaded the shotgun as we tore along the road. We came through a grove of thorn trees to the top of a long slope. The strip was about a mile away, but it might as well have been fifty. The Chinese jet was already turning at the end of the strip to face down the runway. The whine of its engines increased as the pilots ran up to full power.

"You guys in position yet?" I said when Virgil answered my call.

"Negative," he said. "But, man, that plane is not going anywhere."

The ridge with the airstrip protruded into a wide valley. From their higher position, Virgil and Ziz had a better view than we did from the road. Nelson and I didn't see the gunship until it rose up out of the valley and hovered at the end of the runway, bristling with armament. I handed Nelson the binoculars.

"South African Army," he said. "Rooivalk attack helicopter. Eight anti-tank missiles, four air-to-air." As we watched, the helicopter advanced slowly along the runway toward the jet. "Probably having a word with the pilot on the radio," Nelson said.

When the gunship was a hundred yards from the nose of the jet it settled. Before the wheels had even touched the runway, soldiers in battle dress were leaping out. They fanned into firing position in an arc around the front of the jet. By the time we arrived five minutes later, the Chinese guards were proned on the runway with zip ties on their wrists. A young South African officer paced around snapping orders while two of his soldiers stacked the Chinese submachine guns on the apron. A smaller chopper came in and landed behind the gunship. The officer marched up to me. "Medic!" he shouted over the din, jerking a thumb at the second chopper. "We've been told there's a casualty."

"At the house," I yelled.

"I'll show them," Nelson said and hurried to the second helicopter. It lifted off and headed for the compound.

A major in a rumpled uniform met me at the top of the gangway. "You're Turner?" And when I said yes: "Nkosi," he said. "Signals." Signals meant military intelligence. Nkosi gave me a curious look. "Quite a mess, this. I thought you people were more professional."

"Please don't tell anybody," I said.

Nkosi gave me a long look. "None of my business, really. Above my pay grade. The story will be that we acted on confidential information about a foreign terrorist operation. Later we will apologize to the Chinese government and blame everything on you."

"Works for me."

"That's the spirit," he said, and stood aside so I could enter the rear cabin. "You've got two minutes. Then we have to realize our grave error and let the lady go."

Mei was sitting at a desk at the far end of the lavish cabin, her hands folded in her lap and her eyes watching me as I came in. Lapis lazuli clips held her thick black hair in place, so I guess she carried spares. She wore a pale blue silk top and a sapphire choker.

"You can kiss those drives good-bye," I told Mei. "We'll have a court order for them by tomorrow, and Hassan will be in jail while we file the extradition papers."

"Oh, no," she said. "Never happen." Not a hair was out of place. Her expression was a blank page. Mei was never in a rush. She ran the most powerful and secretive hedge fund in Asia, and did it with marble aplomb. Her twin brother was a babbling idiot thanks to what we'd put him through, and she had helped us. Butter wouldn't melt.

"You have no friends in Africa. These soldiers will release us," she said calmly. "I will pick the drives up on the way home. The South Africans will have them waiting for me at the airport."

I didn't doubt it, but I wanted her to think we cared. The data on the drives was useless without the black box. The Chinese would spend months ransacking the data for a formula that wasn't there.

"If Tabitha dies, I'll kill you, Mei."

I don't know why I said it. I hadn't meant to. It just came out. Mei gazed at me placidly. Nkosi stuck his head in the door and told me to wrap it up.

"I wished no violence," Mei said. "It is not my way."

I stood up. "Sure it is. But that's OK, because it's my way too."

53

E xtra serrano," Tommy said to the Pastraminator woman.

"I know," she snapped, because that's what we always ordered. We never varied. The Pastraminator, available at Murray's Cheese on Bleecker Street, is more a cult than a sandwich. Its members come from every corner of the five boroughs to witness the miracle that happens when pastrami, sauerkraut, jack cheese, jalapeño (optional serrano), and chipotle aioli get shoveled into a couple of slices of rye, stuck in the Pastraminator machine, and fused into a single entity.

We took the sandwiches, grabbed some beer, and headed up to Minetta Triangle, the wedge of greenery shoehorned into the acute angle between Minetta Street and Sixth Avenue.

"The *Wall Street Journal* says Van Kees is launching a lab-grown diamond line," Tommy said, sitting on a bench and unwrapping his Pastraminator.

"That's right," I said. "It's a natural for them. Van Kees has the expertise, great brand recognition, and they won't have to share the profits the way they do with mined diamonds."

"But why compete against real diamonds? That's their main business."

"All Van Kees is doing is taking a piece of the action from people who were already competing against them."

"And the ones they're making—I guess you can tell them from real diamonds?"

"Well, Van Kees can. They're the ones who make the machines. That's the real story. The biggest diamond company in the world, who created the modern diamond business, who know the most about how to fake the structure of a diamond, are also the ones who make the machines that everybody else uses to catch the fakes."

Tommy thought for a minute, then said, "Huh."

"Exactly."

The little thicket where we sat felt like its own world. A sliver of peace hived off from the frenzy of the city. But nothing is really hived off from the frenzy. It's dangerous to think it can be. It will tempt you to forget what's out there. Hassan. He was out there. I had some people looking for him in the Cape. Even if there had ever been a chance of extraditing him, and there hadn't, it's not what I'd have wanted anyway. I wanted to kill him. Hassan had said my abiding sin was needing to know every detail. Not now. Now my abiding sin was the deep desire to kill Hassan. Not a day went by that I didn't think of it. I took pleasure from it, or at least comfort. That was my sin. And it made me alone.

The cops had closed the file on Lou and Coco. Their remains were buried in the Chatham Square Cemetery, a tiny Jewish graveyard on the Lower East Side. I'd gone and sat there for an hour and remembered all the bad things Lou and I had done when we were young.

The news about the undetectable fakes was buried too—deep in our files. There had been less than a dozen stones all told: the ones that Lou took, plus a few that Van Kees had fed into the trade to see if they'd be spotted. They weren't. Little Teddy said they would never attempt it again, that the knowledge was too dangerous. But of course she'd try. How could she not? No chance of being caught when you're the one selling the technology that does the catching. And it's not like you need another Joos to learn the tricks. AI will learn the tricks.

Joos was in the Du Toit family plot at the Moederkerk in Stellenbosch. Marie was still on ice in Antwerp.

The Bulgarian girl with the shot-off head was incinerated by the City of New York. The dog walker's body returned to Missouri. That's where she'd come from to make her fortune in the city. Mrs. Goodwell was still in the fridge at a morgue in Fulham, southwest London.

"Hey," I said, "thanks for getting the Recces out of the slam in Jo'burg."

Tommy nodded absently. He was still thinking about Little Teddy.

"Did she say anything about the Lucifer stone?"

"When I talked to her at Elandskop, she was still in shock. It was hours before her lawyers arrived, and I think she was telling the truth. She thought it was crazy to try to pass off such a stone. But for Teddy it was an obsession—a way to stick his finger in the diamond world's eye."

Tommy nodded. "A diamond was a diamond if Teddy said it was."

"And Lou needed the money, so he went along with it. But I think he knew the Lucifer was a step too far and got cold feet."

"And Teddy snapped," Tommy said, getting to his feet. "When you've got one foot on the dark side, not so hard to go all the way."

"You should put that on a T-shirt."

We dropped our bottles in the recycling, crossed Sixth Avenue and headed west on Bleecker Street. One of the benefits of pedestrian travel with Tommy—well, the only benefit—is the way the sidewalk clears. Even in a powder-blue bowling shirt with ivory piping and "Babe" stitched on the breast, a ripple of menace preceded him. We made it from Sixth Avenue to Seventh without so much as brushing another sleeve.

"Just ticking the boxes again," Tommy said as we crossed the street, "you were a little vague about who got what, quantum-computing-wise."

"The Chinese have the drives from Joos's laptop," I said. "That means they have his inputs and a bunch of data, but we have the actual AI thingamajig that ran the reactor."

"So we leave the Chinese in the dust?"

"All I know is the guys at DARPA have been doing handstands since they got it."

The Defense Advanced Research Projects Agency had collected the black box from Lily when she got back to New York, and had carried it across the runway to a waiting Gulfstream. I'd sent them the Lucifer when I got back.

"Put that DARPA stuff in your final draft," said Tommy. "Use words like *crucial* and *strategic* and get China in there as much as you can. Our funding review is coming up."

I opened the window to let in the cool air from the alley. The ping of the arriving elevator and the sound of squeaky wheels announced Frankie's morning round. I finished another 16-B and shoved it in the outbox as she came in and parked the cart and sat on the windowsill. She lit up a Kool and blew the smoke out into the alley.

"Too bad about Tabitha," she said. "Where is she now?"

"Still on Diego Garcia."

"Yeah, I don't get that. The middle of the Indian Ocean. Couldn't they just bring her back?"

"She was bad. The venom and the loss of blood. She went into shock and flatlined twice in Jo'burg. The plan was to take her out to Germany, and they sent a sort of flying hospital down to get her.

When they got there, she was worse. They were worried about the length of the flight. Twelve hours to Wiesbaden or five to the base on Diego Garcia. That's what it came down to."

She took a last drag and flicked her cigarette into the alley. She dug the paperwork from my outbox and dumped it in the cart. "You might as well give me the ones you're hiding in the bottom drawer," she said. "I'll take care of them." I handed them over and she added those to the cart too before she said, "That surveillance you asked for?"

"Uh-huh?"

"So Tommy cleared it, and MAUREEN went through all the footage from the auction house on the day the Geneva white was sold. We IDed some diamond dealers—I sent you a list. But it sold to a telephone bidder, so I asked for bank tracking."

"And you couldn't find a matching payment."

"No."

"It's called structuring," I said. "The buyer broke up the payment into smaller amounts to avoid detection."

"I thought you already figured out it was Tabitha."

"Yes, but she had help. Otherwise you'd have a picture of her sitting there in the sales room with a bidding paddle."

"Why does it matter?"

"It matters because whoever helped her didn't do it for nothing, and I want to know what they got in return."

"Maybe get MAUREEN to track the phone bid? The search authority is still in place, so I can run that for you myself."

"No. It'll be a nominee, too well buried to find. But let's try this. At some point there was a physical transfer of the diamond. The white had to get from the auction house to Tabitha. Someone had to wrap it up and deliver it to the buyer, or whoever acted for the buyer. Get MAUREEN to blitz all the traffic out of the auction house that day, and blitz the hotels, the trains, the buses, the airport—wherever any of those people went. I want MAUREEN to hold Geneva upside down and shake. The buyer's in there somewhere."

"Done."

"Thanks," I said.

"It's me who should be saying that. Thanks to you, the transfer came through."

"London?"

"I'll hoist a pint for you at the Dove."

"I need to find more space," Lily said that night as she inspected the new crop of lettuce in her vertical farm. "I should move this somewhere else."

Lily's triplex penthouse at the Santa Clara had terraces on each floor. They wrapped around three sides of the building. Each terrace was stepped back from the one below, giving the building its famous wedding-cake appearance. On one side of the penthouse, Lily had cocooned the whole three stories with glass in what amounted to a single greenhouse. The plants grew in trays, watered by a system that dripped nutrient-laced water down from a single feed point at the top.

You don't expect to find a farm, even a vertical one, on the most expensive real estate in Manhattan, and Lily was fighting a very public battle with the Santa Clara's co-op board. It was still in court, which was where Lily liked it. She found it invigorating—and profitable. Americans love stories about orphans who make good, and if you dress the girl up with elvish ears, you can take that image straight to the bank.

The press ate Lily up, and Slav Lily's Crimson Flavor Grenades (her tomatoes) and Slav Lily's Genuine West Side Super Crinkle (lettuce) sold out as soon as they hit the shelves. Still, it couldn't last forever. So before the image of the plucky Russian girl beating back selfish billionaires to provide New Yorkers with environmentally sound food could start fraying at the edges, Lily played her master stroke. She launched Slav Lily's Real Snow Diamonds with the slogan: "No carbon footprint when Mother Nature makes the stone!"

"The snow diamonds thing—that's where you were going all along," I said. "All this lettuce, that's just to associate you with the idea of a green product."

"It's a post-truth world. People don't buy products, they buy whatever story they want to tell themselves. I help write the story."

I'll say. She'd written one for me. In that story, Lily agreed to help Alex, and Alex paid her back by writing a report accusing Mei of serious crimes. My bosses took the report to the Canadian government, pointing out that threats to our security were threats to Canada's. The Canadians forced Mei to sell her share in the northern mine. Guess who got it.

What bothered me about that story was how quickly it traveled. My report went up to the cabinet and breezed right through. Nobody got back to me to check things out. You could hear the rubber stamp go *thwack*. I had the feeling they'd been waiting for it. Even the Canadians. And if they had been waiting, someone had prepared them. Someone deep enough in the game that they were actually there ahead of me.

My phone pinged. The delivery guy from Motorino was on his way up. I went to the elevator and collected the pizzas. I popped them in the oven to keep warm while I set the table on the terrace overlooking Central Park. I went back in for the pies. When I came out again, Lily was sitting at the table, her diamond-spattered T-shirt twinkling in the light from the antique carriage lamps.

I took a slice of the soppressata super picante and one of the margherita. I left the cremini for Lily. She preferred it, and so did the dog. He'd end up with most of it.

"You are brooding, Alex," Lily said. "Are you thinking of her?"

"Tabitha? No. She'll be fine."

"Of course she'll be fine. She is made of titanium. I'm not talking about Tabitha. I meant your daughter. You have hardly spoken to her."

Lily endured my silence for a moment. She watched the dog hoover up the cremini. Then she said, "I told Annie we'd come out this weekend."

I didn't want to see Annie. Lily knew that. A gulf had opened between us. I didn't know how to bridge it, or really want to. If I left it, maybe the gulf would grow so wide it could never be filled in and I wouldn't have to try. Time and space would bury the pain. But even as I thought that, I knew it wasn't true. You can't bury people you love without burying the lemon-colored room and the drawing she made when she was four, giving her dad a bright blue face because that year blue was her favorite color. Bury that and you're gone too.

We left early, to make a day of it. Lily had a new Porsche Cayman. Aqua, black inside. We shot through the midtown tunnel and up onto the Long Island Expressway at quantum speed. My phone buzzed in my pocket. I took it out. Message on the secure server. I logged in and went through the access protocols while Lily vaporized the traffic.

The message was from Fort Meade. Frankie had arranged for the search to come straight to me. MAUREEN had sifted through hundreds of people until she'd settled on the old guy with white hair and a jacket with black lapels, and followed him from the auction house to the airport on the night of the sale. I swiped through the stills she'd isolated. No surprises in the shots from inside the terminal. Dilip and Vijay, Lou, half a dozen other dealers I knew. Nobody was getting a handoff from black lapels. Then the surveillance moved outside. Geneva's Cointrin airport has some of the heaviest private jet traffic in Europe, so it took a minute to get through all the footage as the auction-house messenger—that's who he was—made his way past the parked Gulfstreams and Learjets and Citations until he got to the one with the steps down and the warm light from the cabin spilling out. By that time I was ready for it. You have to be. It's not personal. It's just what we do. That's what I told myself when I saw the Dassault, and framed in the light from the cabin, waiting for the white, Lily.

"What a glorious day," she shouted now, the wind whipping her dark curls as she snapped the stick up into fifth. "Let's go by Sag Harbor. We can take the ferry to Shelter Island. I packed a picnic!"

"Great," I said, thumbing a quick note to Tommy. Lily had got the white for Tabitha, and Tabitha had got the mine for Lily. We had a watch on Lily and yet we'd missed her trip to Geneva. Go ahead and guess why. We'd missed it because Tabitha knew about the watch and therefore how to duck it. Tell MAUREEN to pull them both apart, I wrote.

"I do love you, darling," Lily said.

Of course she did. We were made for each other. I reread what I'd written and pressed SEND.

ACKNOWLEDGMENTS

I have too many friends in the diamond business to thank them all, but I want to single out Paul Zimnisky, the respected analyst, and Don Palmieri, an urbane diamantaire and accomplished forensic investigator, whose Gem Certification & Assurance Lab, now partnered with the Israeli firm Sarine, is a fixture of the New York diamond district. For their help in explaining certain technicalities, thanks to Daniel Twitchen, a scientist and executive at Element 6, the De Beers-owned diamond-technology company; Emmanuel Frisch, a physicist at Nantes Université; and Wuyi Wang, vice president of research and development at the Gemological Institute of America, the world's leading diamond lab. None of these experts are responsible for any blunders, nor for the liberties of fiction.

Special thanks to my editor, Leslie Wells; publisher, Jessica Case; and agent, Michael Carlisle, for his early enthusiasm. To Stephanie Wood, Paul Maloney, Greg Latimer, Mary-Lynne Reardon, Cathrin Bradbury, Ian Pearson, and Ellen Vanstone—many thanks for the encouragement and feedback.

As always, my deepest gratitude is to my wife, Heather Abbott, an indefatigable and merciless reader, whose support has meant so much.